Isle of Larus

Kathy Sharp

Copyright © 2013 by Kathy Sharp
Photography: Ersler Dmitry
Artwork: Crooked Cat
Editor: Maureen Vincent-Northam
All rights reserved.

Isle of Larus: 978-1-909841-05-5
No part of this book may be used or reproduced in any manner whatsoever without written permission of the author or Crooked Cat Publishing except for brief quotations used for promotion or in reviews. This is a work of fiction. Names, characters, places, and incidents are used fictitiously. Any resemblance to actual persons living or dead, business establishments, events, or locales, is entirely coincidental.

Printed for Crooked Cat by Createspace

First Purple Line Edition, Crooked Cat Publishing Ltd. 2013

Discover us online:
www.crookedcatpublishing.com

Join us on facebook:
www.facebook.com/crookedcatpublishing

Tweet a photo of yourself holding
this book to **@crookedcatbooks**
and something nice will happen.

To Bill and Molly Blunden,
with love

About the Author

Growing up by the sea in Kent, back in the 1960s, it was Kathy's ambition to become a writer. Time passed.

She married, moved to westLondon, and had a daughter. She continued to write, and had a small book or two on countryside and nature subjects published. She worked for many years as a desktop publisher for Surrey County Council, and as a tutor in adult education.

And then, one day, she visited a friend who had just moved to the Isle of Portland, Dorset, and fell in love with the place. She has now lived in the Weymouth and Portland area for eight years, and still loves it. The wonderful Jurassic Coast, and Portland in particular, were the inspiration for her first novel, Isle of Larus.

Kathy also sings with, and writes lyrics for, the Island Voices Choir on Portland, and is a keen member of local writing groups, as well as enjoying studying the local flora.

Isle of Larus is Kathy's first novel.

Acknowledgements

Grateful thanks to my family and friends for help and encouragement, and special thanks to everyone who read the book for me.

May I also thank everyone at Weymouth Writing Matters and Off the Cuff writing groups, and the Dorset Writers' Network. It wouldn't have happened without you.

And finally, many thanks to all at Crooked Cat Publishing, for making this fantasy a reality.

Kathy Sharp
Dorset, July 2013

Isle of Larus

Part One
'Come the Ships...'

4

Prologue

There is no such place as the Isle of Larus. Let's get that straight from the beginning. And no such time as the people in this story are living in, if you get my drift. Is it some sort of parallel universe, then, you ask? Well, yes, sort of; a salty little world of its own. Quite like ours, in many respects, but with several quirky features, as we shall see.

Sometimes our universe and theirs bump together and get glimpses of each other, with interesting results. And sometimes their universe produces interesting results all by itself. We shall see some of that, too.

So no Larus then? No such place? Not really, no. But you try telling that to the people who live there. It's very real indeed to them. And the trammels and troubles of life and interpersonal relationships are just as exasperating whichever universe you happen to inhabit.

6

Chapter One
The Four Guardians

Rufus the Hermit sat high on his chilly rock, contemplating the sea. He couldn't actually see it, for he was blind, but he communed with the deep in a very profound way. It was a strange job, he often thought, being a guardian of the island. But who was he to question his fate? His calling came from the Spirit of the Sea itself, and it called often. Some people, notably the Reverend Pontius, said this was bordering on the sacrilegious, all this sea-communing. But most people said what did the Reverend know about it? He was an offcomer and couldn't truly understand the need of islanders to be on the right side of the Spirit of the Sea.

So, week by week, people came to bring offerings of food to Rufus. Some he ate himself, just to keep body and soul together, you understand, but the rest he threw carefully over the cliff as gifts for the Old Man, as they affectionately called the Spirit of the Sea. In return, people asked only that Rufus would intercede on their behalf. Could the Old Man see his way clear to give them a couple of days' good fishing, perhaps? And Rufus communed with the spirit, as one old man to another.

As with many old men, the Old Man was capricious and unpredictable. Benevolent father one minute, bloody-minded, querulous tyrant the next. Rufus understood. He felt that way himself when his bones ached. So there the hermit sat facing east, as craggy and shrivelled as the rock he sat upon, old as the hills and a fair bit more weatherworn.

Meanwhile, over on the western side of the island, the Reverend Pontius, the second guardian, was huffing and puffing in annoyance. A solid man in late middle age, the Reverend had strong opinions on many things, and the Spirit of the Sea was one of them. Weeks of bad weather had seen a steady stream of supplicants heading across to that unkempt and straggly creature, the hermit, bearing gifts of food. There was nothing surreptitious about it, the Reverend noted, it was completely open and blatant. That was the most annoying part of the whole unholy thing. Surely *his* spirit, the Spirit of the Sky, was enough for anyone?

The islanders accepted the Spirit of the Sky, nodded sagely and said it was a very good thing, and that they would come and worship as required. But the Spirit of the Sea was far more ancient. And they had to deal with it on a practical basis, day to day. It affected their very livings. The Spirit of the Sky seemed more concerned with the hereafter, and that didn't put the fish on the table. It was only common sense to hedge your bets, and keep both old and new deities happy. They didn't say this in front of the Reverend Pontius, partly out of politeness, but mainly because he kept them extra-long at prayers if he heard any mutterings. Nonetheless, his contribution to the island's care was valued rather more than he knew.

On the southernmost tip of the island lived another whose job concerned the practicalities of the sea. Rissa the ship warden, the third guardian, dwelt by the great rock, and felt her patience tried by both the hermit and the Reverend. Did either of them really do anything productive? The question was always rhetorical for Rissa. Her own job was clearly the most important on the island, never mind all that god-bothering.

Every morning at first light, Rissa went out in her scarlet gown and faced the wind. If it blew her skirts over her head, there was a gale. If it blew her flat on her back, they had a tempest to deal with. Some people, especially that prissy twit Pontius, said this was unseemly. No woman should be displaying her undertrappings in that fashion. Rissa said her undertrappings were pretty formidable, given the general state of the weather, and what did it matter anyway if there was no one there to see?

Everyone else said that Rissa was the wise woman of the weather, was spectacularly accurate in her predictions, and who cares how she compiles her statistics. It was also known to all, but rarely expressed aloud, that Rissa had another useful role in her guise of ship warden. If a ship came in too close, or looked likely to fall foul of the lee shore on the western side, Rissa would be out in her scarlet gown, doing her bright best to warn them off. But sometimes there was nothing to be done and a wreck was inevitable.

When this happened, Rissa let it be known, and everyone would go and help if they could. There was never any deliberate wrecking – the Spirit of the Sea would not look kindly upon it – but if the boat were doomed, there was no harm in helping themselves to the useful parts of the wreckage. They rescued the ship's people when they could, and gave a decent burial to those they couldn't. After all, they had a real parson and it was all done properly, with a headstone and prayers. Surely the remains of the wreck and cargo was a fair return for this service.

There was more huffing about on the northern side of the island by the harbour. Captain Castello, this time, guardian number four. Not a sea captain, as he regularly informed anyone who would listen, but a captain of artillery. So there. Any fool could build a boat and call himself a sea captain, but a captain of artillery was a force to be reckoned with, in every respect. Rissa looked down her nose and said that two old cannons and a popgun scarcely constituted artillery. Captain Castello said that Rissa should keep her opinions to herself. The two cannon and the popgun, in point of fact an ancient musket, were the Captain's great pride. They lit up his life. Literally. His whole being existed to polish their metalwork. Their gleam was legendary, and the Captain would have slit his own throat for shame should a smudge or thumbprint have remained. However, as Rissa acidly pointed out, these guns had never been fired in anger, not by Captain Castello, anyhow. The Captain said the harbour was the island's lifeblood, and lifeblood must be robustly defended. Just because no bad men had ever set upon the island, it was not sensible or safe to assume that they never would. Most people agreed with this. But there were some that said the defeat of any invader was more likely to be from being blinded by the piercing brightness of the cannons' metalwork than from any shot they could fire.

Nonetheless, the Reverend Pontius was prevailed upon to come down and bless the artillery every quarter-day. He made quite a ceremony of it, which greatly pleased Captain Castello, and the two offcomers felt a bond of fellow feeling in their love of order and cleanliness. And a bond of disapproval for that impossible harridan Rissa, and the grubby old hermit.

In idle moments, some people wondered if there wasn't something going on between Rissa and Captain Castello. The fact that they were so rude to each other positively proved it, some said, for what couple argues more long and loud and aggressively than a mated pair? Everyone thinks the four guardians are as old as time, people would say, and Rufus surely was, but Rissa and the Captain? No one knew for certain how old they were, of course, and neither was exactly young, but Rissa was still a handsome woman – imperious, they said. A little stout round the middle these days, and a terrible temper on her, of course, but striking with all that black hair. An excellent match for the Captain, really, if only he'd take the bull by the horns, so to speak. At any rate, people enjoyed arguing out the likelihood of it all, and some relished the excuse to keep an eye on the movements of them both to see when and where and for how long their paths crossed.

Occasionally fierce rumours were spread, saying the pair had been closeted together, or seen arm in arm. These stories would inevitably come to the notice of the two protagonists who would be indignant to the point of incandescence in denying them. There you are, people would say, proof positive!

The island – their island – was not large. The Reverend Pontius knew he could walk right round it in a day, if he got a move on. Not that there was any great point in walking right round it, but it did give a feel for the size and scope of the place. It mostly consisted of tall cliffs, with little, inaccessible coves. And my goodness, did the wind whistle across the top of it. What made it special was its harbour. This was formed by a set of little islands that were strung out in a great circle to the north. They were wave-washed and wind-battered places, occasionally underwater at the highest tides, but they gave just enough shelter from the worst of the weather, so the waters of the harbour were reasonably calm most of the time. This was enough for the island's fishing boats. They could operate within the calmer waters of the harbour, or retreat to it from outside in harsh weather. It didn't make for a very exciting economy, but it was adequate, and supported a steady population. No wonder, as the Reverend thought to himself in his darker moments, that the Spirit of the Sea still held so much sway. Had it not been for Castello, he would have felt he was the only civilised person among this community of sea-worshipping heathens. Still, this was his vocation, chosen for him by the Spirit of the Sky, and he must do the best he could with it. The Spirit sends his strongest champions to the most difficult places, he said to comfort himself. But it didn't comfort him very much.

He remembered the first time he had seen the island, *our* island, he would call it now. It had appeared as a distant blue-grey bump on the horizon, over a still stretch of blue-grey sea. The sea was so still, indeed, that the boat's crew had taken to oars, with much complaining, and the Reverend had stood in the bows, out of the way, watching the image of his soon-to-be home coming slowly closer. Isle of Larus, he had thought, experimentally. Home. There was to be no going back, he knew, and his insides quailed with gritty fear. He did not know how welcome he would be.

At long last, a little breeze had blown in, and to everyone's relief the sails filled, and they made faster progress. Pontius remembered being unable to decide whether the island was an incredibly beautiful place or a hopeless, desolate rock. He still couldn't, for that matter. It somehow managed to be both at once. The boat had slipped into the harbour as the sun sank, and he had been deposited on the quay with his trunk. He recalled the feeling of being cast away in a hopeless desert. He still felt like that, too, sometimes, though it had been, oh, years and years ago. He found it harder and harder to remember how many. The islanders had taken him under their collective wing. Adopted him like a half-drowned puppy that had washed in, he often thought, and treated him indulgently. But he still wasn't entirely sure whether he was really welcome. Accepted well enough, yes, but did he truly reach these people, or would they just as soon pitch him into the sea given half a chance? The Reverend did not know the answer to that, either.

Captain Castello's first view of the island had been rather different. He had seen it through a frond of seaweed. It had been a strange entrance. He had been washed up in a very battered boat, more dead than alive. A rather tall man, lean, and possibly quite athletic in his youth. The islanders had already pronounced him dead when he opened his eyes and saw faces peering at him through the bladderwrack. It was hard to say who got the bigger fright. Some people ran off shouting that a merman had come ashore, or some such nonsense, he recalled. The more sensible folks had cared for him and tended his wounds, and he had recovered well. For all that, his memory was damaged, and he never did know what had happened to him, or how he came to be in the boat. Little flashes of memory came to him. He knew his own name, and that the trunk they found in the boat belonged to him, and had been bought in a ship sale, but that was all.

When his strength returned, he began to wander about the island, peering into doors and over cliffs looking for he knew not what. Until he found the castle. When he saw the old cannon there, he felt a grateful rush of recognition, and immediately knew he was a captain of artillery. Guns were his area of expertise, he said, although the exact details of what you did with them were a little vague. They certainly needed to be kept clean, and these were filthy, so Castello set to organising and polishing the ordnance. The islanders had paid no attention to the castle or its cannon for years – they had simply forgotten how it came to be there. Castello seemed to be the fellow the castle had been waiting for, and they were happy for him to make it his own, so there he stayed and in time was accepted as one of the island's guardians. Just how long ago that might have been was unclear now to the Captain.

Sometimes details of his past life came back to him. He knew how to sail a boat, for instance, but he had no idea *how* he knew. He was a military man, he reasoned, and, besides gun polishing, he did a bit of marching up and down in the weatherbeaten uniform he had found in his trunk. On the whole he was not unhappy, he told his friend Pontius. It would just be nice to know who he actually was. "You are the northern guardian of the island," said Pontius. "Is that not identity enough for you, old friend?" In general, yes, it was.

Chapter Two
The Wreck that Wasn't

It was Rissa who saw the strange boats first, of course. She had climbed up to the top of the great rock and stood there like a beacon, her scarlet skirts billowing. A strong gust caught her and made her stagger. The wind was freshening very quickly and there was ugly cloud in the south-west. It was time to send round a warning. She gathered her skirts to climb down, but something caught her eye. There were two little ships racing, yes racing, with the wind behind them, straight into the western wall of the island, which was all toothy rocks, as any seagoing man would know. Rissa stared and squinted. They were very strange ships indeed. Sailing boats, to be sure, but what fashion of rigging was that? And why were they so shiny? Shiny white hulls, white as a gull in winter. She gaped at them, and then pulled herself together. At such speed they would strike soon. Effortlessly surefooted, she climbed down off the rock and trotted a little way round the headland to see where they would make their sorry end, for she was quite sure this was inevitable. Right under the black pinnacle, most likely. Rissa frowned. That was the most difficult place to reach, even for the islanders.

But they must do what they could. Rissa trotted back to find her runner. There was always a child, boy or girl, employed at the headland to take news round the island. They were fleet of foot, these wiry young islanders, and Rissa paid them in sweetmeats. Extra if there was a wreck to report. The boy ran off like a hare to tell the Reverend Pontius, who would ring the chapel bell and alert everyone. Soon every able-bodied person would be rushing down with ropes and grappling irons, and high hopes of good pickings.

Strange it was, as Rissa said later, how they raced each other blindly into the rocks, just as if they couldn't see the island at all. Very strange.

As it turned out, there was no opportunity to ask the crew what kind of seamanship they called this. There was nothing to be done at all, because there was no sign of the ships when people reached the cliff top. The predicted storm blew everything asunder, for sure, but it was odd that not a scrap of wreckage ever came ashore. Not so much as a plank. It was all very curious, and the whole business was the talk of the island. Everyone was annoyed at being called out in such weather for nothing, and some doubted Rissa's sanity. Others defended her: the warden had never been wrong, either in her weather predictions or in spotting incoming ships. Her reports had always been utterly reliable, and hadn't everyone benefited from her wreck warnings? Remember the brandy barrels that washed ashore, the year before last?

Rissa herself steadfastly insisted that the boats had been there, heading for certain destruction. Could they have turned in time, escaped back out to sea? Never, said Rissa, no chance at all, and unless they sprouted wings and flew, they must have struck the rocks. But then there would be wreckage, people murmured.

There was a strange story a day or two later that came from Old Billy, who had been up visiting the hermit at the time, and swore blind he saw two white boats heading off the east coast. The *east* coast? Nonsense, people said, and anyway everyone knew that Old Billy liked a drink or five and was unlikely to make a reliable witness to anything. He and Rufus were probably both legless. Or Old Billy was, at least, and Rufus as a blind man, could hardly corroborate the story.

Life ran on quietly after the rumpus of the non-existent wreck had subsided. Since no further information was forthcoming, there was not much more to be said. The islanders gave a communal shrug and carried on with the normal business of life. There was fish to catch, fields to be tended and gossip to be gossiped, and most people found that was more than sufficient to be going on with. They were philosophical about most things, and were happy to accept that unexplained events were simply the will of the Spirit of the Sea. Or the Sky, if they were talking to the Reverend. The hay crop had to be got in. Boats and nets needed to be kept in good repair. There would be time for idly speculating on what it all meant when winter came, if they hadn't forgotten all about it by then.

The Reverend Pontius found himself uneasily concerned with the attitudes of the other three guardians. Rissa, though she was very sure of her facts at the time, was at heart an islander, and seemed to have accepted the whole business as just one of those things. She couldn't explain it, so she simply put it behind her, all rather too easily for the Reverend's liking, and went calmly back to her work. He admired her fortitude, but secretly thought she was not to be too heavily relied upon in the common sense department. Once an islander, always an islander, indeed.

Captain Castello, on the other hand, as an offcomer, might have been expected to show a little more concern. The Reverend always found him to be levelheaded enough. On the day of the non-wreck, he had dutifully trotted up to the cliff top, tenderly cradling his musket in a leather bag. He always brought it to wrecks, more for show than anything else, but it gave proceedings an air of official security, and him a sense of having done his job properly. On discovering there was no wreck to secure, the Captain had gone off in a bad humour, muttering about the risks of getting salt spray on the metalwork. Subsequently, he had little to say about it all, and just seemed to assume there had been a mistake, though he certainly didn't dare say as much in front of Rissa. Castello is going native, thought the Reverend Pontius, if it can't be explained he ignores it these days.

In fact, the Captain had been rather more alarmed than he made out. Things appearing and disappearing suddenly certainly did not constitute normality, as far as he was concerned. He was a man who thought in terms of solid objects and all things measurable. And he was in charge of the island's defence. How can you defend against things that keep disappearing? It was all mighty unsettling, but he would have been strung up by his thumbs rather than admit it, so he simply redoubled his efforts in keeping everything at the castle shipshape. It might not help, but no one could say he hadn't made the effort.

And as for Rufus, well, words failed the Reverend. There he sat on that cliff looking as serene and unconcerned as you please. What sort of a guardian was that? Silly old besom. An islander again, so what else could you expect? Sitting up there taking free food in exchange for nonsensical predictions. It irritated Pontius that people set so much store by the hermit's sayings, for all that they occasionally turned out to be correct. It was bound to happen sometimes, wasn't it? He had said nothing very helpful about the-wreck-that-wasn't. Or anything much at all, at least in the Reverend's hearing. If you couldn't predict or explain something as peculiar as *that*, then what was the purpose of sitting up there?

Pontius sometimes thought, in uncharitable moments, that everyone on this island, excepting himself, was barking mad. His own response to the non-event had been to spend a great deal of time on his knees communing with the Spirit of the Sky, and, in more practical moments, to put a stout bar on the door of his chapel. If there was anything out there that shouldn't be, he wanted to make sure it stayed outside.

Chapter Three
The Shiny Ships

It was weeks later that Pontius was disturbed from his devotions in the little chapel by a considerable hullabaloo outside. There was shouting and hurried footsteps, and in burst Captain Castello, wild-eyed and dishevelled.

"Boats! Shiny white boats… in the harbour!"

"My dear Captain," said the Reverend, a little rattled. "Calm yourself. What is all this?"

"Invasion! We are being invaded… hundreds of them. Hundreds!"

The Reverend was a lot more rattled at this. "In *our* harbour?"

A considerable crowd pushed and shoved its way into the chapel, and somebody began ringing the bell. Cheeky, thought the Reverend, to do that without asking. Cheeky. But an invasion was an invasion.

"Captain, you should not be here, you should be tending to your cannon. You must tell us what to do. You must lead us."

"Lead you? But I don't know how. I don't remember. Perhaps I've never done it!" said the gallant Captain, faintly, and collapsed on the step of the pulpit with his head in his hands.

This was no good at all, thought the Reverend Pontius. A voice from the crowd said, "We must send to Rufus the Hermit, send gifts, tell him to ask the Old Man to send great waves to beat down these invaders."

18

Everyone agreed this was worth a try, and people were swiftly delegated to find food and take it to the hermit.

Rissa appeared, clearly annoyed at not having been the first bearer of exciting news. "What are you all in here for? Send some of the lads to keep watch for me on the great rock. Better still, put watchers on every cliff top, so we don't get taken by surprise like this again."

This was another practical thing to do, and people ran off to organise the lookouts.

Rissa was only partly appeased. "Do we actually know that these ships are an invasion?" she barked at the remaining group. "They could be traders. They could bring us wealth."

No one had thought of this and there were mutterings. How are we to know, people asked fearfully. Rissa shook herself impatiently. "I'll go and ask them."

"But Rissa, they could be pirates, ruffians. They could try to… interfere with you!"

All eyes were on Rissa. "Not in *these* undertrappings," she snorted, and stomped off towards the harbour. The crowd dispersed to test their doorlocks, bury their treasures and hide their daughters in the haylofts.

Captain Castello still sat silently weeping with his head in his hands. The Reverend Pontius patted him on the shoulder, not unkindly, and said, "Old friend Castello, you must rouse yourself. Have you left your cannon unprotected?"

"No," said the Captain, looking up. "I left Lineus the fisherman on guard."

"There," said the Reverend. "You *do* know what to do. You've already done it. Lineus is a stout, reliable fellow. This is the moment you've waited for all these years. Go and show them how to prepare powder and shot. The island needs you. This is your great day, and they look to you for leadership."

The Captain dried his eyes, and ran his hand nervously through his greying curls. "My great day… look to my cannon." He was up and rushing off to the harbour directly, his back straight and a distinctly military determination in his eyes. Pontius watched him go and then fell wearily to his knees and began to pray fervently to the Spirit in the Sky for guidance. I really am getting far too old for this sort of thing, he said secretly.

Down at the harbour things were pretty confused by the time Rissa arrived. The shiny boats were out in the harbour, just as Castello had said, lots of them. But no one had attempted to come ashore, or even approach the quay. They were sailing round in great circles and didn't seem very interested in the island at all. This was a relief, since there was thus no fighting to do, but it also presented a bit of a problem. How was anyone supposed to go and demand to know the intentions of these invaders, when there was no actual invading going on?

Rissa was a little puzzled to know what to do. On the walk down from the chapel she had been steeling herself to go and stand before them, block their way, with a crowd of islanders at her back, and force these strangers to explain themselves. "If they're not coming in, I must go out to them," she reasoned aloud. "Prepare your best boat. Now."

There was a hesitant silence from the crowd on the quay. She knew what they were thinking. Why go out to these boats? Nothing had happened. There was nobody ashore who shouldn't be. No rape, pillage or criminal damage had occurred. Why go and invite trouble? But Rissa's long experience as guardian of the south had trained her to anticipate trouble before it happened, to give fair warning.

"Best boat. Now," she said again, and started forward, though she had no particular idea where to go, the harbour not being her usual habitat.

They led her to the edge of the quay, and she peered about inquiringly. "Down below," said someone, helpfully. "The *Brothers Three* awaits you, Lady." She wasn't entirely sure this

20

showed due deference, but never mind.

Rissa looked down over the edge of the quay. A large fishing boat was tied up at the bottom of a ladder, sending up wafts of antique mackerel. It was low tide. The full horror of the situation hit her. It was low tide; the boat was at the bottom of the ladder; she must climb down the ladder to reach the boat. Clearly it had not occurred to anyone that a woman who routinely climbed up and down a large rock in a gale was likely to be bothered by this prospect. But, she thought, the rock doesn't move. Both the ladder and the boat appeared to be in motion. Her head reeled, and she seriously considered suggesting they wait until the tide came in. But that would take hours. They could all have had their throats slit by high tide. "The Spirit of the Sea protect me," she breathed. ("Ha!" she could hear Rufus saying, if he heard.)

People were beginning to snigger. The lady warden, who had been telling everyone what to do in that officious way of hers two minutes ago, is afraid of going down a ladder. Afraid of showing her knickers, is she? Rissa looked around desperately. Further along the quay was a flight of wooden steps. "Bring the boat up to the steps," she said. "I will embark there." There were further sniggers. Rissa felt she was losing her grip.

"Lady, we cannot. The water by the steps isn't deep enough. The boat will run aground."

Captain Castello had just reached the quay, and jog-trotted past on his way to attend to the artillery. "Take a small boat to the steps," he cried impatiently as he went, "and carry the lady to the larger boat that way." Rissa could have kissed him, except that it would have caused the biggest outbreak of gossip ever. Quite a few knowing looks were exchanged, as it was.

"Do as the Captain says, you idiots, we're wasting time." And she gathered up her scarlet skirts and walked purposefully towards the steps. Soon a suitable small boat had been brought to the steps, and Rissa installed in it without mishap. She was

21

rowed round to the fishing boat. Her entry onto the larger boat was a little undignified, but she managed well enough and sat down regally among the nets and discarded fishtails. Now then, she thought, let's get down to business.

Captain Castello was approaching his destination. He liked to think of it as a castle, but it was just a wall with holes, really. More holes than wall, if he was honest. He had kept his spirits up all the way from the chapel by chanting to himself, "My great day... look to my cannon," but had been distracted by Rissa's distress and was now chanting, "Carry the lady to the larger boat," instead. When the chant transmuted itself into, "Carry the large lady to the boat," he stopped, straightened himself, and realised that he would shortly be facing a group of people expecting orders. Clear, incisive orders. To be given in a proper military fashion. He'd never done such a thing, at least not in this life, on Larus. Castello's military experience was largely confined to polishing metal. But the people *under his command* (he really brightened at that phrase) knew even less than he did, so all he had to do was sound decisive. *But supposing we have to fire the guns...?* He tried to shove the thought aside, but it was persistent. He'd watched guns being fired, hadn't he? He thought he had, and it seemed simple enough. He certainly had a rough idea of how to do it... Anyway, provided it made lots of noise, did it matter if they didn't manage to hit anything? He was hazy about the practicalities of aiming a gun. And provided he didn't demolish his own wall or blow his own foot off... There seemed to be too many 'provideds' for comfort.

For a moment the wild and unworthy thought occurred to him that he could stand back as commander and let someone else put the match to the touchhole. He could blame another for any mishaps that way. But no, command meant taking responsibility. It was a very worrying notion, but somehow inspiring, and he jogged on. If this was truly to be his great day, he must be steadfast. He must protect the island or die in the attempt. He must be heroic. "The Spirit of the Sky protect me!" he muttered.

Up on the east cliff, Rufus the Hermit was receiving visitors. There were many, he thought, and their agitation was tangible. The air around him seemed to heat up with all this anxiety. He sat very still and serene while they bounced around him, all gibbering at once. At length he held up a withered hand for silence, and the gibbering ceased. "Mr Rufus, your honour, a great calamity has befallen... they're in the harbour, in *our* harbour... we have brought offerings..."

Rufus turned his head to the voice. "Calm yourselves. I know of this." No one queried how he might know. Rufus just knew things, and that was that. "I have communed with the Spirit of the Sea. The spirit knows the whereabouts of all ships, alive and dead, and says there are no ships in our harbour that should not be there."

This statement caused further consternation. No ships in our harbour that should not be there? What could that mean? Was the Spirit of the Sea, may he protect us, having an off day? This was no time to do it, if he was. Had the quality of recent offerings not been to the Old Man's taste? Or was it Rufus? Was he finally going gaga? People had been wondering quietly for quite a while if all his wits were collected in the same crab pot. Had he finally slipped over the edge?

"Mr Rufus, your honour! We know there are strange ships in the harbour. How can the Spirit say that there are none that should not be there?"

"'Tis a great conundrum," said Rufus thoughtfully. "But that's what he said."

Shouting broke out: "The Old Man is angry with us!"

"Appease him with the offerings!"

"Don't be so damned silly," said Rufus, unconcernedly. "The Spirit isn't angry, he's just being impenetrable. It happens. But have you considered this: if there are no ships in the harbour that shouldn't be there, then perhaps these strangers *should* be there. Think on that, children." And he felt around for the nearest dish of offerings and helped himself to a morsel.

The Reverend Pontius would have been deeply worried had he heard what Rufus had to say, but as it was, he had been on his knees for some time, and the iffy vertebra in his back was giving warning twinges. He knew that if he didn't get to his feet soon he would have to be lifted off to his bed still in the kneeling position, and he didn't fancy the idea at all. But still, this *was* a bit of an emergency, and the Spirit of the Sky was not being very forthcoming with apt advice. Or anything at all, really. He had always felt that his position as western guardian of the island was a little tenuous. What had he to offer, after all, beyond a little pastoral care?

The chapel doubled as a school for the children, and he taught them their letters when they could be spared from helping in the fields or gutting fish. Attendance was quite good, in general, and sometimes the adults came along too. They enjoyed the Reverend's 'stories' of the strange doings of people in other places and times. Geography and history, he called them. But they were stories, all right, and no one knew whether they were true or just made up for entertainment purposes. Still, the Reverend prided himself on the indubitable fact that all the children, and most of the adults, could read and write reasonably well. That was an achievement, from his point of view, but did anyone really value it, apart from himself? Pontius sensed the irrelevance of it all to the islanders. Sometimes he thought his only role of any real value was to ring the chapel bell when there was a wreck.

One of the lads suddenly put his head round the chapel door and said breathlessly that the lady warden had gone out in a mackerel boat to challenge the invaders, wasn't that a sight to see, and would his reverence like some help, maybe?

"Yes, yes," said Pontius. "Help me up," and dismissed the boy. He needed some more thinking time, as well as the opportunity to get his knees working again without an audience.

He had had the opportunity during his fruitless wait for a word from the Spirit of the Sky, to consider recent events, notably the peculiar incident of the two ships that vanished when they were supposed to be wrecking themselves on the rocks. Hadn't Rissa called them 'shiny white ships'? And what was it the Captain had said, when he burst in? Something similar. 'Shiny boats' wasn't it? There was clear evidence here of a connection, was there not? And somewhere at the back of his mind was that mad story spread by Old Billy of two white boats appearing off the east coast at the time the wreck should have been happening. The old fool was probably drunk as a skunk, but still, it was a lead, of sorts. The Reverend prided himself on his logical turn of mind, and secretly fancied himself as a detective. To begin, then, he would go and interview Rufus. "This is also *your* day, Pontius," he said to himself, as he set off. "Let's see if we can't get to the bottom of this."

But he had not gone far when he met the group of offerings-bearers who had just returned from the hermit's cliff. They told him he would be wasting his time talking to Rufus. The hermit had completely flipped his wig, if you'll pardon the expression, your reverence. Was talking nonsense. No sense at all, ought to be locked up for his own safety. Had said there were no ships in the harbour that ought not to be there. His very words. What do you think to that?

Pontius thought it very worrying indeed, but he wasn't about to say so. He had decided that Rufus would be his first port of call, and call he would. At least that way he could decide for himself whether the fellow had genuinely gone off his chump, and cross him off the witness list if that was the case. Everyone was looking at the Reverend, many of them eating the offerings they had brought back with them. Pontius put on what he hoped was his most severe and wise expression, said he was going to see the hermit anyway, and to stop scattering bits of food around or we'll have rats everywhere.

"Good afternoon, Reverend," said Rufus as Pontius puffed up the cliff. It was unnerving, the way the hermit always knew you were there before you'd said a word. One could be forgiven for thinking his blindness was a pretence, had his eyes not been merely empty sockets. Pontius sat down to get his breath back and assemble his thoughts in some sort of order. Rufus sat in silence, waiting. That was unnerving, too, the way he made you feel flustered and improperly prepared, just by waiting quietly.

"These ships in the harbour, Rufus. People are very confused. I was told you said there *were* no ships in the harbour. Forgive me, colleague, but that is not good sense. Many people have seen them. Are you feeling quite well?"

"Perfectly well," said Rufus. "And I said there are no ships in the harbour that *shouldn't be there.*"

Then logically, thought Pontius, they should be there. Does he mean we are fated to be invaded? That it is meant to be? This was such an unpleasant thought that he kept it to himself. "Does this mean we should not attempt to fight them off, then?"

"No need," said Rufus, conversationally. "No need at all, I don't think."

The Reverend fought down irritation. Dash it all, why couldn't the hermit just talk sense for once? He thought of Captain Castello, down at the harbour tending his guns by now, struggling with equal quantities of heroism and blind terror. What about him – *he* needs to know whether there's any need to fight. And Rissa, heading out to them in a fishing boat, a perfect target in her scarlet gown.

"Do you mean that they will not attack us?"

"They cannot," said Rufus. And left it at that. Pontius didn't know whether this was reassuring or not, and was about to give up and leave, when another thought occurred to him.

"Rufus, you remember the day of the wreck – of the wreck that never happened. Rissa saw shiny white ships racing towards the pinnacle. I heard a tale that Old Billy was up here with you and saw shiny ships. The ships in the harbour are shiny, too. Do you think all these sightings are connected?"

"Oh, yes," said Rufus. "And they *should* be here, indeed yes."

Captain Castello was learning the hard way that you couldn't train a gun crew in haste, especially when you hardly knew what you were doing yourself. The islanders were very willing, valiant even, but they were fisherfolk. What did they know of guns? The Captain himself felt a deep antipathy to the notion of disturbing his perfectly balanced, spotless pile of cannon shot in order to put one into the cannon's mouth. And as to the organising of gunpowder and the match tub, everyone was so interested to see what happened when the two got together, that there was considerable danger of blowing themselves up without firing a shot.

"Silence!" bellowed the Captain, with a volume of voice he hadn't known he possessed, and the babble, and pushing and shoving, and curious peering, stopped obediently. "Watch and learn," he said sternly, and proceeded to load the gun himself, hoping to goodness he was doing it all properly. When he had finished, he walked around the cannon, peering out through the gap in the wall and muttering something about 'maximum elevation', which he thought he had once heard mentioned by somebody preparing to fire a gun. He looked at the cannon, in an appraising sort of way, and looked out to the harbour. Perhaps they wouldn't need to fire at all. Perhaps the invaders would go away. Perhaps Rissa would frighten them off. But to hide behind the skirts of a woman, even one so formidable, was an unworthy thought. Castello was ashamed. Perhaps a shot across the bows would do it, then. A show of strength was all that was needed. Now, Castello, now is your moment.

The Captain strode across and took the match from the tub. There was a sharp intake of breath and everyone rushed towards him to get the best view. The Captain was bowled over by the onrush, the match flew out of his hands and landed impossibly neatly on the touchhole of the cannon.

Out in the harbour, the *Brothers Three* was progressing slowly, fighting the incoming tide. It was an old boat, but seaworthy enough. Its owner Ligo was the grandson of one of the original three brothers, and he was a sailor seasoned with salt, and one of the steadiest men on the island. To him, his boat was a member of the family and he loved it dearly. Rissa was rather less impressed.

She was just wondering what exactly she would say to the invaders when she reached them. Would they even speak the same language? What would she do if she couldn't communicate? A more uncomfortable thought struck her: supposing they attacked without bothering to communicate at all? The fishing boat was completely unarmed, unless you counted a few mackerel lines and a broken crab pot. Ligo was a stout fellow, but who knew what weapons these strangers might have at their disposal? They should have borrowed Captain Castello's musket. At least they could have waved that about and looked a bit more warlike. She was finding it difficult to remain indignant, and becoming fearful. Could they have come to trade? She doubted it greatly. Ahead, the white boats were still circling unconcernedly. "Give me the strength to stay angry," Rissa said softly.

From somewhere among the white ships, there came a very loud, blasting sound. Rissa went rigid with fright. The white ships turned as one to face in one direction, and paraded past the *Brothers Three* as if it did not exist. There was another blast. Were they being fired upon? The white ships gathered speed. They were *racing* each other, thought Rissa, just like the two I saw beneath the pinnacle. She absolutely did not know what to make of it.

They were now uncomfortably close to one of the white boats. And very strange it was, too. A little smaller than the white ships she had seen under the pinnacle. Sleek. Beautiful, even, its white flanks glowing. But what purpose could a vessel of that type possibly serve? It would carry very little cargo, and it certainly didn't look like a fishing boat. And there was a woman. Was it a woman? Yes, but in very strange dress. Where were her skirts? What had she done to her hair? Waving her arms, she was. Shouting. Were they being warned off before an attack? Rissa stood up, trembling. "I am Rissa, ship warden and southern guardian, Isle of Larus," she said loudly. "What do you do here?"

A moment later a cannonball whizzed past Rissa's astonished nose with a whistling roar, crashed straight through the far side of the *Brothers Three* and hit the sea with a great splash. A moment after that, the sound of the cannon fire reached her. "They fired on us! They fired on us!" somebody yelled.

The boat slewed round, sails flapping, while Ligo and his crew moved everything loose, including Rissa, onto the side opposite the damage. "I suppose a craft this size does not carry a lifeboat?" she called lamely. That was too foolish to merit an answer. But a little foolishness was only to be expected, under the circumstances, she thought.

It took a while for everything to be brought under control, but at length it became clear that the *Brothers Three* was not about to sink. Ligo was distraught at this heartless breaking of his wonderful boat, but the damage was high up, and not much water had been taken aboard. Nonetheless, there was a splintered gaping gap. And the wind was rising. Instinctively,

Rissa stood up, shaking, faced the wind, and prepared her weather forecast. "Increasing," she said. "It'll get worse. We must go ashore before it does. Make repairs."

The crew didn't need telling twice, and the boat was carefully put about. As it turned, the outer part of the harbour swung back into view. "Lady, they're gone!" said Ligo. "All the white boats… gone!" And so they had.

Up on the hermit's cliff, the Reverend Pontius had heard the cannon fire. "What was that great noise?" he said, stupidly. "Are they firing on us?"

"Ah," said Rufus, with a small smile, as if that answered the question.

"What do you mean?" asked Pontius. "Are we under attack? Must I ring the chapel bell? Give warning?" He really hated the way Rufus made him feel: like an impatient child asking a silly question. What the devil did the fellow mean?

"The Spirit of the Sea has received the cannon shot. Carried it to the depths. There is nothing to fear."

Nothing to fear? Cannonballs whizzing about the place, and there was nothing to fear? Pontius realised he must get himself down to the harbour and see for himself what was going on. As he turned to leave, another thought struck him and he said, "But you told me the white boats cannot attack us."

"So I did," said Rufus. "So I did."

The Reverend huffed in exasperation and set off. Blithering old fool, he thought, leading me all round the houses like that when there's an emergency going on. Nonetheless, he thought through the things Rufus had told him, as he hurried down towards the harbour. If the hermit is right, and the white boats cannot attack us, then where did the firing come from? "Oh, my goodness!" he said to himself. "Castello!"

Reaching the harbour, the Reverend found a large crowd assembled, practically everyone on the island had come down, and there was much excitement. People were shouting, waving their hats, chanting. What was that they were chanting? Pontius tried to make it out as he elbowed his way through. "Make way, I am the Reverend Pontius. Allow me to pass if you please."

Nobody was pleased to allow him to pass, and somebody boxed his ear with a waving hat as he pushed through the crush. And then the chanting was loud and close. "The Captain got rid of them! The Captain got rid of them!" And there was Captain Castello, being carried shoulder high, his jacket torn and his face blackened with powder, and wearing the smuggest grin the Reverend had ever seen. "Captain, have you fired your guns?" yelled Pontius. Castello gave a modest nod. "And are the white boats truly gone?"

Another modest nod. Or was it condescending? Women were crowding round the Captain, calling out ridiculous things like 'my hero!' and his nods became visibly less modest at all this adulation. The story of the Captain's triumph was being embroidered second by second for the benefit of those who had not been close enough to see at the time. The Captain had fired a gun. No, a *broadside*! Into the middle of the white boats it went, frightened them witless it did. Turned tail and ran, the lot of them, screaming for mercy they were. Such a brave man, our Captain. *Such* bravery! In the face of overwhelming odds… just him against all those boats, armed to the teeth they were. Bristling with cannon. But he saw them off, every last one of them.

Suddenly everything fell silent. Sailing in to the quay was the *Brothers Three*, with Rissa standing at the bow like a scarlet figurehead, glittering fishscales scattered over her skirts like sequins. "It's the lady warden!" Everyone had forgotten about Rissa's diplomatic mission in all the commotion.

The boat glided up to the quay, and people gasped when they saw the shot-damage. "The invaders have fired on our lady warden! Look at the boat! The scoundrels!"

With a thunderous look, Rissa gathered herself, and scrambled up the ladder, skirts or no skirts. People at the front of the crowd called out a commentary to those at the back. "Half the boat blown away! Ought to have sunk by rights! The lady is white as a sheet."

Castello looked warily at her and began, "We have seen off the invaders with our artillery, Lady. They must be cowards to have attacked an unarmed boat. But never fear, they are gone now."

Rissa was silent. Too silent, thought Castello. And then she asked, "How many shots did you fire, Captain?"

Castello thought this safe enough ground, and grinned at her. "One shot, Lady. We saw them off with just one beautifully aimed shot."

Rissa's face became a slightly darker shade than her gown. "Beautifully aimed, was it? Beautifully aimed right through the side of my boat, you nincompoop! The white boats didn't fire on us, *you* did. The shot came from here. I saw its exact trajectory as it whizzed past my nose!" Her voice had risen to a shout.

The grin slid off Castello's face, and Rissa turned to the men still carrying him on their shoulders. "Put that idiot down this minute."

He was deposited on the ground rather too quickly for comfort as everyone backed away from Rissa. They had all seen her in a rage before, and it was wise to give her plenty of sea room. The commentary was passed through the crowd again for the benefit of those at the back, though most of them could hear Rissa quite clearly for themselves. "Says he almost killed her, the dunderhead..." "Couldn't aim a cannon at a big barn door..." "A menace to decent folks..." "Says he's a puffed-up, self-important twit..." And so it went on. The Captain, to his credit, stood silent and shame-faced throughout, his great day lying in tattered ruins. It was Pontius that rescued him in the end, pushing through and taking him by the arm, just as Rissa discovered a dead mackerel entangled in her skirt and looked ready to beat the Captain about the head with it.

"Enough, Lady," said the Reverend, with more authority than he felt. "He's suffered mortification enough. Come, old friend." And he led Castello, who looked close to tears, away.

Well, there was plenty to gossip about that evening, for sure. The Captain had broken the lady's boat, and nearly the lady herself, too. Everyone laughed, but they also appreciated the enormity of it. How close they had come to losing their wise woman of the weather and ship warden. And how could they trust their captain of artillery now? Said Captain had retreated to the chapel with the Reverend Pontius in indecent haste, while Rissa stamped off to the great rock to assess the weather, with the parting shot that at least somebody round here should be displaying a little competence in the workplace.

Castello took up his old place on the pulpit steps, with his head in his hands. "I'm a failure," he said bitterly. "In the island's hour of need. A nincompoop. A joke. And I nearly killed my Rissa."

Pontius felt there was little he could say to comfort his friend in the face of these obvious truths, so he held his tongue. But then a thought struck him. "But, Captain, they went away. After your shot, even if your aim was a little out of true, the shiny boats went away. Perhaps you really did see them off, after all."

The Captain brightened. "Perhaps I did, Reverend. Perhaps I did. I need more gunnery practice, that's all."

Somehow, the Captain's sad statement of culpability was heard and transmitted all round the island. Not the part about being a failure and a nincompoop, but the part about having nearly killed *his* Rissa. This had not come from the Reverend, who would not have repeated a careless remark made in anguish, and he was righteously cross about it. "The damned walls have ears in this place," he muttered.

Castello lay awake, in torment. The juicy rumours about him and the warden had reached his ears, inevitably. They say he loves her... passionately regrets the cannon shot... she hasn't spoken to him since. All true, thought the Captain, sadly. Of course he loved her. He always had. Worshipped the ground she walked on, even when she was threatening to smack him in the face with a mackerel. He tried so hard to impress her, and it all went wrong time after time. And now she wouldn't even speak to him. Wouldn't even shout, swear or wave a fist at him. Rissa had retreated to the great rock and proceeded to ship-watch and predict the weather with her usual perfect accuracy. That magnificent woman in her scarlet gown. The Captain sighed.

On the plus side, it had been pointed out by others that the shiny ships had indeed disappeared after the cannon shot, and that he might have been responsible. Others said it was more likely the proximity of the fishingboat that did it. The jury was out on the matter, but Castello felt disgrace weighing heavily upon him. She will never be mine, now, he thought sadly. Never.

Chapter Four
Mother Culver's Archive

It was all unutterably peculiar. The Reverend Pontius, not being a native of the island, had long been used to the curious ability for double thinking that every islander had. Strange ships in the harbour, things appearing and disappearing, and all they can do is gossip about the Captain and the warden. Nobody seemed over-bothered about the shiny ships – they were gone, and that was that. Had nobody stopped to consider whether they might return, and do some real damage this time? Could they have been sizing the place up for a proper invasion? Why did no one on this island seem to give any consideration to past and future? Why was now all that seemed to matter to them? If you asked them about the past, they talked about the brandy barrels that once washed in. They remembered *that* all right. No wonder, thought Pontius, that he had such trouble convincing them of the benefits of the Spirit of the Sky. *That* spirit was most concerned with the future. The Spirit of the Sea was far more relevant to them: it concerned tonight's dinner. It was a puzzle to know what to do with them.

The Reverend shook himself out of this fruitless philosophical discussion and decided he must approach the whole thing a bit more scientifically. From the beginning, now. What was the history of it all? His own experience took him back only a few weeks, to the point when the two ships 'sailed through' the island. But had anything like this ever happened before? Long ago, maybe? How to find out?

The Reverend was getting into his stride now, and the answer was with him directly. Of course. Mother Culver, keeper of stories. Up until now, he had given her a wide berth, done no more than politely passed the time of day. She was an ancient woman, who might just possibly dabble in witchcraft. Not the sort of person a respectable parson should be seen with. She was neither respectable nor respectful, in his experience. When he had asked her to attend his services for the Spirit of the Sky, she had accused him of peddling mumbo-jumbo. Pontius had thought that a bit rich, coming from her, but had said no more. She was much cherished by the islanders, so he had decided to simply ignore her, and turn a blind eye to the whole thing.

However, keeper of stories she was. How far back did these histories go? Were they just made up so the gullible would bring her gifts? Was any of it likely to be reliable *evidence*? The Reverend did not know, but decided that these were testing times, and any port was worth a try in a storm.

Mother Culver was Rissa's closest neighbour on the southern end of the island, and the two were occasionally considered to be in cahoots, though no one could quite say how. The old woman gave Pontius a long considering look when he appeared at her hovel. "Ha, Reverend," she said quietly. "So it is you, indeed. I had thought to see you here soon."

Confound these people, thought Pontius. How the devil do they always know what you're thinking? "Mother," he said, as politely as he could. "You are faring well, I hope."

"Well," she said, simply. "But you, you wish to know histories, I divine."

The Reverend decided there was no purpose in beating about the bush, and began his enquiries directly. "You have heard the strange tales of our shiny ships, Mother. Is there anything in your histories that tells of anything similar happening? Maybe a long time ago?"

"Perhaps there is, Reverend."

Pontius realised this was likely to be a long interview, so he took a seat on a little stool. Was he going to have to go through all the old woman's mad stories to reach one or two little nuggets of doubtful fact? Probably. But it had to be done.

The Reverend looked up, and found Mother Culver staring most intently at him. This was very discomforting, for she had a gimlet eye, but after a short while he realised she was actually staring straight through him, seeing something else completely. Pontius had never heard any of Mother Culver's stories, and he was unprepared when she began to sing softly:

Come the ships on bright and summer's day
White of wing and curious of sail
Plunge they to the rocks in deadly way
Strike they must, as if at winter's gale…

"You just made that up, you cheeky old baggage!" exploded Pontius. But she had not heard him, and sang on.

Strike they must, but strike they never do
Gone they are within the blink of eye
Through they go, they sail the island through
See them, brother, to the east they fly…

She shook her head. Pontius thought she was laughing at him, and jumped to his feet, bristling with indignation. "You are nothing but a charlatan, Madam," he said furiously. "I'll have none of your rhymes!" And stamped off in a temper.

Mother Culver watched him go, wagging her head gently from side to side. "Mayhap you'll be back, Reverend," she said quietly.

"Poppycock," said the Reverend Pontius as he walked back to the chapel. "Poppycock," he repeated, more to reassure

37

himself than anything else. How could he have believed for one moment that the old crone would take him seriously? Well, he certainly wasn't about to take *her* seriously. No indeed. But on the other hand, could she have invented something so apposite, so quickly? Maybe she could, after years of making up such stuff to pay for her dinner. Either way, that line of enquiry was at an end.

But later, when he lay awake in the small hours, the Reverend had to admit there might just have been something in it. He couldn't remember all the words she had sung. He had been so furious. What was it that nagged him? *Strike they must, but strike they never do.* That sounded as though the whole thing was, well, a regular occurrence. And that other line, what was it? *They sail the island through.* And reappearing to the east, just as Old Billy had said. Nonsense, he thought, she knew what I had come for. She was making fun of me, that's all.

Rissa stood to attention on ship-watch. She had kept to herself since the debacle at the harbour. It had not been her job to go rushing out to sea in a smelly boat. But, blast it, they were such a lily-livered bunch, flapping about and gaping like a lot of beached codfish. No more of that, she told herself, I'll do my own job, and no more. To tell the honest truth, she had been badly frightened in the boat. She liked solid ground under her feet. Storm and tempest she could cope with, but not all that unruly rolling about that boats do. It had given her a horrid heaving feeling in the gizzards. Nasty. And, she had to admit, the arrival of the cannon shot had been a relief, in a way, curse that fool Castello. They had been approaching the shiny boats, and she had had no idea what to do next. She had seen the strange woman on the nearest boat very clearly. They were being challenged, and the next move would surely have been an attack. The *Brothers Three* had quite clearly been incapable of outmanoeuvring the strangers, which all seemed so fleet and responsive and quick to turn. Rissa was sure they would not have survived a confrontation. The breaking of their boat had at least provided the perfect excuse to forget the mission and turn for home. She was blameless and vindicated. People had said she was brave. Brave! If they had known of the terrible fear that had paralysed her, they wouldn't have called her brave. They'd have laughed behind her back, looked for the smallest error in her weather-watching, and called it confirmation. See, the lady warden has lost her nerve, she is no longer reliable. Rissa couldn't bear the thought, and worked diligently to ensure the perfection of her forecasts. She had discovered a great weakness within herself, and she liked it not at all, and had retreated to her little white house near the great rock. It was a perfect little house, with a wobbly roof and a storm porch on the lee side. Its windows faced west and east, with none on the south side, which would have been both draughty and constantly caked with salt. Some said it was scarcely roomy enough for Rissa and her considerable wardrobe of scarlet gowns, but she felt safe and happy there, even if the cupboards did bulge a bit.

Presently, a figure approached slowly. It was clearly her neighbour, Mother Culver. Oh no, thought Rissa. She really didn't fancy the idea of company, not right now

"That Pontius fellow was here," said Mother Culver, taking a seat on a convenient boulder. She was generally a woman of few words. None at all would have suited Rissa, just at this moment.

"Ah," she answered, at length, still carefully scanning the horizon. "And he wanted what?"

"Histories, of course," said Mother Culver, with a girlish giggle.

"He didn't like them?"

"No. Went off in a tantrum. Stamped his little foot, he did."

"What did he hope for? Information about the shiny ships,

I suppose."

"Yes. And I sang him the best song in the archive. Spot on, I thought. Didn't stay to hear the rest of it though, which he'd have liked better, I venture."

Chapter Five
The Wreck that Was

At the harbour, Captain Castello was inspecting his guns and castle. He had to do something to keep his mind off his troubles. But it wasn't helping greatly. Indeed, he was feeling even worse. The brave Captain rather liked to wallow in adversity, repeating his worries over and over to himself, and looking for new ones, too. For all that, he had to admit the artillery was in very good fettle. In his distress, he had cleaned and polished everything to perfection. The gun had come to no harm when it was fired, and actually seemed to have rather benefited from the exercise. This meant the Captain had cared for it and loaded it properly, which was good news, considering he had no idea how he had learned to do it.

Still, he was sitting on the gun's back, idly kicking it in the trunnions, and considering the shortcomings of the castle. If the shiny ships had fired back, the wall would have been demolished with one well-aimed shot. He preferred not to think of well-aimed shots, since he hadn't achieved one yet. And as for his living quarters…

He had never paid much attention to his home. Home! It was a room, and not a very bright or attractive one at that. It was built into the cliff behind the castle wall, perhaps starting life as a fisherman's store. And it was not suitable at all, not one bit. Not now. He had thought so much about Rissa. But what did he have to offer her? Nothing but a dingy dungeon behind a broken wall. She'd never leave her little white house for *that*, would she? Castello sighed, and sighed again. He sighed a lot, lately. And what worldly goods had he to offer? Two cannon and a musket. And a wooden sea chest full of musty old clothes he had picked up at a ship sale. He must take a proper look at it. Take an inventory. Smarten things up. Then the idea hit him.

"I must rebuild!" he said aloud. "Make a proper castle, with proper battlements. And proper living quarters, with draperies and comforts and cushions. That's what I must do."

The Captain had no idea how he would do it, or with what materials, but he knew this was the way forward, he felt it in his bones. Surely the people would help, now that they had seen the danger of invasion. He must persuade them that a proper castle was just what they needed for their future safety and security. This was a good defensive position, with its back to the wall of the cliff, and was worth developing. Something altogether more impressive was needed than the present arrangement. If it was impressive enough, the white boats would hesitate to attack, or even come into the harbour ever again. If it at least looked as if it held lots of artillery, the island would look capable of defending itself. He would draw up a plan and set it before them. And Rissa would be impressed, wouldn't she? Might she not be tempted by the possibility of becoming the lady of a proper castle? Castello risked a small smile.

The chapel bell was ringing erratically through the sound of the storm. The Reverend Pontius, who had been visiting a sick parishioner, broke into an undignified run at the sound, with his heart in the grip of great fear, and his hat clamped firmly onto his head. What now? Had the shiny ships returned? He hoped they had not, with all his being. In the bell tower, which doubled as his living quarters, he found a small girl clinging frantically to the bell rope, and being jerked off her feet between clangs. She had kicked his little table over and broken his best basin. "What is it, Marila?" he yelled over the din. "What's happened? Come down off that." And he set her on her feet.

"A ship-wreck, Reverendness. A real one this time."

The Spirit of the Sky be devoutly thanked for *that* small mercy, thought Pontius, still in a panic.

"Where has it come ashore? Tell me!"

"Under the pinnacle, the lady says."

Damnation, thought Pontius, it's such a long climb down there. Marila made to start ringing the bell again, but Pontius stopped her. "I'll see to that, or you'll be breaking your neck, or the rest of my furniture. Go and tell your family – tell everyone you meet where the ship is to be found, and that it's real this time. Tell them I said so." Let's hope it *is* real this time, or my reputation's shot to pieces, thought Pontius as the girl sped off, and he began ringing the bell again.

Everyone was soon turned out on wreck-duty and, on arriving at the cliff top, all were relieved to see a very real barque battering herself to pieces on the rocks below. The two surviving crewmembers were relieved, too, when they were hauled ashore. By the time the rescue was complete it was nearly dark, and it was generally agreed that the picking-over of wreckage could wait until the morning. Several brandy barrels had washed in and everyone was looking forward to a jolly evening of celebration.

The survivors and the brandy barrels were manhandled up the cliff equally carefully, and soon everyone was gone except Captain Castello and the Reverend Pontius. The Captain retrieved his musket from a niche in the cliff and they set off up the path together.

The wreck had given Castello an idea. He felt ready to confide in his friend, and so happily agreed to come into the chapel and take a nip of the brandy that would already be waiting in a little flask. Even a summer storm could leave you chilled to the bone, after all. The two of them sat

43

appreciatively sipping the brandy and enjoying its comforting interior warmth while the wind rattled through the belfry, causing an occasional soft, tinny clunk from the bell. They sipped, but both knew perfectly well that just about everyone else on the island would be pouring the stuff down their gullets by the mug full, and were unlikely to be up and about much before midday tomorrow. They also knew that there was a fairly free and easy first-come-first-served custom, as far as wreckage collecting was concerned, on the understanding that everyone took only what they really needed.

Castello rarely took much from wrecks at all, and so he thought himself entitled to get to this one early and take his pick of anything worth having. He did have a need for it, after all, and he told the Reverend of his great plan to extend and rebuild the castle for the security of the island. And, who knows, he said shyly, to provide him one day with married quarters. To that end, any stout timbers that washed ashore might come in very useful, and maybe even some of the cargo, if there was anything worth having... but he couldn't manage these things alone. Would the Reverend be so kind as to assist? Pontius smiled sympathetically. It was good to see his friend, who been so low and downcast, sparkling with enthusiasm for this new plan. Of course he would help. They talked on until Rissa suddenly put her head round the door, a little dishevelled, and announced that the wind was dropping, and it would be fine in the morning, and she was going home to bed, so there. The door slammed and she was gone. Pontius and Castello were left staring at each other. Calm weather and a fine day in prospect. Perfect. They left the brandy flask unfinished and agreed to meet at the pinnacle at dawn.

Castello barely slept, and was up before first light. Rissa's weather forecast was proving accurate, he was pleased to note, and he headed for the quay. The brandy had done its work, and there was no sign of anyone else at all. The Captain set about borrowing a boat. There was just enough breeze for a sail. It would be the easiest way of carrying back anything he might find at the wreck. He was a good sailor, though he rarely needed to use his skills, and soon he was heading out of the harbour and skirting the eastern side of the island, which was the safest way to get where he was going. He was enjoying the freedom of it, watching the tip of the sun appearing on the horizon and knowing he was taking the first step towards achieving his goal. Nonetheless, he hoped fervently that he didn't bump into any shiny ships. Not now, please. He took the boat close in to the southern tip of the island, safe enough today, and caught a glimpse of an astonished Rissa coming out of her house. The Captain gave her a smart salute, and sailed on.

At the pinnacle, he found Pontius already waiting and busy tending to a body that had washed ashore. Castello made the boat fast, and clambered ashore to assist. When everything was properly done, they looked around at the wreckage. There were certainly lots of timbers in surprisingly good condition, some of them with iron fittings, which was even better. Castello was just wondering aloud how to transport these to the boat when something caught his eye. Wedged between the rocks, high and dry, was a bronze cannon. He gave a gasp of delighted disbelief. How many times had he seen a wreck and thought bitterly of the beautiful ordnance and shot that had surely sunk straight to the bottom of the ocean, beyond reach forever? He was at the gun's side in a moment, laying hands on it to be sure it was real. It was perfectly real, and apparently undamaged and, what's more, its wooden gun carriage was still loosely attached. He sat on the rock and let his imagination run away. Himself, resplendent, in charge of three cannon. Did that count as a broadside? It does, it must! A real force to be reckoned with. And worth rebuilding a castle for, was it not? He tore himself away from the beautiful gun. He and the Reverend couldn't possibly move it alone; it would have to wait until the island got over its collective hangover. Still, the cannon wasn't going anywhere. He'd stand guard over it if he had to. Castello looked around in a state of deep satisfaction with his lot. "The Spirit of the Sky is truly with me today!" he said.

Meanwhile, the Reverend Pontius had spied a large trunk afloat. He had managed to grapple it alongside the rock he was precariously perched on, and shouted to Castello to come and assist. "Reverend, you'll never guess what I've found," said the Captain, bursting with his news.

"Never mind that," said Pontius breathlessly, cutting him short. "Help me with this trunk."

Castello came and looked. It was a strong piece, for sure. Expensive. Worth having for itself. A bit of a clean up and it would look well in his imagined married quarters. So he swallowed his great news, and worked with the Reverend to haul the thing ashore.

The sun was high up, and one or two figures were beginning to appear on the cliff top by the time they had the trunk secure. The pair of them sat down on it and mopped their brows, before taking a fortifying swig from the Reverend's brandy flask. Still, it was a job well done. Castello considered the next move, and decided he must empty the trunk if they were to have any chance of getting it onto the boat. It was securely locked, but he had brought tools and was sure he could open it without undue damage. The Captain took his time over the job, while Pontius took a breather. It was such a beautiful trunk, and he really didn't want to damage it. The question was, had the water got inside it and spoiled its contents? At length the lock was undone, and Pontius came to help lift the lid. The trunk was full to the brim with rich fabrics. Out came, one after another, hangings so richly coloured and embroidered with gold thread that they seemed to have a natural glow all their own. Castello stared in amazement. The weight of them was astonishing. No wonder the trunk had seemed so heavy. He and Pontius laid them carefully in the trunk's open lid. None of them seemed to have any water damage at all, and the trunk was quite dry inside. Astounding! At the very bottom of all this was something encased in a fine bag. They lifted it out and opened it. Inside was a scarlet uniform with golden epaulettes. A military man's uniform. Castello gasped at the sheer finery of it.

"The Spirit of the Sky surely meant this for you, my friend," said Pontius.

As the day progressed, the items of the wreck were removed to safety. Bleary-eyed, the islanders wandered down in ones and twos, and lent a hand. Castello insisted on taking the trunk and its indescribably precious contents round to the quay in the boat himself. No one else, to be honest, set much store by it, when he said, truthfully, that it was full of wall hangings. Most of the islanders would have preferred a box of good blankets, in all honesty, and were happy to let the Captain take the trunk away. Another boat was brought to carry the larger timbers round to the castle, and all the smaller broken fragments of timber were carried off to join the communal heap of wood available for repairs and winter fuel. Nothing, but nothing, was ever allowed to go to waste. There were some useful bits of spar and rigging from the unfortunate ship, and they were soon pressed into service in order to move the cannon and its gun carriage. They were resourceful people, these islanders, and they had soon rigged up a little crane to hoist the gun carriage out of its resting place. It was stoutly made, and nothing too important had been broken, and it could be trundled up the cliff one way or another. However, as evening drew on, it was decided it was now too late to move the cannon. Castello was distraught, convinced it would evaporate in his absence, and ultimately announced he could not leave it and would be spending the night beside it. So the gallant Captain slept among the rocks under a tarpaulin, with his arm round the cannon, dreaming of himself standing

47

beside the splendid gun in a scarlet uniform, a lady in a scarlet gown beside him, gazing up adoringly.

Mother Culver's histories were generally regarded as cracking entertainment, and little else. The notion of history was not a great presence in the collective island understanding. That was the whole problem, of course, thought the Reverend Pontius to himself as he approached her hovel once more. No one here took much notice of the passage of time. Once people reached adulthood they simply stopped counting years, and when they reached an advanced state of decrepitude, they were counted as old. As simple as that. How on earth, thought the Reverend, am I supposed to instil a proper respect for the hereafter in people who pay so little attention to time? These ideas had occurred to the Reverend many times, but this was the first time he had regarded the islanders' attitude as anything other than a confounded nuisance and minor obstacle. Now, he realised, it was dangerous. If you kept no history, you were never forewarned. You were always unprepared for the future. And so, reluctantly, he had decided to try once more to get some sense from Mother Culver. She had seen him coming from some distance, and was waiting. Wisely, he had brought her a gift, a little flask of brandy he had set aside, and she had fallen upon it with rather unseemly delight, the Reverend thought. He sat down and tried to be as companionable as possible.

"Tell me, Mother," he said, "that rhyme you sang me when last we met…"

"The song from the archive, you mean?"

"The archive?"

"Yes," said Mother Culver. "The archive. Passed down from one keeper of stories to another, it is, down all the years."

"And just how many years old is this, um, song?"

Mother Culver regarded him quietly. Was the fellow mad? No one knew such things. The archive just was. The songs just were. At length she said, "No idea."

Pontius tried to contain his irritation. Think like a detective. Ask obvious questions first. "You did not witness a coming of the white boats yourself, before now?"

"I did not."

"Was it in your predecessor's time, perhaps?"

"I know nothing of that. I only know the songs of the archive."

Pontius felt he was going round in circles, and began to suspect she was making fun of him again. But he pressed on. "Do you know if this has happened many times before?"

"You must ask the hermit. He knows more."

The Reverend sighed. Blind leading the blind, he thought, and back to the beginning. It had scarcely been worth the gift of brandy. He rose to leave, trying to think of a civil word of farewell, but she stopped him.

"There is more of the song, Reverend. You did not stay to hear it last time."

Pontius hesitated, and she began to stare at him in that disconcerting way again, and then softly sang:

Come another day, they come once more
Turning in the harbour circles wide
Race they as the dolphins race before
The bow of boat a-punching of the tide…

Oh brother, though your heart is full of fear
See them close and clear or see them not
A champion of the island shall appear
And see them off with single lucky shot…

This was such a perfect description of the appearance of the white boats in the harbour, that he again thought she was making it up, and stomped off despite his resolution to hear her out.

49

"But Reverend, there's more…" called Mother Culver after him, not very loudly. But Pontius didn't stop. He'd heard enough. His heart pounding with fury – or was it disappointment – he headed home.

Chapter Six
Fort Resolute

Unaware that he had just been described as a Champion of the Island, Captain Castello had all the reclaimed articles – he jibbed at the word 'booty' – neatly stashed at the castle. Even the cannon. Oh, especially the cannon. Comfortably seated on its carriage it needed only to be cleaned and polished and it would be ready for action. The Captain was tempted to jump straight in and start cleaning it up, but he restrained himself, deciding that a full inventory of everything he had brought back would be the proper methodical approach. Once he knew what he had to work with, he could start on his plans for a new, improved castle. So he patted the cannon affectionately on its bronze behind, and went to find a scrap of paper and a measuring stick.

Who would have thought, Castello said to himself, later, that so much timber could be contained in one not very large ship? And that so much of it could survive more or less intact? It was good oak, too, and not at all wormy or splintered. No wonder Ligo the fisherman had needed to make so many trips to bring it all back. And, among other wonders, Ligo had found a timber with the ship's brass bell still attached. There were a few dents in it, but nothing serious, and Castello was thrilled. Another warning bell for the south of the island. And something beautiful to polish. It was inscribed *Resolute*.

Lots of ironwork had been brought back attached to timbers, too. How had that survived? It would all need careful attention to prevent it rusting. But that was the Captain's speciality, and he smiled happily in anticipation. He had, of course, given the pick of the spars and rigging to the fishermen for repair of their boats, but there were oddments left over, and he listed them carefully. And then there was the trunk. But he would save contemplation of that until it was dark. For now, there was much work to do.

His first and most urgent job was to attend to all the metalwork, and he set himself to polish and preserve it all. As he worked, he began the plans in his head, thinking through the best ways to use the materials he had and, looking at the beautiful bell, a splendid idea struck him. "I shall call this new castle Fort Resolute, after the ship that made it possible," he said aloud. He really liked the sound of that. Captain Castello, commander of Fort Resolute.

When darkness fell, and his eyes strained, Castello retreated to his room, and stood looking at the trunk. He opened it, reverently, and took out the glorious golden wall hangings, one by one. They were even more beautiful by candlelight. "Make any room look like a palace," he murmured. "Even this one." And he held one of the hangings carefully up against the wall.

At last, he came to the bag containing the precious uniform. He had insisted on the trunk being moved with everything inside it just as it had been found. How he had shouted at Ligo for nearly dropping it! But here it all was, safe and sound. He took out the uniform, breathlessly. It was so unlikely to fit him, but he was handy with a needle (again, he had no idea how he had acquired such a skill) and he was sure it could be adjusted. Gingerly he picked up the gorgeous scarlet jacket, and slipped it on. A little on the large side, maybe, he reckoned, but not very much. The quality of the cloth, the stitching, the style, were exquisite and expensive. What manner of man had this belonged to? Had he perished aboard the *Resolute*, or was he in some port awaiting its arrival?

No matter, thought Castello, I shall wear it with pride. He set the glowing coat aside, and burrowed into the bag, finding breeches, finely made shirts, boots and a hat. They were all admired in turn, and then carefully repacked. As he lifted the bag to return it to the trunk, something caught his eye at the bottom of the box. Another bag, slender this time. Castello opened it and drew out a sword, complete with belt and scabbard. An officer's sword. Speechless, he drew the blade along his finger, immediately drawing blood. It bites, then, he thought. The blood flowed, and he flapped about, careful not to get it on any of the clothes or hangings. "I am doubly, triply blessed," he said contentedly. "And resolute."

Rissa was shouting at the top of her voice as Mother Culver approached the little white house by the great rock. She had come out to her washing line and found a wild goat eating her best underskirt. The washing-prop was the nearest weapon that came to hand, and she brought it down smartly on the beast's rump. The goat trotted a few steps, then turned and stared insolently, a trail of scarlet fabric dangling from the side of its mouth. Rissa moved forward, menacingly, and at length the animal turned, still chewing, and trotted off down the cliff path in no particular hurry. Seeing Mother Culver, she replaced the prop under the line and inspected the tattered remains of the skirt.

"Ruined! That brute will end its days in a cooking pot, if I have my way."

The old woman took a seat on a rock. "Your Castello is mightily pleased with the wreck, I hear."

"He's not *my* Castello," said Rissa, warily. "You have news of the wreck, do you?" She had not gone down to the pinnacle, this time. In fact, she could hardly bear to look in case the wretched boat had turned out to be unreal again. People would bring news of it, soon enough, and so they had. Two crewmen rescued, one in a bad way, two bodies washed

53

ashore. The Captain down at the wreck at the crack of dawn gathering timbers and goodness knows what else. She had regretted her harsh words to him after the fiasco at the harbour. Still, she thought, you could be forgiven for getting a bit shirty when you've nearly been cut in two by a cannonball, however good the intentions behind firing it.

"Well, whosoever he belongs to, he's strutting about down at the castle in a fancy hat, and says we must all call it Fort... what was it? Yes, Fort Resolute. All on account of a few pieces of timber and another gun."

"*Another* gun?" said Rissa. "Something else to be a menace to decent folks with, I suppose!"

Nonetheless, she couldn't help a tiny smile. How like Castello to make such a meal of a few bits of wreckage. Still, she thought, it'll keep him happy. The knowledge of his sad despair had weighed upon her. He does his best, after all. It's just a shame he makes such a muck of it.

Mother Culver was obviously in a gossiping mood. "They say he slept all night down under the pinnacle with that gun. Refused to leave it. And he brought back a trunk, too. Gave Ligo a princely dressing down, he did, when the fellow dropped it. Told everyone it was full of cloth hangings, and they let him keep it, but no one knows for sure what's in it. I'll warrant that Pontius does, though. Thick as thieves, those two."

Thick as thieves. There was an idea, now. If Rissa wanted to let it be known that she had forgiven Castello his mistake, which she did, a word in the Reverend's ear, subtle-like, would be a good place to start. She didn't want to tell the Captain herself, publicly, but she knew that bad feeling among the guardians was bad for the island. At least, that's what she told herself.

Mother Culver was still musing about the trunk. "Very heavy they said it was. Could be full of gold bars, some say, for what use that would be to him here. Going to build his fancy fort out of gold bars, is he?"

"Now, Mother," said Rissa. "The Captain's a bit pompous at times, but he's not a liar. You shouldn't spread that sort of gossip." Mother Culver said nothing to this, but nodded very knowingly.

At the castle, that is to say, the Fort, the Captain was also considering the contents of the new trunk. The rich hangings were infinitely more precious to him than gold and, if he were honest, the uniform and sword most precious of all. He had been unable to resist the temptation of going out wearing the fabulous hat with its golden cockade, and of selecting a piece of timber on which to inscribe 'Fort Resolute, work in progress'. Both these changes had been duly noted by passers-by, and Castello had decided this was now the time to unveil his plans for the new fort to a grateful populace. The Reverend Pontius had encouraged him, and assured him the islanders would support the new initiative. But now that it came to it, the Captain's courage rather failed him. He would visit Pontius, show him the full revised plan, ask his advice, and probably ignore it, and then enlist his support in presenting the whole thing after Sunday prayers.

The Reverend Pontius was having a busy day. The Captain had arrived early and used up most of the morning in presenting his rather overblown plans for the new, improved castle. Still, the Reverend had to admit that Castello had done a thorough job. Apart from the timber retrieved from the wreck, he had toured the island and commandeered every loose block of stone and brick available and had them all conveyed down to the castle. Every piece had been measured, labelled and listed to show where it fitted into the plan.

The Captain's plan showed a semi-circular gun platform, to be built using the stone from the old wall, which was to be demolished, and trimmed with oddments of brick. With three guns, he reasoned, he could cover every entry point into the harbour. Pontius thought that the Captain's ability to aim the guns might be the weakness in this strategy, but he kept the thought to himself. The timbers of the *Resolute* would form a substantial protective stockade between the guns, and last, but not least, there was to be a new house close by the gun platform. The house was a good size larger than most on the island. Castello said this was necessary for receiving visiting dignitaries. The fact that visiting dignitaries were as rare as hens' teeth seemed to have passed under the Captain's radar. "We must look as though we mean business!" as he said more than once. In return for the islanders' help in realising this plan, Castello would train three gun crews to man the cannon, with proper drills and practice twice a week. One of the rescued sailors from the wreck had said he could obtain supplies of powder and shot, to be exchanged for salted fish, so they could afford some practice.

Pontius really couldn't fault the plan, the meticulous use of available materials, or the look of raging enthusiasm on his friend's face. But he was worried. Supposing the islanders wouldn't help, wouldn't let the Captain have his fabulous fort? Wouldn't swap fish for cannon shot? It would destroy him utterly. Then, thought the Reverend, as Castello left, I must see that they do!

The Reverend was just steeling himself for a return visit to Rufus, as suggested by Mother Culver, when Rissa put her head round the chapel door. They hadn't spoken for a while, and they greeted each other formally. Castello had left his plans spread on a pew, and Rissa eyed them curiously. "What's this, Reverend?" she asked.

"This," said Pontius, "is the Captain's plan for his new fort."

Rissa stared. She couldn't help it, she was impressed. The attention to detail was amazing. "I hope it comes true for him," she said without thinking.

"I hope it comes true for us all," said Pontius. "A fort with three cannon, properly manned, would bring us security, would it not?"

"Indeed, Reverend."

They regarded each other gravely for a few moments, the islander and the offcomer. Both were wondering if the other could be trusted. Pontius was the first to take the plunge. "Lady, I beg you not to speak against this plan. The Captain is a good man. He will work tirelessly, and he will secure the island for us. I know he can be vain and silly – which of us is perfect? – but he needs a purpose, and this is an excellent one. We will present the plan to everyone after prayers on Sunday. The people listen to you. If you say it is sound, they will accept it. I myself shall speak in favour of it."

Rissa considered. "I will think about it, Reverend. I do not know yet whether I shall speak in favour of the plan, but I shall not speak against it. I promise you neutrality, at least."

Pontius bowed politely. Rissa prepared to leave, and then turned. "Oh, and if you should see the Captain, please tell him he is forgiven for nearly shooting my head off. It's a mistake anybody could make."

Chapter Seven
The Prophecy

A bramble had snagged the Reverend's coat as he stumbled along the cliff path to see Rufus. "Damn and blast the thing!" he muttered as he tried to unhook it. His language had really deteriorated this last few weeks. Five minutes later there was a tear in his coat and he had dropped the offering of bread and cheese he had brought for the hermit. One of the island goats had appeared and made advances on the food. Still hooked up, Pontius had waved his arms about in an attempt to chase the animal off, and that was how the tear had happened. He managed to rescue the cheese, but the goat made a sudden dash and grabbed the bread, running off up the nearly sheer cliff with it. "I have brought you some bread and cheese," he said to the hermit, when he reached the end of the path. "Well, some cheese, anyway. There was a goat..."

"Ah," said Rufus. "Never mind, Reverend."

"I wanted to speak to you about the white boats," said Pontius, getting straight to the point.

"Ah," said Rufus, again, unhelpfully. "And what does the Spirit of the Sky say on the subject?"

"Very little," said Pontius, truthfully. "However, Mother Culver..."

"Yes," said Rufus, "I heard you had visited the good Mother."

There was nothing very good about her, Pontius thought. She was an evil old bag, and a witch to boot, quite likely.

However, she had said, and sung, some disturbing things.

"She sang to me," said Pontius, glad that Rufus could not see the worried expression that was undoubtedly settling on his face.

"She does that," said Rufus.

"Do you set any store by these songs of hers, by the archive, as she calls it?"

"Oh, yes," said Rufus. "All true, in general."

"It seems… that is to say… I couldn't quite make out…" Pontius struggled to find the right question. "I got the impression, from the songs, that the white ships have come here before. Do you know if that is true?"

"Oh, yes," said Rufus. "Not in my time, of course. But, yes, they have come before. And again, I expect."

"Again?" said Pontius, aghast. "Could you be a bit more specific?"

"This is not the only 'now'," said Rufus slowly. "There are many. Sometimes they overlap a little, the Spirit of the Sea says."

The Spirit of the Sky forgive me, thought the Reverend, but I shall strangle him if he goes off into one of his whimsies. More than one 'now'? What on earth could it mean?

"This is the crossing point, come to us again," said Rufus, conversationally. "Between one now and another. It happens, er, *now and again*."

These islanders will be the death of me, thought Pontius. How he wished himself back having a nice practical talk about bricks and mortar with Castello. "What must I do, colleague?" he asked, defeated.

"Why, seek out Mother Culver. Be sure to hear it all. Contain your impatience. All is well."

I am careering back and forth across this island like a shuttle in a loom, thought the Reverend Pontius, crossly. But would the warp and weft he produced show a pattern that made sense of it all, that was the question. Whatever the answer, he was pretty sure Rufus was wrong. All is not well. Not well at all. Not by a long chalk. The Reverend was a worried man. Half way to Mother Culver's, he realised he was still clutching the cheese he had taken for Rufus, and forgotten to put down. Ah, well, it would do equally as a gift for the old woman. His interview with Rufus had upset his equilibrium, as usual. All that stuff about multiple 'nows' was very unsettling. Surely now was now, and that was that. Nonetheless, he had to admit that the white boats resembled nothing he had seen or heard of. There was something about them that seemed to belong to another time. And all that sudden appearing and disappearing. Not what things normally did in the here and now *he* was familiar with. And why was the Spirit of the Sky, who so often answered his questions in his prayers or in his sleep, so silent? Just as if he had been blocked off, he thought.

On reaching Mother Culver's, Pontius handed over the cheese, rather shamefacedly, for the wrappings had been torn, and there was the hint of a goat's tooth mark on one side. Rufus would have been none the wiser, but the old woman looked askance at it. She took it anyway, and it vanished into her apron pocket.

"Well, Reverend," she said at length. "Would you hear the end of the song, then?"

"If you please," said Pontius, quietly, unable to meet her eye. "The hermit recommends it."

"Ha! Does he, now?" she said vehemently. There was no love lost between Mother Culver and Rufus. She believed she was entitled to be a guardian of the island, too, on account of the archive. He used her like a servant, she thought, sending people down to her for answers. Had he not the answers to these questions himself? No? Then who should be guardian, of the two of them? She should, of course. But the Reverend, looking very discomfited, was still awaiting his song, so she began to sing.

Come they thrice, oh come they one time more
Bring forth your champion, set him to the fore
The means to keep us safe within him lies
By giving of himself in sacrifice

Forget, forget, forget, time out of mind
For many a year you will not see their kind.
But now and then the island wakes from sleep
To please the spirit of the boundless deep

Boundless deep? And anyway, it's not boundless, thought Pontius, irrelevantly. It has edges. It's just big. These islanders, they think that just because they can't see anything but sea around them, that it goes on forever. Have all my geography classes fallen on stony ground? He struggled to bring his mind to bear on the matter in hand.

What could it all mean? Trying to make sense of this stuff was like having your brains pickled in vinegar, packed in like a jar of samphire. "Is that a history, Mother?" said Pontius, slowly. "Or a prophecy?"

Mother Culver wagged her head contentedly. "Both, brother."

The Reverend was even more worried now. What was that alarming part about the champion of the island – Castello, if he wasn't mistaken – sacrificing himself to save us? He certainly wasn't going to tell *that* to the Captain. And if the song were to be believed, the white boats would return, perhaps soon. True or not, he was damned if he was going to be caught unprepared. Even less would he let his friend be caught unprepared, and he set off directly for the harbour.

Passing the time of day over the garden fence was not the sort of activity that Captain Castello normally indulged in.

61

Still, as he remarked to Ralham, his neighbour, these were not normal times. It was as if the island and its inhabitants had been given a shaking. Old certainties, solid until a few weeks ago, seemed to have melted and shifted. Ralham wholeheartedly agreed. It had long been understood that he would marry his other neighbour's daughter. But now he just wasn't sure that it was the right thing to do. She was a charming girl, no denying it. But things had changed with the coming of the white boats. Horizons broadened. "In fact," he said, "I'm with you, Captain. I want to learn to fire the guns. Make the island safe."

Castello was delighted with this show of solidarity. He had thought the hardest part of his great plan would be to persuade the islanders that it was worth giving up time and effort to guard against something that might never happen. And here was somebody volunteering without even being asked. The Captain began to explain his great plan to his new ally, embellished with a few glimpses of future glorious battle, victorious and without loss, naturally. Ralham listened, entranced, and Castello was about to go in and fetch his drawings, to demonstrate the layout of the gun platform, when he saw the Reverend Pontius, looking cross and dishevelled, approaching in haste.

"Here comes another supporter for our cause," said Castello genially, grinning, but the smile fell off his face when he saw that it was not annoyance on the Reverend's face, but intense anxiety.

"Captain," said Pontius, breathlessly, "a word with you. Will you excuse us, Master Ralham?"

All the way down the hill, the Reverend had struggled to decide what to say to his friend. It was imperative that he should not dwell on the detail of Mother Culver's predictions either to Castello himself, or to anyone else. Especially not to anyone else. If the islanders drew the same conclusion, that Castello was the island's saviour, but only through self-sacrifice, well, they might encourage him to take reckless chances. Walk into the very jaws of death. He simply could not let that happen, whatever the cost. If Castello were lost, he, Pontius, would be alone. There, that was the nub of it. Selfishness, not concern. He could not face a future on this desolate rock without a friend. What the Spirit of the Sky would say, he did not know. But since the spirit seemed to be on an extended leave of absence at the moment, he set the thought aside. The important thing was to see that all was prepared for the third coming of the shiny ships. He still struggled to find the right words.

"Castello, old friend, how goes progress on your plan?"

"Well enough," said Castello. "But your reverence didn't run all the way down the hill to ask me that. Here." He ushered Pontius into his room, and found a seat for him. The Reverend mopped his brow, took a few deep breaths, and calmed himself.

"No, indeed. I have come to warn you. There is a... a prophecy. It says the white boats will return to us once more."

"A prophecy, brother? What prophecy? Since when have you set store by prophecies?" Castello was alarmed. This was not like the Reverend at all. "Do you mean this is a prophecy from the Spirit of the Sky?"

"If only it were," said Pontius, and buried his head in his hands.

"Not from the spirit? Then from where?"

Pontius looked up, and Castello was horrified to see there were tears in his eyes. "The Spirit of the Sky has forsaken me. All I have to work with are the islanders' mad stories." Castello opened his mouth to pooh-pooh such tales, but Pontius stopped him. "This prophecy foretold the first two visits of the white ships. Very clearly, Captain. There is no mistake. And it says they will come once more. I beg you will pay attention and give it credence."

"The shiny boats will come again? When?"

"I do not know. The prophecy is vague as to timing. But come they will, I truly believe."

They stared at each other. "Must I go and hear this prophecy, then?" asked Castello, perplexed.

Absolutely he must not go and hear it, thought Pontius. "No need, friend, no need. The important thing is that we must be prepared. At least this time we are warned."

"Yes," said Castello, slowly, thinking that a little more detail would have been extremely welcome. What *could* they do against these invaders?

Pontius thought it important to keep the Captain's mind off the prophecy and on the anti-invasion preparations. "Yes," he said firmly, straightening his back, "we must make a plan."

A plan. This was something the Captain could do, and he put his mind to it directly. "Well, with your permission, Reverend, I will present my plans for the development of Fort Resolute after prayers on Sunday as we intended. The rebuilding works may have to be postponed, but we can start training our gun crews immediately. There is space for our new gun as things are, and the sooner our men are trained, the better for us all. Ralham has already volunteered."

The Reverend would have fallen on his knees to thank the Spirit of the Sky for this positive response, if he had thought anybody was listening.

"Yes, Captain, that is just the thing. Just the thing. And tell me, is Ligo's boat fully repaired following its, um, accident last time?"

"It is," said Castello. "Perhaps we could strengthen it a bit. Add a little more cover for the crew, in case we need to go out into the harbour again. Maybe equip a second boat as support. Lineus' boat, the *Mergoose*, perhaps."

"Splendid," said Pontius. "This is all good. The sooner the better. I know I need not ask you if your guns and shot are prepared."

Castello bowed his head modestly. Of course they were.

"Reverend, I must begin work on this immediately. There is no time to be lost. I shall go and commandeer a working party to tend to the boats. And we may be able to use some of the timbers from the wreck to shore up the castle wall. I hope I may tell them I have your blessing in this venture."

"Of course you may," said Pontius, close to tears again. "Oh, and, Captain," he called as Castello made to dash out of the door, "The lady says she forgives you for the cannon shot. I think she may speak in your favour on Sunday." A big soppy smile spread across Castello's face, and then he was through the door and gone.

The Reverend Pontius saw himself out and walked slowly along the quay, trying to arrange his thoughts. What to do next? It was important in these trying times, he thought, that the four guardians should work together, as far as possible. Of the four, the only one who might be unaware of the prophecy was Rissa. Rufus always seemed to know everything anyway. So the Reverend's next job was to see that the lady warden was fully informed: she might need to increase her little tribe of lookouts. He sighed and set off on the long trudge back up the hill. Perhaps, he thought, she already knew of this 'song' of Mother Culver's. She and the old woman were quite close and spoke frequently. But surely she would have said something? But then, no, Rissa was an islander. She may well have heard the song and taken it no more seriously than anyone else had.

Pontius was loath to be the one to bring her this disturbing news, but it was important that she should understand the urgency. Could he get away with leaving out the part about the champion of the island? He would try to, he decided, as he puffed along the steep track.

On the southernmost tip of the island, Rissa was compiling her evening forecast, and making her final watch for lost ships as the sun sank. It was clear and set fair – very pleasant weather, and she was just telling this to her runner so the word could be spread to everyone, when she spotted the Reverend Pontius approaching. Here comes the Reverend, *again*, she thought. Something in his demeanour put her on guard, and she sent the lad off with the weather forecast directly.

"Lady, I must speak with you," said Pontius, unhappily. "You may know… there is a prophecy afoot. The white boats are fated to come back a third time. We must all make ready." There was a long space while Rissa digested this. If she knew the full content of the prophecy, her face did not betray it.

"Coming when?" she said at length.

"I do not know, but perhaps soon. You will want to warn your lookouts, no doubt. The Captain is already making preparations. We must not be caught off guard."

Rissa's eyebrow shot up at mention of the Captain. "I have told him of your forgiveness, Lady. He is heartened."

She gave an inscrutable little smile. "I will strengthen the lookout, Reverend, and make sure there are runners ready to inform everyone. Leave it to me."

Pontius bowed, and without another word, turned wearily homewards. The moment he was out of sight, Rissa walked determinedly into the gathering darkness, heading for Mother Culver's house. She was sure the old woman must be the source of this prophecy, and sensed that the Reverend was not telling her the whole story. There was only one way to get to the bottom of this mystery.

Mother Culver was surprised to find the warden at her garden gate so late in the day. Rissa pressed a little vial of brandy into the old woman's hand. "Now, Mother," she said, "sing me the song you sang the Reverend. All of it." And she folded her arms expectantly.

It was full dark when Rissa strode along the path to the hermit's cliff. A true islander, she thought nothing of walking by a sheer drop at this time of night. Normally, she would scarcely give Rufus the time of day, the old scoundrel, but this was different. He had the ear of the Spirit of the Sea, and she needed an answer from that entity. The hermit was actually surprised to see her – a first time for everything, she thought – but listened quietly while she repeated the essence of Mother Culver's song. Rissa had come to the same conclusion as the Reverend Pontius: that Castello was the 'Champion of the Island' who must sacrifice himself to save them.

"So the question is, colleague," she said, "must this be? What does the spirit say?"

Rufus had a long think, so long that she thought he had fallen asleep, and nudged his elbow.

"Just resting my eyes, Lady," he said testily. What nonsense, thought Rissa. He hasn't got any eyes.

"The spirit says there is more than one kind of self-sacrifice, and that it will happily accept any variety. Do not fear, Lady. All is well."

"Is that all you can tell me, colleague?" she asked. But he really had fallen asleep this time.

Chapter Eight
The *Brothers Three* and the Great Bird

The sermon that Sunday was necessarily brief, and very well attended indeed. The chapel was packed with people unable to move their elbows, or sitting on each other's laps. Standing room only, in fact. If only, thought the Reverend Pontius, resignedly, it was so full every week. Secrets were very hard to keep on this island, and word rapidly spread that the Captain was having work done on some of the fishing boats with a view to converting them to battle cruisers ('battle cruisers'? thought the Reverend, how things do become exaggerated!) in advance of the imminent return of the dreaded shiny ships. The Captain would be unveiling his full plan for increased national security after prayers on Sunday. Everyone knew this by Saturday evening, and everyone had come to hear all about it. And so they would, if the Reverend would just get done with his pontificating. The level of talk in the chapel grew so loud that Pontius admitted defeat at an early stage, and made way for the Captain.

Castello took the pulpit and looked nervously round at the many expectant faces. You could have heard a pin drop, thought the Reverend, and after the way they talked right through my sermon, too. The Captain continued to look around. For effect? wondered the Reverend, and then realised his friend was looking for Rissa. She was not there.

Castello began, hesitantly, "Friends, you have all seen the shiny ships." Nods of agreement. "I am going to show you my plans for defence of the island, in case they return, which it seems they may." Gasps of astonishment. "I have made detailed designs for the rebuilding of the castle, which I will show you." Uneasy silence – they all knew the castle wouldn't rebuild itself. "And I will offer to train three gun crews, chosen from among yourselves, to man our three cannon." Dead silence, broken by the door flying open, and Rissa sailing regally in, wearing her finest scarlet gown.

The interruption allowed chatter to break out, and Castello knew he must keep their attention. "Find a seat for the lady!" he bellowed. "You there, Ligo. Clear a space for her." Ligo leapt up and bowed politely to Rissa, offering his seat.

"My apologies, Captain," said Rissa, sitting down. "Pray continue."

Every head, which had swivelled round to see her, swivelled back again to Castello. He cleared his throat and began to explain the plan for the semi-circular gun platform 'elegantly trimmed in brick', the stockade 'in stout oak', and the new house 'for the welcoming of visiting dignitaries'.

"Of course, I cannot achieve this alone," concluded the Captain. He knew this would be the tricky part. "I shall need your help, friends." They looked doubtful. Very doubtful. "But consider this: I have already acquired the necessary materials, and I shall work side by side with you. Together we will create a fort to be proud of. Fort Resolute, named for the ship whose timbers shall provide its very fabric." Castello was quite pleased with this eloquent turn of phrase, but the islanders still looked doubtful. They were clearly considering the amount of work this was going to need.

"But first, we must become a fighting force. Before the shiny ships return, I will train you to man the guns. Our very security is at stake. Master Ralham here has already volunteered, and will be my first gun captain. Who will join us?" There was a huge, almost tangible silence, which went on far too long. The Captain had played his trump card, and feared it was not enough.

"Captain, I will volunteer," said Pontius getting to his feet.

There was another silence, and then Ligo the fisherman stood up. "We can't have you firing guns, Reverend, at your age and what with your bad back. You couldn't lift the cannon shot, sir. You would do yourself a mischief. I will take your place."

A moment later Ligo's brother Lineus was on his feet. "Me too, Captain."

"There," said Castello, "I have my three gun captains! Who else will join us?" After another moment of silence, pandemonium broke out, with everyone talking and shouting at once, and pushing towards the pulpit to see the plans and volunteer their services. The Reverend Pontius was politely shoved out of the way, and the Captain very nearly bowled over by the onrush, silently thankful that he had prudently made a second copy of the plans, since the first seemed likely to be torn to pieces in the confusion.

In the midst of all this chaos, the chapel door was flung open and Pontius was aware that someone was trying to push through the crowd making squeaking noises. He elbowed his way towards the sound and found a small child, one of Rissa's runners, pulling fruitlessly on the sleeves of the adults. With difficulty, he hoisted her out of the crush. "Now then," he said, setting her on a pew, "What's the matter?"

With a great intake of breath she squealed, "They're back, they're back! The shiny ships! In the harbour…"

There was a long, becalmed moment while everyone took in this new development, and then a noisy stampede for the door. Pontius, Castello and Rissa were carried along in the rush, not managing to disentangle themselves until they were outside. The three guardians stared at each other in alarm. Anxious glances were exchanged. Pontius and Rissa were painfully aware of the content of the prophecy, and concerned about what might happen to Castello. More anxious glances.

The Captain hesitated and then visibly made a decision. He straightened, and then strode off, shouting, "Ring the bell, Reverend! Keep a good watch to the south, Lady!" Pontius and Rissa turned to each other, frowning. Pontius knew the ringing of the bell was superfluous at this stage. Everyone already knew the news. In fact, the ship's bell at the castle could be heard clanging tinnily in the distance. He said that just to keep me out of the way of any danger, thought Pontius. Rissa, who already had lookouts all round the island, thought exactly the same thing. She was beside herself, wringing the folds of her skirts, and looking around in breathless distress, and then turned to leave.

"I cannot let him, Reverend," she said. "I cannot let him sacrifice himself." And she ran after the Captain.

By the time Captain Castello reached the harbour, he had reasoned that he could not risk firing the guns this time. He was distraught that the white ships should return before he had had a chance to put his grand plan into action. The gun platform unbuilt, the gun crews untrained; they were simply not ready. They had been saved last time by a lucky shot, no more. He had put the fact that it had been all more or less accidental out of his mind, but it was now forcing its way in again. "I must not endanger anyone else," he said under his breath. "I must face this alone."

Ligo and Lineus were waiting on the quay. "Are we to use the guns, Captain?" asked Ligo.

For a long moment Castello looked out to the harbour, where the shiny ships were circling silently. They really were quite small, he noted, gratefully. Far too small to carry cannon. "No," he said, decidedly. "Find your crews and prepare your boats. I will go out to parley with the white ships." And with that he disappeared into his room. There were a few things he needed to take with him.

By the time Rissa arrived, the two boats were nearly ready,

71

although they looked not much like battle cruisers. There was no sign of Castello at all, so she took her opportunity. "You there, Ligo. Get me aboard; I will go out to the shiny ships."

"You, Lady?" said Ligo, looking up in surprise from the deck.

"Yes, me. What is the matter with you, man?"

"But…"

"But nothing. Get me aboard at once and stop dithering before we are all murdered in our beds."

"But…" said Lineus, from the other boat, moored alongside.

"Any more buts and I'll knock your silly heads together! Get on with it at once."

The brothers looked at each other and shrugged. These guardians were all a bit mad. A crowd was gathering and watching with interest. Rissa was just working herself up to begin some serious scolding, when silence fell. She looked around in consternation, and beheld an amazing sight. There was Captain Castello wearing the most amazing get-up imaginable. An absolute vision in red and gold braid, glowing in the afternoon sun. Golden cockade on the hat. Gleaming boots. The full works, in every sense. The vision strode purposefully forward and halted before her. The uniform had brushed up pretty well, he thought privately, as he took a stance to show off the sword at his side. For extra effect he drew the sword, to a gasp from the crowd. It flashed gloriously, and he was almost distracted into waving it about. But no, this was serious. He sheathed the sword again, and bowed.

"Why are you here, Lady?" he said sternly, or as sternly as he could manage. "You are neglecting your duties at the great rock. Which I clearly told you to attend to."

"I am going out to the white ships. I will speak with them this time, if you promise not to fire cannonballs at me, Captain," she said defiantly.

"Lady, I cannot allow it," said the Captain firmly. "It is unthinkable that I should hide behind the skirts of a woman, even such a brave one as yourself."

"But…"

"No buts!" There was clearly to be no arguing with him. Rissa held his gaze for far too long, then admitted defeat, inclined her head slightly, and stood aside, eyes modestly downcast, mainly to hide her worried expression. And very becoming, too, thought Castello, thinking he had finally won an argument. *But now I have work to do. The Isle of Larus has need of me!*

This rather pompous thought would not have sustained the Captain as long as it did had he known all the facts of the matter. His newly acquired habit of gossiping over the garden fence with his neighbour and gun captain-to-be Ralham had produced some interesting information. Pontius' visits to Mother Culver were events so novel that they were freely discussed, and the Reverend's interest in a particular story of hers was well known. "It's a prophecy, they say," Ralham had said. "A champion of the island will save us from the white boats when they come back." The crucial part involving self-sacrifice seemed to have been lost in translation somewhere along the way, and Castello had immediately known that the champion of the island must naturally be himself. Why hadn't the Reverend told him? It stood to reason, didn't it? So his refusal to let Rissa go out to the white boats was not quite as gallant as it appeared. Oh, he wanted her kept safe, sure enough, but he also wanted to be sure that it was he who was acknowledged as the champion of the island. He would never live it down if she were the one to see off the white boats for good and all. All his plans for the fort, for gun crews, for battle cruisers – all would lie in ruins if he allowed a woman to face the white boats in his place again. He would have to leave the island, put himself in exile; such would be the shame. He set all these uncomfortable thoughts aside as he prepared to embark.

"Ralham," said the Captain, "bring me my musket." And Ralham scampered off to fetch it, basking in reflected glory. "Ligo, Lineus… are we ready to put to sea?"

Ligo and Lineus glanced at each other with suppressed grins, and then saluted smartly. The Captain climbed aboard, mightily pleased at this show of respect, received the musket from Ralham, and chose a place to stand where he would not obstruct the working of the boat, and where everyone on the quay would get an excellent view of him in his splendour. Soon the *Brothers Three* and her consort the *Mergoose* were making their way out into the harbour. I am the commander of a naval flotilla, thought Castello, contentedly. Is admiral of the fleet taking it too far?

The crowd on the quay were cheering. Rissa watched in dignified silence, and then extracted a dainty handkerchief from her sleeve and waved it. The Captain saluted her. There were some that said there had been none of this saluting nonsense before the coming of the shiny ships. It was all very military, and so on, but was there really any need for it, at all?

At the chapel, the Reverend Pontius was on his knees, once again. He had been left at a loss when everyone had gone to the harbour. He had rung the chapel bell for a while, as he had been instructed to, more for something to do than anything else. Now he prayed fervently to the Spirit of the Sky to help him, to show him the way forward, and, most specifically, to help his friend Castello, who did not know what he was letting himself in for. The spirit had nothing to say, and the Reverend creaked to his feet and walked sadly out of the chapel door, thinking he should head down to the harbour. Outside, he came nose to beak with a large seagull, perched on a gravestone. He stared at the bird, and it stared back. Could it possibly be a sign, he thought? Could the Spirit of the Sky have sent a bird to show him the way? The bird turned to face the wind and flew off lazily across the churchyard. I am becoming a superstitious old fool, he thought, as bad as that hermit throwing offerings over the cliff. I asked for spiritual guidance, and practical help. My spirit would not send a *bird*, would he? And the Reverend limped off towards the harbour, his back twingeing painfully, and his head equally sore with fears for his friend.

"Oh, Reverend," said Rissa, rushing up when Pontius finally arrived at the quay. "He has gone out in the fishing boat. I couldn't stop him."

I find that hard to believe, thought Pontius, though her distress was evident.

The improvements to the *Brothers Three* had included the building of a forecastle on the bow. It gave the boat a certain presence and, Castello hoped, would afford a little more protection to the crew, including himself. The sheer weight of timber had unbalanced the boat so much, that they had been obliged to build up the stern to match. The boat sat much lower in the water consequently, and it had been necessary to relocate some of the rigging. The whole thing had proved a confounded nuisance when they were out fishing, but no one was complaining now, halfway across the harbour with the white ships circling ahead. There were an awful lot of them, the Captain observed, uneasily, however small.

"What orders, Captain?" said Ligo, at the tiller. Castello was both delighted and dismayed. Delighted at being asked for orders; dismayed because he didn't know what orders to give.

"Steady as she goes," he said, non-committally, and hoped that would do. He was also wondering about the weapons. He would not be able to use the sword and the musket at the same time, he realised, and he was damned if he'd hand either of them to anyone else. The musket had never been fired, and he had no idea whether it would work properly. Nonetheless, as they neared the white boats, he brought out the powder and musket balls he had brought with him, and made a great show of loading the thing. Ahead of him, one of the white boats was hoisting a flag – no, a sail. A great blue sail, blue as the sky. The Captain had never seen anything like it in all his born days. The sail filled, and Castello couldn't help thinking of Rissa's skirts billowing in the wind. The boat bounded forward. Effective, thought the Captain, with the part of his mind that wasn't scared witless. Curiosity and fear are often close neighbours.

As they approached the nearest boat he made his way nervously forward and took up what he hoped was a warlike stance.

He took out the sword and held it aloft. "I am Captain Castello, Commander of Fort Resolute, Isle of Larus!" he bellowed, and waved the sword menacingly.

People in outlandish dress were peering over the side of the white boat as it sped past. They looked surprised, or possibly frightened. Frightened! They were scared. The good Captain took heart and brandished the sword again. Had they heard him? "I am Captain Castello, Commander of…" he began again, but the rest of the sentence was drowned out.

Out of the sky came a most terrible, terrible sound. It was so loud, neither the Captain nor his crew could find words to describe it when they returned home. Louder than the loudest gale. Louder than thunder. And such a wind as beset them. A whirlwind. And above them, a great, terrible bird was hovering. A bird as big as a boat. Bigger. An immense russet and white, three-legged bird. The Captain dropped his sword and grabbed the musket, for what use it would be against such an apparition. But he had to try. A gap had opened up in the great beast's side, and a man – was it a man? – yes, a man clothed in a brilliantly coloured costume and a very strange hat began to descend on a rope. Was the bird disgorging a previous meal to make room for another, thought the Captain,

76

wildly. Am I about to be eaten? The man on the string was dangling very close, just above the *Brothers Three*, and was clearly shouting, though Castello couldn't make out was being said. Screaming for help, probably, Castello thought. He felt like doing the same thing himself. They stared at each other. This was very serious. Castello aimed the musket towards the bird, closed his eyes and squeezed the trigger. There was a huge bang.

The Captain found himself on the floor, his ears ringing, struggling for breath. With a great effort he propped himself on one elbow, and saw the musket beside him, smoking, its barrel distorted and broken. He flopped back down, and gasped until his breathing eased. It was the recoil from the gun that had winded him. He felt over his ribs looking for damage. No breakages, but a lot of bruises to come, for sure. It seemed very quiet. At length, Castello sat back up again and looked around. The *Brothers Three* and the *Mergoose* were all alone in the harbour. Not only that, they were about to collide. Ligo and the rest of the crew were picking themselves up but not in time to get the boat under control. There was a rending crash, which threw everyone off their feet again. For a terrible moment, Castello thought his punishment for failure would include death by drowning, which he greatly dreaded. He would rather have been eaten by the great bird, all things considered, than spend eternity alone on the cold, dark bed of the sea.

On the quayside, the crowd had continued cheering and saluting up until the appearance of the great bird, when a horrified silence had fallen. Rissa fainted clean away, out cold on the cobbles, and was tended by the Reverend Pontius who fanned her face with his hat, and called for smelling salts. Both of them thus missed the crucial moment when the white boats and the great bird disappeared, and had to rely on hearsay subsequently. When Rissa sat up and smacked the Reverend's hat out of the way – rather rudely, he thought – to see what was going on, there was nothing to see but the *Brothers Three* and the *Mergoose* tangled together.

"What happened? What happened?" she said, trying to get up.

"Lady, I think the Captain shot that great bird!"

"Vanished, it did. Must have shot it to pieces."

"The shiny ships, they're gone, too! The Captain scared them off!"

Aboard the *Brothers Three* it was becoming apparent that the castellations on the bow had proved very strong indeed. Too strong for the *Mergoose* anyway. She had been rammed amidships and was severely damaged and listing. Lineus was frantic. If his boat sank out here, she would be beyond recovery. Both crews understood this immediately, and did what they could to save her. In the end they succeeded in taking her under tow, gently edging in towards the quay and safety. Castello worked alongside them, doing all sorts of damage to his glorious uniform in the process. He didn't want to lose half his fleet in his first battle.

At length, the *Mergoose* was so low in the water that she ran aground. Small boats were putting out from the quay to assist. She was safe enough here and they could tend to her properly at low tide. Lineus stood on the sunken deck, clinging to the mast and up to his knees in water, the very picture of a captain going down with his ship. Still, she wasn't about to go down any further, and he was soon in one of the small boats directing salvage operations. The *Brothers Three* cast off the tow, and headed in to the quay.

Castello had been so absorbed in the rescue he had paid no attention to anything else, and was taken aback by the sight and sound of the celebrations on the quay. Everyone was jumping up and down, shouting, clapping, saluting and throwing hats in the air. Rissa was still sitting on the cobbles. "Perhaps you should put your head between your knees, warden," said the Reverend Pontius, desperately.

"Don't be ridiculous," she snapped. "That's indecent."

That's rich, coming from her, thought the Reverend, not for the first time.

Captain Castello was looking sadly at the wreckage of his musket. He wouldn't look much of a returning hero waving that about, but his sword had survived undamaged and unsullied, so he drew it and brandished it. This drew great cheers from the crowd, so he waved it again. He had mislaid his hat in the confusion, and his uniform was considerably the worse for wear. No matter, he thought, I have been in battle. The odd smut and rip is only to be expected. His ribs felt as though he'd taken a mule kick, and he was rather pleased to discover a long bloody scratch on his face where he had collided with something when he fell. These were the sort of polite war wounds he could happily admit to. As soon as the boat was safely tied up at the quay, he ran nimbly up the ladder and presented himself to the crowd. He drew his sword and waved it again, to great cheers. He was loving every minute of it, shameful thought though it was.

People were shouting, "Hail Castello, our hero!"

"Let us build Fort Resolute!"

"Isle of Larus forever!"

He took it all in gratefully, waved the sword a few more times, for the benefit of the crowd, and then sheathed it, before turning to Rissa, who was still on the cobbles. He bowed to her gallantly, and offered her his hand. And his heart, too, he thought, if only she would have it. She allowed him to help her to her feet, and shook out her skirts. Her hands were black with dirt from the ground, and she brushed them together nervously.

"Captain, you are hurt!" she said, tracing the cut on his face with her fingers and leaving a trail of dirty fingerprints. "Oh." She took out her handkerchief and dabbed at the dirt and blood. It was quite a deep cut, and the Captain fervently wished it might leave an enduring scar.

Was this the calm before the storm, he wondered, nervously. Was she about to start yelling at him for insisting on going out to the white boats in her place? For stealing her thunder, maybe?

There was a silence. Rissa looked up at him through her eyelashes, with the tiniest smile. Was she... was she *flirting* with him?

"Captain," she said, quietly. "Tell me, sir, do you have a first name, and may I know it?"

First and last names didn't count for much on an island where everyone knew everyone else, and no one had ever asked him before. Castello still wasn't entirely sure whether he could trust her not to start shouting at him and calling him names. Nonetheless, she could use *this* name, if she wanted to.

"Why," said the Captain, "it is Hugh."

"Hugh," she repeated. "I don't believe anyone else on the island has *that* name. I like it very well."

Castello smiled, contemplating a future of happy enslavement both to his fort and his lady, and he boldly kissed her grubby hand, to violent cheering.

Chapter Nine
The Last Laugh

The Reverend Pontius was extremely gratified. Chuffed to bits, in fact. The island was safe, the white boats had come as predicted, and been seen off, and were unlikely to return in the near future, though he planned to go and check on that before too long. His friend Castello was an entirely happy man, the toast of the island, and engaged to wed the lady warden. A very happy outcome for them both, though somewhere in an uncharitable corner of his soul, the Reverend couldn't help thinking that they richly deserved each other. The Captain was vain, his lady a termagant. Their union was sure to make life interesting for everyone else. The Captain was further blessed with the knowledge that his projected plan, Fort Resolute, was about to be built, according to his exact specifications, by a grateful populace. It was never a bad thing, thought the Reverend, as he went to see the work in progress, to be prepared.

Castello greeted him warmly. He was in his shirtsleeves, checking building materials off a list. "Ah, Reverend, you have just missed Rissa – that is to say – the lady warden," he said. He couldn't quite bring himself to refer to her as 'my fiancée' yet. "She was here giving her approval to the plans for the new house."

Giving her orders, more likely, thought Pontius to himself.

"I never... I never had the chance to thank you, Reverend, for your support that day," said Castello, shyly. "You showed such bravery in volunteering to stand beside me on the gun platform, despite your age and infirmity."

Age and infirmity, indeed, thought Pontius. The cheek of it. But he kept the thought to himself and nodded amiably, and then drew a delighted smile by saying, "It would have been an honour to have served beside you in such a cause, Captain."

Later, the Reverend clambered along the path to the hermit's cliff. There were a few points he would dearly love to see cleared up. Rufus was sitting silently, peering sightlessly over the ocean. As usual, the hermit was aware of the Reverend's presence before he announced himself and, as usual, the Reverend was irritated by it.

"Well, Reverend, to what do we owe this honour?"

"Colleague, I need to make sense of what has happened these last days and weeks. Can you enlighten me at all?"

"Ah," said Rufus, genially. "Well, sir, the Spirit of the Sea, while he has our best interests at heart, you understand, is sometimes, shall we say, a playful entity." Playful? There was no answer to that, so Pontius sat in silence.

"The Old Man, as the people call him, likes to give the Isle of Larus a glimpse of other worlds. And other worlds a glimpse of the island, too," said Rufus, cryptically. "It's the spirit's way of testing our mettle, you know."

"He sends the shiny ships to test our mettle? Our bravery and ingenuity, you mean?" said Pontius.

"Indeed," said Rufus. "There is no harm in it, but the spirit feels it does you all good to be given a good shake-up, now and again. Also it provides hours of innocent amusement for the spirit himself. Most entertaining, he says."

"And what of that great bird?" said Pontius. "Surely that was sent by *my* spirit, the Spirit of the Sky."

"Not my department," said Rufus, unhelpfully. "But perhaps you are right. It did come from the sky, after all. Did your spirit not give you a sign that all would be well?"

The Reverend was too ashamed to admit his recent lack of communication with the Spirit of the Sky. But he remembered the bird in the churchyard. Had it been an omen after all? "Perhaps your spirit and mine have both been at work, colleague," he conceded at last. "And the prophecy? It says that a champion of the island will sacrifice himself. And yet everyone came back safe and sound."

"The lady warden knew of the prophecy," said Rufus. "She tried to sacrifice herself in the Captain's place. He refused to let her do it, and went out to face the danger himself. They both offered to sacrifice themselves for the island and for each other. It's all very neat and tidy, when you think about it." The Reverend wasn't convinced, but it would just have to do.

"And what of us, dear colleague?" asked Pontius. "How have we proved our mettle?"

"I have no need to prove anything," said Rufus. "I am the spirit's familiar. And pretty good at it, too, if I may say so."

Pontius was dumbstruck and outraged by this total lack of modesty, and couldn't think of a suitably withering reply, so he said nothing.

"And as for you, Reverend, you have proved yourself a true champion of the island. You stood up and offered to help when others, true islanders all, held their peace. The spirit is much pleased with you." Pontius wasn't sure that he wanted to please the Spirit of the Sea, but again said nothing.

"Oh, and by the by," said Rufus. "If you find yourself with an hour to spare, now and then, might I recommend some further visits to Mother Culver? Hear her archive through. She has much to teach. Write it all down, perhaps. Gain wisdom. And then share it with everybody." Pontius nodded, getting up to leave.

"Oh, and Reverend," said Rufus, quietly. "Be aware the spirit may send further tests of our mettle." But Pontius was already half way down the path and did not hear.

Was it truly a good idea to indulge Mother Culver in this way, thought the Reverend Pontius to himself, as he picked his way back down the cliff. Scattering stories round the island, putting ideas into people's heads. Is it wise? But then, is it not what I do, every Sunday, in the chapel – telling stories, planting ideas? Is there really any difference, if the intention is good? This was one of the very many things he did not know. Perhaps only time would be the judge. As he plodded wearily on there came an echo from the cove below. Just a wave running over the sandbank, he thought. Or was it watery laughter?

AND WHAT *OUR* WORLD MADE OF IT ALL...

From The Western Clarion:

Man sees Non-existent Island
- Champion Yachtsman tells of spooky experience

Champion yachtsman, James Fortune, 31, spoke for the first time today about his terrifying ordeal in the English Channel last week.

"To be honest, I don't really want to talk about it, but people are saying I'm crazy, so I need to clarify things."

Still looking visibly shaken, Fortune gave *The Clarion* exclusive details about what happened.

"Well, Liam (Beddowes, his teammate) and I were sailing side by side. Visibility was good, conditions were good. Wind freshening. Nothing out of the ordinary. And suddenly, out of the blue, there it was. An island. It was so close I could see the rocks. I didn't have time to do anything. Just stared at it in horror. Sheer cliffs. Jagged rocks."

"Just when I thought we were going to strike at full speed, it – it disappeared. Just like that. I looked up and it was gone. Nothing but sea, exactly as it should have been."

"We sailed on eastwards and, the moment I got my breath, I turned and looked back – and there it was again. But we were on the east side. Just as if we'd sailed straight through it. Gave me the right creeps, I can tell you. A moment later, and it was gone again."

Fortune's teammate, Liam Beddowes, who was sailing alongside, was reluctant to comment. "I didn't see anything myself. Or anything out of the ordinary. The marker buoy was just where it should have been. We were just where we should have been. Everything was just where it should have been. But I did see Jimmy's face, and believe me, it was the face of a man about to crash into rocks. Scared the life out of me."

A spokesman for the British team said, "All the team members have been under a great deal of pressure in the run-up to the Championships next month. There was a full investigation following the incident reported by James Fortune, particularly since it took place on the course competitors will be following, but nothing was found. There were no reports of fogbanks, squalls or anything else that might have explained the phenomenon. In light of Liam Beddowes' comments, we are satisfied there is no danger to anyone. On his return, Mr Fortune was examined by doctors and placed under sedation for several days. We wish him a speedy recovery, but his participation in the Championships is now in doubt, and team reserves are on standby.

Asked if the mystery could be explained by the presence of an uncharted island the spokesman said, "Don't be ridiculous. How could there be any uncharted islands? This is the English Channel, not the Bermuda flipping Triangle."

From The Western Clarion:

Yacht fired on during sailing championships

Maria Jacobs, leading member of the British team in the current sailing championships, taking place in the English Channel this week, claims her yacht was fired on.

Ms Jacobs, 29, said, "We were just about to start the race,

when I saw what appeared to be a fishing boat, under sail and approaching us. There was a woman in the boat wearing fancy dress – a long red gown – and I thought it was some sort of environmental protest. No one else on my boat seemed to have seen this, and the fishing boat was heading straight in among competitors. I waved and shouted to warn them off, but they continued to approach. Just as some sort of collision seemed inevitable, I saw a cannonball fly across the fishing boat and smash into its far side. This was very worrying, as the cannonball would have hit my boat had it continued any further."

"I was so astounded I just stared for a moment. Then I yelled to my crew, thinking the fishing boat might need assistance. But when I turned back it had simply disappeared."

Asked whether she thought the boat might have sunk, Ms Jacobs said, "No. There simply wasn't time. And there was no wreckage or anyone in the water. Absolutely nothing. And as to where a cannonball might have been fired from in the open sea like that. Well, I just can't explain it."

No other member of Ms Jacobs' crew saw anything out of the ordinary, nor did any of the other boats' crews.

A colleague, who asked not to be named, commented, "She's nuts."

This latest incident follows the strange event in the same sea area three weeks ago when champion yachtsman James Fortune reported the sudden appearance of an uncharted island during a practice session. Mr Fortune has since been stood down from the British team and sent for 'long-term rest' to a sanatorium in Hampshire.

Both the British sailing team and the organisers of the Championships declined to comment on this latest phenomenon, but a spokesperson for HM Coastguard stated, "All fishing fleets were aware that racing was taking place in that sea area, and there were no reports of any vessels having strayed too close. There were similarly no reports of any vessels being damaged or lost."

Asked if there were any possibility of a cannonball having been fired, the spokesman stated, "There were no unauthorised vessels in the vicinity. Ms Jacobs was obviously mistaken. How could anyone be firing cannonballs? This is a sailing regatta not the Spanish Armada."

From The Western Clarion:

Man Blows himself up with musket at sailing championships

Competitors are threatening to withdraw from the current sailing championships fearing terrorist activity following yet another strange event in the English Channel yesterday. A rescue helicopter was called out by yachtsman James St John when two unknown vessels approached his boat. Mr St John, 33, stated: "I saw two sailing boats approaching, one of them with a very strange structure on its bows – like an old-fashioned galleon. There was a man in an extraordinary outfit standing on the boat waving a sword. I had to make a split-second decision, and I decided to call for help. This could have been something really serious."

Neither Mr St John's own crew, nor the crews of any other boat would admit to having seen anything. Mr St John continued, "The SAR helicopter was with us very quickly and came in close over the two boats, and lowered a man on a winch. I saw the man with the sword blow himself up with a musket. Yes, a musket. You'd better ask the helicopter crew, they must have seen him. I've nothing more to say." Apparently both boats then 'disappeared'.

HM Coastguard said the matter was under investigation and refused to comment further.

The leading vessel was seen by Mr St John to carry the

name *Brothers Three*, Isle of Larus, but there were no further identification markings. An official stated: "No vessel matching its description is registered to any port. And there is no such place as the Isle of Larus. Somebody is having a laugh."

The Clarion Investigates...
Investigative journalism at its most incisive

Cannonballs, Muskets, Invisible Islands?
What is going on in the English Channel?

Silence has descended on the English Channel once again with the conclusion of the recent sailing championships. No one's admitting to anything, but there is no doubt some very strange things have been going on out there. Race officials and HM Coastguard have been reluctant to comment on the hard-to-believe reports that have come in. There was talk of sending in a naval destroyer to restore order at one point.

First, yachtsman James Fortune reported an uncharted island suddenly appearing in his path during a practice run. His teammate Liam Beddowes saw nothing, and it was thought that Fortune was suffering from hallucinations brought on by stress and exhaustion.

But soon afterwards, yachtswoman Maria Jacobs reported seeing a fishing boat struck by a cannonball in the same sea area.

And five days ago, yachtsman James St John, reported two strange boats, one carrying a man who proceeded to blow himself up with a musket. There has been much talk of eco-terrorists, and even suicide bombers, but no group has claimed any responsibility for these attacks.

Despite the news blackout that has followed, *The Clarion* has unearthed some amazing information.

A cannonball has since been found in the nets of a trawler working the same sea area recorded in Ms Jacobs' report. It was in pristine condition, and showing no signs of having been in the sea more than a few days. It has been taken to a secret location for a full forensic examination.

An unofficial source at HM Coastguard has disclosed that a musket ball was found embedded in the fuselage of the search and rescue helicopter despatched in answer to Mr St John's emergency call. The source further stated that members of the aircraft's crew had been forbidden from discussing the matter with anyone until further notice, although it is said that the winch man is under sedation.

For all that, it is rumoured that Fortune, Jacobs and St John, now all retired from competitive yacht racing, are planning to collaborate on a book chronicling their extraordinary experiences, with lucrative film rights to follow.

Did they witness something supernatural? Or was it all an elaborate money-making hoax? They will, of course, deny this. But they just might be laughing all the way to the bank.

Part Two
'Comes a Thief...'

92

Chapter One
The New Beginning

The lady warden, Captain Castello's lady, was in an interesting condition. Everyone said the Captain must have anticipated the wedding by quite a long way, judging by the size of her, possibly even on the day he defeated the shiny ships. The Reverend Pontius huffed and puffed about it a bit. A woman as strong-minded as the warden should have been perfectly capable of keeping the Captain at arm's length until after the wedding, he thought, and the fact that she hadn't only went to show that she was indeed the shameless hussy he had always thought her, and no better than she ought to be.

Other people took a more relaxed view. It was nothing unusual on the Isle of Larus for a bride to be pregnant before the wedding. As long as there *was* a wedding, nobody thought too much of it. The Reverend's attempts to persuade the islanders that this was a scandalous way to behave had met with blank incomprehension. So the fact that Rissa had been, if not the size of a house, at least the size of a substantial shed on her wedding day bothered no one but the Reverend. For that day, and that day only, she had abandoned her scarlet gowns and appeared in an ivory silk confection trimmed with an enormous bow at the back. She resembled nothing so much as a giant perambulating wedding cake. The Captain wore his full dress uniform, complete with sword. Everyone agreed it was a splendid wedding, though the bride was clearly tetchy with morning sickness. By the time the happy couple had emerged from the chapel, she had hit him over the head with her bouquet for asking once too often if she was quite well, and been mildly sick in the font. He took good care to keep the sword well out of her reach.

The rituals for the Spirit of the Sky having been observed, husband and wife processed to Rufus' cliff so the hermit could bless the union on behalf of the Spirit of the Sea. Rissa, as an islander, had insisted on this. Just about everyone on the island followed them along the cliff path to watch, and for a short time the four guardians were together – a rare event – the Reverend Pontius having caved in under pressure to attend.

After the wedding, the two had settled uneasily into married life of a sort. Rissa had refused to leave her little house at the southern tip of the island. She insisted, too, on continuing her work as ship warden and wise woman of the weather. How could she not? She was a guardian of the isle and had essential duties to perform, and perform them she would, as best she could. The Captain, as the northern guardian of the island, understood. Besides, he really had nowhere to accommodate her at present. His plans for the transformation of the old castle into the new Fort Resolute were finalised, and work had begun. But it would be some time before his new house was completed, and it was easier to let his wife stay in her own familiar surroundings for the time being. He would be able to persuade her to move down to the fort when the sumptuous apartments he had in mind were a reality. At least, that's what he told himself.

For the moment, he was really more anxious about Rissa's health. She was no longer in the first flush of youth, though it would have been more than his life was worth to say so, and it seemed to him a distinctly dangerous business for a woman of her years to be having a child. In fact, you could quite easily have knocked the Captain down with a guillemot feather when she blushingly announced the news. Rissa herself, despite her bad temper as her pregnancy progressed, seemed largely unconcerned with the dangers. None of the island women were very bothered about it, and in fact death in childbirth was a rare occurrence.

When Rissa's travails began, Castello had hastened to her side, hoping to comfort her. It soon became apparent that he wasn't being very successful at it. He was astounded at the immoderate language she used. Where on earth had she learned such words? The Captain wasn't entirely sure he knew what they all meant, which was probably just as well. And when he put his head round the bedroom door to ask how she did, she had lobbed a water decanter at him with astounding force, to judge from the crash. She was a remarkably good shot, too, hitting the door on the exact spot occupied by his left ear a moment earlier. He filed that information away for future reference, and idly wondered whether he shouldn't recruit her into one of his gun crews.

At length, Mother Culver, in her capacity as midwife, emerged and waved him in. Rissa lay exhausted, her dark hair dishevelled, a tiny, red-faced, swaddled bundle cradled in her left arm. And another one in her right arm. Castello stared in amazement. "There are two!" he said.

Rissa didn't even bother to open her eyes. "Of course there are two," she said wearily. "Twins. Boy and girl."

"Are they identical?" asked the Captain, without thinking it through logically.

"How can a boy and a girl be identical, you blithering idiot?"

They were not a bit identical, as it happened. The little girl had scraps of fair hair and when she opened her large pale eyes, Castello felt he was looking at his own mirror image. The boy had thick black hair and was unmistakably Rissa's child, both in looks and temper, and he wailed furiously when the Captain tried to pick him up.

The happy pair had at least managed to agree on the naming of the twins. Castello named the girl, and Rissa the boy. The Captain looked tearfully at the squawking bundle and said, "We will call her Lara, as she is a creature of the Isle of Larus, like her mother."

"Pompous twit," said Rissa, and took a more traditional approach in naming the little lad Petrus, after her late father.

With this agreed, Castello had stepped outside Rissa's house to find a considerable crowd enjoying the spring sunshine, some with picnics.

"Ah," he said, unprepared, when everyone looked at him expectantly. "Erm – my lady wife has presented me with twins, a son and daughter. They will be named Petrus and Lara."

As usual, everyone seemed to know all about it already, but there was good-natured cheering, and polite enquiries after Rissa's health. The men slapped him on the back, some of them privately thinking the Captain deserved some sort of medal for extreme bravery.

One of them was undoubtedly the Reverend Pontius. He was delighted to see his friend settled with wife and family, of course. But he couldn't help wondering whether Castello had taken on rather more than he could cope with. Still, it was done, and the Reverend wished them all well. He happily baptised the babies in the chapel font (mercifully cleaned out since the wedding), on behalf of the Spirit of the Sky, and was sulkily aware of a second baptism, with seawater, performed by Rufus on behalf of the other spirit. Ah, well, he thought, resignedly, at least I got there first.

The Reverend had promised himself a private visit to Rufus the Hermit, to make quite sure that another visit from the shiny ships wasn't imminent. He had put it off over the winter, as the cold weather had played havoc with his bad back and flared up the rheumatics. It wasn't sensible, he had thought, to make matters worse by clambering about up a cliff in the bitter east wind. But now that the spring was come, he really couldn't justify further delay, and set off for his visit. Rufus looked more ragged and scrawny than ever, but retained his air of smug certainty.

"I hope you do well, colleague," said Pontius.

"Well enough," replied Rufus. "But you are here to enquire after the shiny ships, not my health. Right?"

"Right," said Pontius. "Would you just kindly confirm that they will not be back?"

"Oh, no."

"WHAT...?"

"They'll come again," said Rufus, matter-of-factly, "But not for many a year. As I said before, Reverend, the Spirit of the Sea sends them to keep us on our toes."

They did that, all right, thought Pontius to himself.

"Each time they come," said Rufus, "the island becomes aware of the dangers that might beset it. We can be a little unworldly, cut off here in the wide sea."

You can say that again, thought Pontius.

"However, each time they return, our castle is rebuilt and the island prepares to defend itself. Rather neat, really. However, the people always forget, and the defences fall into disuse and ruin. So the spirit sends the shiny ships as a reminder now and then."

Pontius was reasonably satisfied with this. "One more thing, colleague," he said as he prepared to leave. "The people on the shiny ships – we can see *them*. Can they see *us*, at all?"

"Ah," said Rufus. "Some of them can. Those that have the Sight." And he turned his empty eye sockets to the sea. "It gives them quite a fright, by all accounts. Oh, and by the way, Reverend, you haven't been to visit Mother Culver yet, have you? See that you do."

That old ragamuffin, thought the Reverend Pontius to himself as he walked back, telling me off like a naughty child. The unmitigated cheek of it. But he headed for Mother Culver's hovel nonetheless.

She was sitting idly outside when he arrived, and he lowered himself painfully onto an old wooden stool nearby. He had a few questions for her, too.

"Mother, I believe you told me that some of your, um, archive pieces are histories, and some are prophecies."

"Indeed, Reverend. And some are both. Oh, yes."

"Like the shiny ships?"

"As you say, Reverend."

"Forgive the inquisition, Mother, but does this mean that your predecessors as keepers of the stories created the histories and made the prophecies themselves?"

"Yes. And so do I."

Pontius was startled by this revelation. He hadn't really thought of the stories as a continuing work in progress. It was very unsettling to think of this scruffy old woman assessing and summarising the things that happened on the island and handing them on to posterity just as she chose. And as for going into a trance, or whatever she did to get prophecies, well, it was just too alarming to contemplate. And witchcraft, to boot, wasn't it? The Reverend wasn't sure about that, but he *was* sure that the island's history was too precious to entrust to this old baggage. And then and there he determined that he would hear as many of the stories as he could persuade her to tell him and write them down. He would also write his own history of the island, as far as he knew it, carefully and logically. No mumbo-jumbo. Mother Culver saw the change of expression on Pontius' face as he made this decision, and watched him intently. "Well then, Mother," said the Reverend at last, "Have you added new stories recently? About the shiny ships for instance?"

"No need," said Mother Culver. "That one is a repeating prophecy. It'll come round again just the same, all in good time. But I have added another."

"Ah, and what is the subject of it?" asked Pontius, trying to sound casual.

"It is a history. It is passing rare for two of the island guardians to marry, and that is a matter that must be recorded."

"Of course. Very proper," said Pontius. He could record all that for himself. It was the older pieces that interested him. "Tell me Mother, are there other, er, prophecies that you think the people should know? To keep them from harm?"

"There is one, Reverend," said the good Mother. And waited expectantly. Pontius sighed and withdrew a small brandy flask from his pocket and placed it before her. She nodded, and then stared vacantly for a moment before starting to sing:

Comes a thief who spins a web of lies
Entangling all the island in its toils
One by one we're caught, as helpless flies
While, spider-like, he makes off with the spoils...

Pontius screwed up his face, trying to commit this to memory. *Comes a thief...* "That is most alarming, Mother. Would you have any idea at all *when* this, um, thief might appear?"

"It's all a little vague, but soon or soonish, I suspect."

"Thank you, Mother," said Pontius. "I shall be on the alert. Good day to you." And he rushed off, wanting to get home to write the prophecy down before he forgot it.

Mother Culver sighed. "He never does wait to hear the rest of the story..." she muttered, picking up the brandy flask.

Fort Resolute was actually beginning to take shape quite well. The imposing residence Captain Castello had envisaged was still no more than a plan, but no matter – the defences were the most important thing, and they were well in hand. The proposed gun platform was already a reality. A broad stone semi-circle on the site of the old castle, now demolished,

99

it was every bit as elegant as the Captain had intended, built of pale stone and trimmed with red brick inserts. He was very pleased with it indeed. The islanders had worked all winter, whenever the weather was too rough for fishing, and it had been finished both sooner, and to a higher standard, than he had expected. Work had even begun on the protective stockade before the spring had come and his working party had had other matters to attend to. The three cannon were in place, and looked so impressive the Captain was thrilled to be in command of them.

Over the winter, too, the three gun crews had been practising their gunnery. Admittedly, it was all a dumbshow – just going through the motions of loading and firing and cleaning. The shot and powder were too precious to use for practice, but the Captain was expecting a trader to arrive before too long, who would provide the island with these supplies in exchange for salt fish. And then they would be able to practise firing at a target. The Captain could hardly wait.

But, in the meantime, life was working out nicely. The islanders had agreed to provide a living for a nursemaid to assist with the twins so that Rissa could continue her important work as ship warden and wise woman of the weather. Aside from the necessities of childcare, motherhood had not adversely affected the lady warden at all. She had recovered quickly and was soon making her perfect weather forecasts again as if nothing had happened. To see her scoot up the great rock, thought Castello fondly, you'd never know she was the recent, and rather mature, mother of twins. And the babies were thriving, very loudly. Yet another good reason, thought the Captain, why she, and they, had remained at her house on the southern tip of the island, while he manned the fort on the northern end. Though there were times when he swore he could hear them even from that distance. For all that, when he returned to his inadequate room in the evenings, he had enjoyed happy daydreams of the future, when the children were older and had stopped bawling quite so much. Captain Castello and his son, Cadet Petrus. Captain Castello and his beautiful daughter, Miss Lara. His son would follow him as commander of Fort Resolute, of course. And his daughter – how could she not be beautiful with such a mother – would follow Rissa as ship warden. He was quite proud of himself for having created two of the next generation of guardians of the isle. With the help of his dear lady wife, of course. If only the shot and powder would arrive, the Captain's happiness would be complete.

Chapter Two
Trade's Increase

A low, slow boat slunk into the harbour one morning, letting the tide bring it across since there was barely enough wind to fill its large ruby-red sail. She was the *Honest Trader*, a bluff-bowed, shallow-keeled, full-bellied sort of capacious boat. The kind of boat that could creep unseen into any shallow creek, and out again, and undoubtedly did. She was so low in the water because she was laden with shot and powder. Salticus, captain and proud owner, had heard that a new market for these commodities had opened up on Larus, and he was very happy to exploit it. There was nothing he liked better than a new market – for the excellent reason that the people who formed it often had an imperfect knowledge of the relative values and exchange rates of different commodities. This was particularly true of islands. This is right up your street, Salticus, my lad, he thought to himself, ripe for the picking, I'd say.

Captain Castello, always watchful, had spotted the vessel as it entered the harbour. There was no surprise at his being first to see it, as he had waited and watched for it so long. The shot – it brings the shot and powder! He was thrown into confusion in trying to decide whether the boat's captain would count as a visiting dignitary, and thus whether there was a need to change into his full dress uniform to greet him. But no, he thought, this man was a dealer, not a leader of men. Nonetheless, he couldn't be greeted in shirtsleeves, and the

Captain hastened to make himself at least moderately respectable. He really wanted to talk to the fellow in private, to make the deal without a great crowd of onlookers interfering and shouting, so he quietly asked Ralham, his most trusted gun captain, to *not* spread the word, and to keep everyone at bay until he had had time to settle the bargain.

And so the Captain stood alone on the quay as the *Honest Trader* approached. He was a little alarmed at the appearance of the vessel's owner, who wore a rather splendid outfit topped off with a jewelled turban. Good grief, thought Castello, perhaps I should have gone for the full dress after all. But it was too late now, for the boat was tying up at the quay. Salticus gave final instructions to his crew, and climbed ashore.

Castello stood smartly to attention, saluted and began his much-rehearsed speech. "Good day to you, Captain, and welcome to the Isle of Larus. I am…"

"Stripe me pink!" said Salticus genially. "If it isn't Hugh Castello, as I live and breathe!" Castello stared at him, speechless, for a long moment.

"Do we have acquaintance, sir?" he said, at last, formally. In truth the Captain had no idea whether he knew the fellow or not. Not since coming to Larus for sure, but before that… He certainly didn't remember Salticus, but then, he had very little memory of anything or anyone before his arrival on the island.

"Well of course we do, though it's been many a year. It's me, Salticus. Don't you know me, Hugh?"

On Larus, only Rissa called the Captain by his first name, and then only in intimate moments. It made him very uncomfortable to hear it being used so lightly by this stranger. But this stranger clearly knew *him*. The possibility of learning the story of his own past was both tempting and terrifying.

"I fear I do not remember you, er, Salticus. I arrived here injured, and I have little memory of anything from my past life."

"Ah," said Salticus thoughtfully. "Then perhaps I will be

able to do you the service of jogging your memory a little, Hugh, my old shipmate."

At that moment Rissa appeared with the nursemaid carrying the babies. She had put that Master Ralham firmly in his place when he tried to prevent her going through to the quay, the cheek of it.

"Oh, er, may I present my lady wife," said Castello. "And my son and daughter. Rissa, this is Master Salticus – he has brought the powder and shot."

"Well, well, you old dog!" said Salticus. "Your servant ma'am." And he bowed to Rissa, whose eyebrow shot up in a worrying fashion.

"Will you excuse us, dearest?" said the Captain. "Master Salticus and I have much to do. Shall we begin the unloading, sir, and I will send for the salt fish barrels, so we can agree the barter?" Castello was desperate to get away before the fellow referred to him as 'Hugh' in Rissa's hearing.

Rissa nodded and retreated, and Castello beckoned to Ralham, who hastened over. "Make up a working party, Ralham, whoever you can find, to help unload this boat. And send a runner to get the fish barrels sent down. Jump to it, now."

"Aye, Captain," said Ralham, suppressing a smirk. But he saluted smartly, all the same, before dashing off. This time it was Salticus' eyebrow that shot up.

"Captain, is it, Hugh? You've come up in the world, and no mistake."

"Purely an honorary title," said Castello, quietly, his stomach churning with anxiety. "Among the islanders, you understand. Now, allow me to offer you some refreshment before we begin our bargaining." And he ushered Salticus into his room. It wasn't untidy, exactly, for Rissa had made 'improvements', but he regretted at this moment not having built his new house yet. Salticus looked around, missing nothing.

104

"Forgive me, sir," said Castello, "but you find us in the midst of building work. Our new gun platform is complete, as you see, but there is much still to do."

"Mm," said Salticus, thoughtfully, stroking his beard. "You seem to have done well for yourself, indeed. And who is paying for all this, if you don't mind my being nosy?" Castello minded quite a lot, and longed to tell Salticus to mind his own business, but he was anxious not to offend the man, not with the long-awaited powder and shot being unloaded as they spoke.

"The islanders do the work – they are not paid – their reward comes in knowing the island is secure."

Salticus' jaw dropped a fraction. "Unpaid, is it? How very public spirited. So is there no currency on Larus, no coinage?"

Castello squirmed as if he were on the rack. He was stricken with the sure and certain knowledge that Salticus was all wrong. Completely and utterly all wrong. And possibly evil. But the Captain couldn't invent a lie. After all this time on Larus he simply couldn't remember how. So he told the truth. "People barter with each other, mostly. There is a small amount of silver in circulation."

"Is there indeed," said Salticus lightly, and took a seat at the Captain's little table. Castello hastily produced a small flask of brandy, and Salticus fell upon it greedily.

"A toast, er, *Captain*," he said, raising a glass. "To trade's increase!" And drank it off at a gulp.

Up at the chapel, the Reverend Pontius was hearing all about the arrival of the *Honest Trader*. He was delighted that the Captain would have his supplies and be able to do some proper gunnery practice. Castello had been on fire with impatience all winter, and now at last his dearest wish was granted. Excellent. The Reverend went over to assist with the loading of the fish barrels – well, more to listen in to all the gossip than to actually assist. But it showed willing. There was wild talk about the ship's captain. He dressed in silks and wore a jewelled turban, fancy that! He must be a Turk, a Rajah, an eastern potentate maybe. Why, he could be a magician, a sorcerer. And the Captain – our Captain – was treating him very civilly indeed. Welcoming him as a visiting dignitary.

Well, thought Pontius, that was all very proper, he was entitled to a civil welcome. But all this magician nonsense…

The cart was nearly fully loaded, and the only horse on the island, Master Ferro's old grey mare, was being backed into the shafts. She was past her best, for sure, but strong and steady and not given to any variety of skittishness. Pontius decided to accompany the cart down to the harbour and take a look at the new arrival for himself. Well all right then, he was curious.

Meanwhile, Captain Castello was having a very uncomfortable time. Salticus was very forthcoming, more so as the brandy flask emptied. Castello was a little annoyed. He had been saving that to share with the Reverend. The trader had lifted off his turban. Lifted it off, like any other hat. The Captain had expected it to *unwind*, but no, off it came in one go, revealing a mop of greasy black hair. As Salticus talked, Castello stared at him, trying very hard to remember something, anything, about the man. He didn't think they could have been friends, however genial the fellow was. The disgusting way he had guzzled the brandy offended Castello's fastidious soul. No, they had never been friends. The trader was relaxed, an easy talker. He was about Castello's age, and must once have been good looking. He still was good looking, to a degree, the Captain observed to himself. The women must have swarmed round him like flies once upon a time. Perhaps they still did. The fellow was a ruffian, no doubt about it. A scallywag. And, my goodness, could he talk!

Castello had begun asking questions, questions about his own history. Not that he really wanted to know all the answers, since he suspected he wouldn't like them, but because he didn't want to tell Salticus anything more about the Isle of

Larus than he had to. So he chose what he thought were the safest enquiries, and pressed on. Had he been a seagoing man, then?

"You jest," said Salticus with a roguish smile. "Well of course you were. We were shipmates together on the *Fulmar* before she sank. That was the last I saw of you. Thought you dead for certain."

"Ah," said Castello. It was as he had always thought, from his skill at sailing. "And did I work the guns?"

"Finest gun captain in the ship," said Salticus. "Top class you were, matey." Again, Castello was happy with this. It explained his love for the cannon.

"And did I fire guns ashore, too?"

"Believe you did. You were an army man, before the *Fulmar* I seem to recall."

It all made sense. Castello couldn't help being flattered and pleased, though he was uneasy about having been a mere gun *captain*. That meant he was not an officer, which was a little worrying. But he swept that aside, a captain of artillery, sort of, by land and by sea – just what he wanted to hear. Only the good Captain could not have found this slightly suspicious.

"And here you are then, Hugh," said Salticus, looking around. "A very comfortable billet. Nice little island. Respected by the natives. Not bad at all, eh, *Captain*?" and he nudged Castello's elbow conspiratorially, and winked. Castello was horrified. But not as horrified as he was at Salticus' next remark.

"And a splendid little family too. You're a lucky man, old shipmate. Magnificent woman, that wife of yours. A right regal beauty." Another conspiratorial nudge. "Long as I don't tell the other one, eh?"

Chapter Three
The Salticus Club

It rapidly became apparent that Salticus was on a mission to make himself amiable to the entire island. Within a matter of days he had shaken every male hand, kissed every female hand, and pressed sweetmeats into every child's hand. This sort of geniality went down well with the islanders, and soon he had a little fan club following him about. Wherever Salticus was, there was laughter and bonhomie, and brandy. He brought little kegs ashore from the *Honest Trader*, and sold drinks at very reasonable prices.

The Reverend Pontius was instantly suspicious. He had a little more experience of the wiles of the world than the islanders, but even so, he could find no evidence of sharp practice. The alcohol was dispensed sensibly. No one was found to be roaring drunk – not even Old Billy, which was little short of a miracle – and the price was fair. Indeed it was on the low side. Salticus was probably making a small profit and the islanders enjoyed their evenings without any serious ill effects and no nuisance caused to anyone. It was all so damned reasonable that it was impossible to criticize, really, without seeming to be a killjoy.

The Salticus Club, then, was a drinking club, but not in the least noisy or dissolute. He led his little band round the isle, meeting at different places each day, so as not to disturb the neighbours.

One evening they met at the southern tip of the island,

close to Rissa's house, but not too close, in consideration of the children. Salticus was at his most genial, and had distributed a few drinks free of charge. "What would you say," he asked no one in particular, "if I were to offer you a wager?"

A perplexed silence fell. A wager? "We do not lay wagers on Larus," somebody said. "They cause bad feeling. Discord."

"Discord?" said Salticus. "Among us? We are all friends here, are we not?" They couldn't deny it. "It is just an innocent diversion I have in mind. A bit of fun." They were wary, but he knew he had their full attention.

"Tell me, do you gents know what a water-devil is? A water whirlwind, that is?" There was another perplexed silence.

"Do you mean a waterspout, Master Salticus?"

"Yes, yes! A waterspout. Do you see them here?"

Yes, they said. Now and then, in the thundery weather, you might see a waterspout. Quite a rare thing, though.

"Yes, indeed, a rare thing. I am willing to wager a silver sixpence," producing one from his pocket, "that a waterspout will be seen, from this spot, before this hour tomorrow." And he laid the sixpence on a rock with a satisfying chink. A long silence ensued.

"Will nobody take my wager?" asked Salticus, with an air of wounded disappointment.

"But we do not take wagers on Larus." There were nods of agreement.

"Surely," said Salticus, "you all make wagers every day. You wager your skill at fishing against the skill of the fish in avoiding being caught, do you not?" That was one way of looking at it, to be sure.

"You wager your assessment of the weather against your need to go to sea. You wager your very lives every day. It is a game of skill – and you are all skilled at it, or you would be at the bottom of the briny and not sitting here at all." There was no denying it, at all.

"But we have our lady warden. She assesses the weather.

And she is never wrong. It is no great wager."

"So you have," said Salticus. "And what I am proposing is no great wager, neither. Let us call on your esteemed lady warden and take her advice in the matter of waterspouts, and then you can decide whether the wager is worth taking. I can't say fairer than that, now can I, gents?"

They agreed he couldn't, and a runner was despatched over to Rissa's house to ask if the lady would care to settle a weather-related dispute. She appeared quickly and approached, looking wary and puzzled.

"My dear madam," said Salticus, bowing low, "perhaps you would assist us?"

"What is it you wish?" she asked, keeping well out of Salticus' reach. He had a leery gleam in his eye that she did not like at all, and she wasn't about to let her hand be slobbered over by the likes of him.

"Why, ma'am, we require a weather forecast. I have offered a small wager to these gentlemen that a waterspout will be seen here before this time tomorrow, and in all fairness I think they should have your advice on the matter."

Rissa considered this. She disapproved of Salticus. She disapproved of the drink he brought and she specially disapproved of gambling, but she could scarcely refuse to give a weather forecast. It was her job, after all. She was torn between her loyalty to the islanders and her loyalty to her job, which up until now had been one and the same. But there can be no harm in telling the truth, she thought. If anyone takes this wager, they are likely to win. I am not assisting him in fleecing anyone.

"A waterspout. Here? Before this time tomorrow? Anything can happen, of course. But this is not the type of weather... Very unlikely, I should say."

"There now," said Salticus, "We have the word of the Oracle. Thank you, ma'am. Now, with all information before you, will anyone take the wager?" And he picked up the sixpence and turned it in his fingers, making it glint enticingly.

Old Billy stepped forward. "I'll take your bet, sir," he said, and produced a silver sixpence of his own. Everyone was astounded. Not at Billy having taken the wager, but at his possessing a sixpence unspent on drink.

"Done!" said Salticus, before anyone could object, and turned to Rissa. "May I ask you to be the adjudicator, ma'am? I know everyone here will trust your word." Vigorous nods of agreement. "We will return here tomorrow evening and you can tell us whether any waterspouts have been observed. And to see full fair play, I respectfully request that you hold the stakes for us, too."

There was another long silence. Rissa shifted uncomfortably. She was aware she had been manoeuvred into something, but she couldn't quite identify what was going on. Salticus was almost certain to lose his money. Presumably, he was unable to conjure up waterspouts on demand, even if he did dress like a sorcerer. There could be no harm in it and no loss to the island. Reluctantly she took the coins and placed them in her purse. Surely it was safe enough if she was there to ensure fair play?

Although Captain Castello knew nothing of this, as yet, he would not have been at all surprised. He had been expecting something to happen ever since the *Honest Trader* had arrived. It had been a surprisingly long wait, and it had played on his nerves terribly. Salticus had told him many things, that first day, most of which left him acutely uncomfortable. Not really a captain of artillery. A mere gun captain on a ship. Shameful enough, indeed, that he had been claiming a rank he was not entitled to all this time, and something he would struggle to live down if it ever became known. But not really illegal, not a crime against man and deity. He had made a mistake in this, perhaps, but he could live with it. The other thing, though, the enormity of it! He could hardly bear to consider it.

Another wife, and, according to Salticus, no less than four other children. Bigamy, betrayal, and he knew not what else. How could anyone forget having a wife and four children? Try as he might, he had no recollection of any such thing. He had felt in his bones that he was a bachelor.

"Oh, yes," Salticus had said, rather obviously enjoying himself, "three boys and a girl. Or was it two of each?"

"But I've been here so long," Castello had replied. "These children must be grown up by now." He couldn't bring himself to say 'my' children.

"They are," said Salticus. "And I believe one of the girls is married and has young ones herself."

A grandfather, to boot. Was there no end to this torture?

"And I believe your dear Mama still lives, though she's pretty frail these days."

"Mama?" Castello said, faintly. A tiny memory stirred, somewhere deep down. Was he remembering his mother's voice? It was all insupportable. He was close to tears with the anguish of it, and with him in this fragile state, Salticus had pounced.

"Now, Hugh, old shipmate," he had said, "I see this puts you in a difficulty. Bigamy and desertion. Unpleasant words, to be sure." He shook his head, while the unpleasant words soaked in. "But we are sailors, men of the world, are we not? A girl in every port, eh?" he had added with a particularly nasty wink. "Never fear, I shall not breathe a word of it, not to this wife or the other one, nor to any of all those children, nor to your sainted mother in her dotage. And no one else on this isle knows, no one but me. Your secret is in safe hands, friend."

Castello would have sooner entrusted his safety to a man-eating shark, but he could only accept Salticus' assurances of silence. What were they worth, he wondered.

Salticus had seemed to read his mind.

"Ah, I see you don't trust me. But consider this: I have no reason to cause you trouble by spreading this sorry story about. What would it profit me? Nothing. You are a customer, after all. It is but a small favour you ask of me, to remain silent, and I am happy to grant it. Happy." He paused for effect. "And it is but a small favour I shall ask of you in return."

When news of the bet filtered through to the Reverend Pontius the following morning, his emotions went through many changes. He was appalled – he was disbelieving – he was appalled again – he was disappointed – he was furious. Gambling? On Larus? Appalling! The lady warden advising the gamblers, adjudicating, holding the stake money? Impossible. She was a guardian. But as the tale was related to him, word for word, he understood that she had done exactly that, albeit reluctantly. He was deeply disappointed in her. How could she have been so stupid as to involve herself in such a thing? But of course, it was Salticus at the bottom of this, was it not? And the Reverend was furious.

He was sorry for Rissa. She had been reeled in and landed like a stately haddock. He was disappointed in her, as a guardian, in being so gullible, but he was not surprised. She was an islander, after all, an intrinsically honest creature, and well out of her depth in dealing with the crafty machinations of such a snake as Salticus.

Pontius decided not to challenge her about it. She must know she had been a fool, and rubbing it in would not help. There was nothing to be done but let the whole thing take its course, let the bet be settled and hope that would be an end to it. Nonetheless, he would be saying some pretty strong words about the evils of gambling in Sunday's sermon. Oh yes, indeed. And as for Castello, what on earth had come over the fellow? Why was he not berating his wife? Why had he not come up to the chapel in a state of indignant fury? Why had he not complained about Salticus bringing brandy onto the island? Indeed, why had there been no word from him at all recently? Surely, thought Pontius, Castello cannot approve of the fellow, or even actually like him. Never. It simply wasn't possible. But word was, the Captain was spending a lot of time with Salticus, far more than could have been necessary for the bargaining over the shot and powder. Could it be they were friends? The Reverend felt a small but unmistakable pang of jealousy. The Captain is *my* friend, said a voice, deep inside. My *only* friend, said another voice. It was true. Their friendship had grown out of adversity, from being the only two offcomers on Larus. How could Castello just turn away from him like this after all this time? Neglect him? Barely speak to him? And with such a one as Salticus. The reptile! Honest trader my elbow, said Pontius to himself, knowing a rat when he smelt one. But what could he do? Patience, I must have patience, and be observant. There is more to this than meets the eye. I must do what I can to support the lady warden; we are both victims in this case, I fear, he thought, and rushed off to do just that.

As Rissa waited unhappily for the appointed hour for the settling of the bet, she had plenty of time to regret her actions. She knew now what she should have done. She should have drawn herself to her full height, put on her most imperious expression and told Salticus that her forecasts were for the purpose of keeping people safe at sea, not for settling bets. She was the wise woman of the weather, not a bookie's runner, and they should all be ashamed of themselves. This was what she should have said, but she hadn't, and it was too late now.

The Reverend Pontius had enquired after her at her house, been politely told she wasn't in, and had found her sitting at the foot of the great rock, staring listlessly out to sea, and idly pulling the flower heads off an innocent thrift plant. She barely acknowledged him when he pulled up an adjoining boulder and sat down painfully. He didn't wish to look down on her in any sense. She looked so pitiful, he thought,

114

collapsed there with the pink flowers strewn over her skirts, and he was furious again with Salticus for reducing her to this.

Normally, in times of trouble, Rissa threw herself into her work. But not today. A battleship could have run aground with all guns blazing and she wouldn't have seen it. This was serious, the Reverend thought, what if she gave faulty weather forecasts, overlooked endangered ships? Lives could be lost. He must support and encourage her.

"I have let myself be caught unawares, Reverend," she said sadly. "I have been – what is the word? – *naïve*."

"You have been nothing but your good, honest self, my dear," said Pontius gently. "You are not to blame. And you have done nothing wrong."

"You are very kind, Reverend. But see what a net I am entangled in. I have given my word, and I must see it through. I am ashamed. How will the people ever trust me again, now I have *colluded* with that snake?"

"You have been duped, as I don't doubt we all will be in the end. Salticus is an evil man. I know it. I can't prove it yet. But I will, rest assured. In the meantime, Lady, I recommend you look to your work. You are important to us here on Larus."

He hoped this might cheer her, but there was no sign of it. Rissa continued to stare at the sea. "Oh, Reverend, there is worse," she said, without taking her eyes off the horizon.

"Worse?" said Pontius, alarmed. Whatever could she mean? He waited quietly for her to continue.

"It's Castello, my husband. I can't understand what's happened to him."

You and me both, thought Pontius, slightly relieved, but said nothing.

"He came in this morning, very early, to see us. Went straight in and kissed the babies, even though we had not changed their clothes. He never comes near them, Reverend, until they are clean and sweet. Never. But today he insisted on picking them up, both of them, as they were. Not a word about the smell. And Petrus was sick all over his gold epaulette. Not a word. By the time we had induced him to put them down, they had both piddled all down his second-best uniform."

This was so out of character that Pontius was shocked. His fastidious friend Castello allowing the children to piddle on his uniform? It was unthinkable.

"And then, what do you think, Reverend? He came over and kissed me in front of the children, in front of the nursemaid. It was just too improper for words." Public displays of affection were certainly not Castello's style at all, thought Pontius, but again said nothing.

"Well," Rissa went on, "As you know, Reverend, I am a reasonable woman, but this was all so unlike him, I fear I lost my temper."

You astound me dear lady, thought Pontius.

"I had been expecting him to come and rail at me for my part in that shameful business with the bet. I was ready to reply in kind, to ask him why he did not fetch his sword and run that Salticus creature off the island immediately, bag and baggage. He said nothing, Reverend. Not a word. So I pitched in with my half of the argument anyway. Asked how he could stand by and see his wife insulted, duped, made a fool of. Involved in a wager. Do you know what he said? He said there was no harm in it. That Salticus was his friend, and had done nothing wrong, and that I should not speak ill of him, and that was an order."

Pontius was shocked again. He didn't know anyone on Larus who would dare give an order to the lady warden, including, and especially, her husband.

"I flew into such a rage, Reverend," Rissa went on.

No surprise there, thought Pontius.

"I shouted at him. Called him a spineless ninny. A big girl's blouse. He wouldn't answer. I threw the chamber pot at him, and caught him such a blow on the knee. He just turned and walked out. I slammed the door after him so hard the gutters fell down, I was in such a passion. But, oh, Reverend, when I looked out of the window and saw him limping away, his uniform all besmirched, looking so destroyed, I could have wept. I have been a wicked woman." And tears ran down her face.

"Dear Lady," said Pontius, daring to pat her hand, "There is wickedness abroad. But it is Salticus who causes it, not you. Compose yourself, dear."

Rissa blew her nose on the hem of her skirt, and turned her anguished face to the Reverend for the first time. "Has my husband not spoken to you? You are his friend. Has he not explained himself at all?"

"He has not. I have scarcely seen him," said Pontius, sadly. "He spends his time with Salticus these days."

"Then we have both lost him, Reverend," she said.

That evening, Rissa looked out of the window and saw a little crowd gathering, with Salticus in the middle. The Reverend Pontius had advised her to settle the bet, as briefly and simply as possible and then withdraw before anything else could be said. This was wise counsel, and she decided to act upon it. Drawing herself up, she shook out her gown and strode across the turf, frowning.

"Ah," said Salticus, grinning greasily, "Here is our esteemed lady. We can now settle our bet."

Don't you 'esteemed lady' me, thought Rissa, her fieriness returning, or I'll knock your silly grinning head off, turban and all. It was good to know she had a supportive ally in the Reverend.

"There has been no waterspout seen or reported," she said, as evenly as possible. "Old Billy wins the wager." And she handed over the two silver sixpences, receiving a gummy smile from the winner for her trouble. She inclined her head to them all, turned on her heel and walked swiftly back to her house.

Sadly, though, the gambling bug had taken hold, assisted by Old Billy waving his money about and crowing about his win all over the island. A small waterspout betting-exchange sprang up among the islanders, and for the rest of the week Rissa endured a succession of young lads knocking on the door to artlessly enquire whether any waterspouts were expected today, at all. She told them truthfully that she thought not, and then boxed their ears for involving themselves in this wicked gambling, which they said was a bit rich coming from her. Some complicated deals were done, and the odds lengthened, but eventually the evident complete lack of waterspouts won out, and everyone lost interest. Salticus took no part. He watched and waited until the time was ripe, until they needed something else to gamble on. It had cost him a single silver sixpence to get the island hooked. An absolute bargain, to be sure.

Although he took no bets himself, Salticus was a mine of useful ideas for things to bet on and generously offered to hold the stakes. The number of barrels of fish landed in a day – a real skill required there, gents – or the simple toss of a coin if you can't wait that long. By the end of the month, they were betting on everything and anything, and the Reverend Pontius was giving some truly tub-thumping sermons on the subject. Bets were placed on how many times he would wallop the pulpit per sermon.

At the height of this madness, Salticus dropped a sudden bombshell. He was leaving. Soon. It was time to move on. No, he could not be induced to stay. The brandy was running low. But not to worry, the *Honest Trader* would return in a month or two.

Poor Castello. Life had become unutterably complex in such a short time. Over a matter of months he had gone from lonely bachelor to father of six. And in the last few weeks he had been obliged to deceive his wife and turn away from his dearest friend. His life, so recently happy, had collapsed in ruins. And it was all his own fault. How could he have forgotten a whole other family? And what ill luck that Salticus should arrive with this knowledge, after all this time. But, then, no, it was not a matter of luck. He had *asked* for a trader to be alerted, to come and bring the military supplies. He had brought this on himself with his vanity, with his wish to impress people. With his wish to be somebody. But he had *already* been somebody. He had been northern guardian of the Isle of Larus, a respected man. He had thrown it all away for powder and shot. It was entirely his own fault. And when Salticus had asked that the Captain do him the small favour of turning a blind eye to any little *enterprises* that might be set up, selling a little brandy, taking a little wager or two, that sort of thing, nothing improper, he could hardly refuse. It had seemed to do no real harm, up to the point when Rissa had been involved. Then it had become truly personal. He had remonstrated with Salticus, who had merely said, "Remember our bargain, Captain." Castello's hands were tied.

The awful scene at Rissa's house had followed, his attempt to defend Salticus, the disappointment on her face, his dishevelled limping away in disgrace. He was no longer her hero, that was for sure. It was all as bad as it could be. But now the swine was leaving Larus.

Castello harboured mixed feelings about Salticus' imminent departure. On the one hand it meant the rogue would not, accidentally or otherwise, be letting slip to Rissa the small fact that her husband was a bigamist and her children illegitimate. This would be a considerable relief to the Captain after living on a knife-edge of anxiety all this time. But on the other hand, it meant the scoundrel might return next month with Castello's wife – his real wife, that is – in tow, and anything up to four of his other children.

When the day came, everyone went down to the quay to

see the *Honest Trader* on her way. Most of them were genuinely sorry to see Salticus leave. He may be a bit of a sly one, people said, but he had certainly livened the place up a bit. Rissa, Castello and Pontius all came down for the occasion, ostensibly to provide an official farewell, but actually to be quite sure the ship was really gone. The Captain gave a short, stilted, uncomfortable speech wishing the *Honest Trader* a safe and prosperous voyage. Everyone cheered, and Salticus came forward. "Friends!" he cried. "My *dear* friends," with a leery glance at Rissa. "My crew and I have greatly enjoyed our happy stay on your delightful island, but it is time for us to move on and do some *honest trading*." Pause for laughter. "I shall keep your needs in mind while I am away, never fear. And when I return, I shall bring something with me that will surprise you all!"

Castello fervently hoped it would not be his real wife and family. He bowed stiffly to Salticus, and handed him down to his boat.

The three guardians stood long after the crowd had dispersed watching the boat as she unfurled her ruby-red sails, made her way out across the harbour and through the channel between sandbanks out into the open sea. Each of them was heartily wishing she might go straight to the bottom of the ocean, or be sucked up by a waterspout, or anything so long as she never returned. And each in turn was ashamed of the thought.

Chapter Four
A Couple of Kings' Worth

For the next half-dozen mornings, Captain Castello spent an unwarranted amount of time at the quay staring out to sea, making absolutely sure that the *Honest Trader* was really gone. He got a bit of a fright on the second day when a red sail appeared in the distance, but it proved to be only the *Brothers Three*. Ligo the fisherman had been impressed by the great blue sail he had seen on one of the shiny ships the previous year, and wondered whether something of the same design might not work on his own boat. He had felt that plain sailcloth would not do for something so innovative, and had done a deal with Salticus to purchase one of the *Honest Trader*'s spare red sails from which to fashion it. The jury was out on whether the new sail improved the boat's performance, but it did make it very distinctive, and Ligo was content.

No harm done, then, but it made the Captain realise how out of touch he had become. Since Salticus arrived, life had largely stopped dead for Castello. He had not gossiped over the fence with Ralham; he had drawn away from his friends and family for fear of implicating and injuring them; he had not even tried his gun crews with live shot. His whole attention had been centred on Salticus, and what he might do or say. But as the days passed, he slowly relaxed. The whole, horrible incident slithered steadily into the past. The islanders had short memories, and it wasn't long before they stopped talking about Salticus. Out of sight, out of mind, it was, on the Isle of Larus, and gone was as good as forgotten.

The Reverend Pontius, however, did not have such a short memory, but he was glad, nonetheless, when people began to think and talk of other things. He was confident that the islanders' enthusiasm for gambling would quickly wane without Salticus to encourage it, and within a matter of days he was proved right. The tone and quality of the gossip he heard in passing changed subtly but steadily, and it soon seemed that all that remained of Salticus was the powder and shot he had brought and the single silver sixpence he had invested, neither of which could be considered a bad thing in itself.

The Reverend had had a lonely time since his estrangement from Castello. There was no point in denying it. But it had not been wasted time, indeed not. He had used the extra leisure to do some serious writing. He had begun one new book to contain Mother Culver's archive, as he had planned. It now contained the *Song of the Shiny Ships*, as he titled it – all six verses, written in his best handwriting. And he had down the *Song of the Thief*, as he called the verse he had more recently heard. He was quite sure this prophesied the arrival of Salticus, and had begun to wonder if there might be more of it. Mother Culver was no fool, he knew, and it was important not to make her suspicious by appearing at her house every five minutes demanding to know more stories. She would certainly not like the idea of her songs being written down. This was a long oral tradition, the Reverend knew, and he must tread carefully. Nonetheless, a visit to hear the next part would not seem unreasonable now.

The book lived under a loose floorboard beneath the pulpit, safe from prying eyes. The Reverend was uneasy at this deceit of the islanders, but it was for their own good, he told himself. And the book was not alone – it had a companion volume (more than I do, thought Pontius, sadly). This was the Reverend's history of Larus, at least as far back as he could rightly remember, and it was coming along well. He had written down everything he could remember on odd slips of paper, and was gradually juggling them into some sort of order. It was very much a work in progress, of course, but progress was being made, which was very gratifying.

Pontius was just packing away the *Book of the Archive* and the *Book of Larus* into their hidey-hole when the chapel door opened and Captain Castello appeared.

"Am I disturbing you Reverend?" he asked, with a shy smile.

"Just a moment, Captain, and I'll be with you," said Pontius, flustered at being caught in the act. In the past, Castello would undoubtedly have asked the Reverend what he was about, with floorboards all over the place under the pulpit, but he said nothing and waited quietly, looking out of the window. In the past, Pontius would probably have shared his secret with his friend, but just now he had no idea whether the secret would be safe, or indeed whether they were still friends. He replaced the floorboards and stood up creakily.

"You are all dusty, Reverend," said Castello affectionately, brushing cobwebs away. Pontius was so pleased to see the Captain, and to hear him speak like this, that he felt his old features stretching into a broad smile. He had almost forgotten how to smile, these last weeks.

"I am on my way to see Rissa, that is, my lady wife," said Castello, as if explanation were necessary. "I have been rethinking the plans for the house at Fort Resolute, Reverend. I have redrawn them – I am thinking of something a bit more substantial. See." And he took a packet from under his arm and spread out a set of plans on a pew. He didn't add that he might need a larger house to accommodate an extra wife and another four children, not to mention a grandchild and an aged mother.

Pontius was delighted with it all. He was so happy and relieved to see Castello back to his old, enthusiastic self.

"There, Reverend," the Captain said, "the ground plan is much the same – there is only so much space, after all – but I have added another storey. There was stone and brick to spare when we completed the gun platform so I won't need to find extra materials. What do you think? Will the people assist me?" he added, with an anxious look.

"Of course, Captain," said Pontius. "They will be happy to help when they can. I shall speak of it after my sermon on Sunday." It would make a welcome change, the Reverend thought, from rants about the evils of gambling.

"You are a true friend, Reverend," said Castello. "But I will build this house if I have to do it single-handed. I shall go and mark out the foundations as soon as I have seen Rissa. I would not wish to waste the light evenings."

When Castello arrived at her house, Rissa had greeted him politely but coolly. Had asked how he did. Would he like to see the children? He would. Goodness, they had grown. No, really. It was quite perceptible. She was looking very well. Was that a new gown? The small talk had faded. He had surreptitiously checked the room for anything she might use as a missile. She had recognised the move, and sat down with her hands clasped.

"Rissa, I, um, have a proposition – would like your opinion."

A proposition? What on earth was he saying? Was he about to suggest their separation become permanent? The pain and disgrace shot across her face, and Castello mistook it for anger. He jumped to his feet, ready to make a hasty exit. The collection of plans slipped from under his arm and scattered on the floor.

"I – I just wanted to show you these plans. New plans. For the house at Fort Resolute. Bigger. More imposing. More modern. But only if you like them. Dear wife." And he ran his hand nervously through his grey curls. It was a gesture she loved, and her heart went out to him. She leapt up and rushed to throw herself into his arms. He took a step back and crashed into the door, thinking she might have a concealed weapon about her person, but one careful look at her face revealed nothing but affection. He kissed her fondly and knew that all would be well between them now.

Ten minutes later the nursemaid came cautiously into the room and was astounded to find them poring over the plans, hand in hand. She had made herself scarce after taking the twins in for Castello to see, but had been unable to resist a bit of eavesdropping. It had given her the fright of her life when the Captain had collided with the door, uncomfortably close to her ear, and she had scuttled up to the twins, fearing an almighty matrimonial ding-dong downstairs. Rissa sent her off to fetch tea, and she went to the kitchen muttering, "They're all mad, these guardians!"

Now that the whole Salticus business seemed to be over, at least for the time being, the Reverend Pontius thought it high time he had another word with his colleague on the east cliff. The Spirit of the Sea always seemed to have useful knowledge on the whereabouts of ships, and Pontius wanted to enquire about the current status of the *Honest Trader*. He rather hoped it might be occupying a comfortable berth at the bottom of the sea. But no.

"That ship is far away, the spirit says," said Rufus, mournfully. "But she is well. Quite intact." He looked nearly as unhappy about it as the Reverend felt.

"And will she return, colleague?"

"She will. The spirit will not prevent it," said Rufus, and buried his face in his hands.

This was so unlike Rufus, who normally affected an air of complete nonchalance, that the Reverend began to wonder if the hermit were ill. At his age... well, you never knew. And living out here in a hopelessly inadequate dwelling on this draughty cliff top in all weathers… it wasn't good at all for an old man. The hermit rather had the appearance of having shrunk in the wash, these days.

The Reverend Pontius, though no spring chicken himself, always felt like a callow youth in the presence of Rufus. It was one of the many things he found irksome, and he had always felt that the hermit did it on purpose. But now he was not so sure. Rufus was just a poor, helpless, blind old man whose self-containment was a natural result of his affliction. And, of course, his ability to commune with the Spirit of the Sea. Ah, well, thought the Reverend, we all have to make our way in the world as best we can. And he resolved to bring Rufus a blanket or two, and any other little home comforts he could find. And as for the return of Salticus – well, he would worry about that when the time came.

The population of the Isle of Larus generally remained pretty steady. Deaths and births seemed to balance out naturally, on the whole. The survivors of shipwrecks very occasionally made their homes on the island, but, in general, they merely waited for the next trading ship to come in, or for a ship taking shelter in the harbour in rough weather, and then moved on. Seagoing men tended to be restless, and shipwrecked passengers had homes elsewhere. The islanders made them welcome while they stayed, and most of them used whatever skills they had to pay their way while they waited.

There had been just two survivors of the wreck of the *Resolute*. One had quietly died a few days later and been respectfully buried, the other, one of the ship's crew, was in good health and recovered quickly. He had been a considerable help to Captain Castello during the building of the gun platform. He knew a good deal about guns, too, and the Captain had learned quite a lot by listening and watching intently. He would have been just the fellow to assist with the building of the new house, but he had left with the *Honest*

126

Trader, so the Captain began work more or less alone.

He had barely got started marking out the foundations when his neighbour and gun captain, Ralham, saw what he was about and came to give a hand with the measuring. They worked companionably, and eventually began to discuss the possibility of some live gunnery practice. Ralham had been quite perplexed at the Captain's neglect of the gun crews since the arrival of the powder and shot. But now, it seemed, he was back to his old self, and keen to try out the guns again. Ralham offered to organise the practice sessions. The Captain need do nothing but say the word. The Captain was happy to say the word. Gunnery practice would commence as soon as it could be arranged.

From that day onwards, Castello spent every spare moment digging out the foundations. He didn't at all mind the hard physical work – indeed he was rather enjoying it – and the islanders were mightily impressed that a guardian should roll up his sleeves and work with pick and shovel like this. In ones and twos they came to assist, whenever they had an hour to spare, and Rissa visited frequently to deliver sustaining meals and make encouraging noises. The ground was hard, and progress was slow, but the outline of the ground floor steadily appeared. And at the same time the sound of cannon fire became so commonplace that people stopped jumping out of their skins and simply ignored it.

The Reverend Pontius, too, came down regularly to see how things were going. He had offered to help but given the increasingly creaky state of his back, Castello wouldn't hear of it.

"No Reverend," he had said, "Just come down before sunset and talk to me while I work. Tell me if I'm digging a straight line." It was all so meticulously marked out that Pontius knew there was no need to do anything of the kind – but he came along anyway, most evenings, and talked to the Captain until darkness fell, and then sat and talked another hour. Sometimes

Rissa came down, too, and all three sat together. It was hard to say which of the three was happiest.

One exceptionally warm evening the Reverend came down the hill mopping his brow and thinking he wouldn't attempt the walk back until well after dark when it cooled down a little. He found Castello and a small gang of assistants, sweating as they worked. It was a little shocking to the Reverend to see his fellow-guardian labouring in the heat like this. But one look at the Captain's face showed he was perfectly happy with the arrangement. Pontius waved and took a seat on a boulder to get his breath back.

The regular, muted ring of picks and shovels on solid ground was suddenly interrupted with a resounding clang. Work stopped while everyone looked to see what had caused this abrupt change of tone.

"Reverend!" called Ralham, "Come and see what we have found!"

Pontius hauled himself to his feet and looked down into the trench. The working party was digging something out.

"What is it?" asked the Reverend, peering down.

"I believe it is an iron chest," answered Castello, standing up and beating off the dust. They sent for a chisel. A crowbar. And by and by an object was lifted out of the trench. It was heavy, very heavy, they said. It took four of them to lift it. It was, indeed, an iron chest.

"Well," said the Reverend. "Let us open it."

Castello insisted on opening it carefully, so as not to damage the chest itself. It was pretty well rusted, and it took a while to persuade the lid to lift. And when it finally did, everyone stood and gazed in astonishment. The chest was full of silver coins. Absolutely full.

"Good grief!" said Pontius, as astonished as everyone else. "Is it... is it full all the way down? I mean, is there anything else underneath?"

Castello pushed his hand down into the heap of coins as far as he could reach, and found only more silver.

"Must be a king's ransom there!" somebody said.

"Indeed," said the Reverend, "A couple of kings' worth, at least, I should think."

They stared at the treasure trove. Someone had buried this, quite some time ago, to judge by the state of the chest. Chatter quickly broke out. Had anyone ever heard of a buried hoard on Larus? They had not. How had it come there? It was a gift from the Spirit of the Sea! Or the Sky (with apologetic glances at the Reverend). It was a wonder to behold. What must be done with it? Did it belong to the Captain, since it was found in the foundations of his new house? There was far more silver in the chest than normally circulated on the island.

"No," said Castello. "This is a gift to us all, to Larus. From whichever spirit." With a wry look at Pontius, who smiled in agreement. "We must hold this as a… a…" There was a word from long ago trying to find its way into the Captain's mind. "A Commonwealth!"

Everyone was very pleased with this. It could be used to buy seed. Or a new ram to revitalise the sheep flock. Or powder and shot for practice.

The Reverend Pontius decided to take charge: "The Captain and I will count the silver. We will hold public meetings to decide what to buy. Things for the benefit of us all. And all shall take part in making the decisions."

Everyone was very pleased with this, too.

"But for now," said Pontius, "we must keep it safe."

"No one on the isle would think to steal it, Reverend!"

"No, indeed. But this is a great fortune, and we must have it secure, all the same." Pontius caught Castello's eye. They were both thinking of someone not currently on the island who would love to help himself to it, given half a chance.

"Let the Captain decide!"

Castello thought for a moment, then said, "Well, it is very

heavy, so it would seem logical not to move it too far. Especially in this heat. Let us keep it in my room, for the time being. I can secure the door. It will be quite safe. And I will open up for anyone who wants to come and see it. If you trust me, that is," he added as an afterthought.

Well, of course they did. Excellent plan. And the chest was duly hauled and hefted indoors.

Word went round like wildfire that a treasure had been found. A king's ransom! *Two* kings' ransoms, the Reverend says, and we can all go and see it. The Captain had his work interrupted by a steady stream of curious islanders arriving to view the hoard. There was an orderly queue outside his door, the first couple of mornings. Castello thought it wise to call down Ferro the blacksmith to repair the chest as far as possible, and put a new lock on the Captain's door while he was about it. With this done, the novelty quickly wore off, and Castello completed the digging of the foundations in peace.

The idea of a 'commonwealth' was perfectly natural to the people of Larus. Things were normally held more or less in common. All the land on Larus belonged to the island as a whole, people said. Different areas were historically used by families, or individuals, and this was usually acknowledged and accepted. When there was a genuine need for a new building, everyone discussed it and decided where it could best be accommodated for the benefit of all. The castle had, in effect, been a 'vacant lot' when Castello arrived, and his inclination to take it on had been welcomed.

The four guardians were likewise held in common to the island, and all four were paid in coin or, more often, in kind, by the whole population. A share of the fish catch, perhaps, or fruit from the island's two stunted little apple orchards, a loaf, a cheese. Whatever they had, they shared with the guardians. It was a successful system, with everyone happy to give a share, and the guardians taking, in general, only what they needed.

They were very much cherished by all the islanders.

Captain Castello, however, was now being considered something of a special case. The building work at the Fort, and the training of the gun crews had him jumping about 'like a herring on a griddle' as somebody put it, and it was decided that the newly wealthy Isle of Larus could afford a housekeeper for him. Obviously, people said, the lady warden had her own important work to do, without managing two households as well. No, the Captain should have a housekeeper, initially to take care of his present quarters, and later to look after the new house and keep it in good order for the reception of visiting dignitaries, when they arrived.

Castello was delighted. But who could be appointed to this important new post? Someone reliable, and preferably someone living conveniently nearby. "What do you think, Master Ralham?" asked the Captain.

"Why, Limanda is surely the girl for this job," said Ralham.

The Captain gave him an enquiring look. Limanda was the daughter of Ralham's other neighbour, Alvan, and it had long been thought they would marry. But Ralham had been reluctant. Castello suspected this was a ploy on Ralham's part to distract the girl from this rejection. Still, if she were not about to marry, she would need some sort of occupation, and there was no denying she lived locally. And so it was arranged. Limanda came to clean and tidy on a regular basis. She received a suspicious glance or two from Rissa in the early days, but she proved to be quietly competent, and everyone was content with the arrangement.

The Reverend Pontius made his weary way up the cliff to visit Rufus the Hermit. He had found a couple of warm blankets, and wrapped them carefully round a dish of hot food. It was more of a consoling visit to one of the old folks of the island than a consultation with a colleague, he thought. He did it for everyone else, so why not for Rufus? The hermit had definitely seemed to be feeling his age, the last time Pontius had seen him, and the Reverend's job included tending to the needs of everyone, guardian or not. As Rufus never left his cliff top, people sometimes seemed to forget he was there, so it was the neighbourly thing to do.

Rufus looked thinner and more worn than ever, but he sat up and sniffed as Pontius approached. The aroma of the food had clearly reached him. The Reverend had the painful thought that the hermit resembled nothing so much as a wretched old dog, chained to a kennel and smelling a distant bone.

"It's only me, colleague," said Pontius, getting the first word in for once.

"Have you brought an offering for the Spirit of the Sea, Reverend?" said Rufus, as self-contained as ever, despite his appearance.

"No, brother," said Pontius. "This is for you. And some blankets too."

"Visiting the poor and sick, are we?" said Rufus. "The Spirit of the Sky will be most gratified, I should think."

The Reverend fought down the impulse to tip the whole lot over Rufus' head. Why couldn't he just say thanks very much, and pass the time of day, like everyone else? Instead, he unwrapped the dish and put it into Rufus' hands. The hermit turned haughtily away. But he began to eat, all the same.

"No doubt you already know that Castello, Rissa and I are on good terms again," said Pontius. "That creature Salticus caused a rift. Entangled the lady warden in shady dealings, he did. And what came over the Captain, I simply do not know. Unless you do, of course," he added, hopefully.

"I don't," said Rufus, pausing between mouthfuls. "But I can guess." The hermit left this interesting statement hanging in mid-air as he continued his dinner. But he declined to elaborate, and finished the bowl in silence. Pontius saw there was going to be no explanation, took a deep breath to repel the impatience welling up inside him, and asked the pressing question that had, if he were honest, brought him here.

"Last time I saw you, colleague, you told me he, Salticus I mean, would return. It has been two months. Do you still think so?"

"Oh, yes," said Rufus, matter-of-factly, and handed the empty bowl back. "Soon."

The Reverend sighed unhappily, and prepared to leave. "Take care, old man," he said resignedly, and set off.

"*You* take care, Reverend," called Rufus after him. "And thank you, colleague."

Chapter Five
The Magnificent Surprise

A completely still day was a pretty rare thing on the Isle of Larus. A breeze and, quite often, a gale, blew more or less continuously, from one direction or another. This was just as well, of course, in a place whose economy depended on fishing boats going out under sail on a frequent basis. The steep sides of the island meant that at least one aspect of it was a-lee of the wind most of the time, providing a little respite from the interminable gusts and buffets, but only down in the depths of the coves. Yes, a really still day was a novelty. When it did happen, the island regained its sense of sound. The cries of the gulls became closer, more intimate and more complete. Normally, the wind ran off with most of the detail, and you would only hear the edited highlights, so to speak. Small sounds, that were obviously always there, became audible again – the rustle of small animals among the grasses, and the swish of birds' wings and of women's skirts. On still days, people realised just how loud they usually were obliged to yell in order to make themselves heard above the continual whistle and moan and rush of air, and it was quite pleasant to converse with their neighbours at a civilised volume for once.

It was just such a perfectly beautiful, still morning the following week when Captain Castello came out to look at the building works, as usual. The foundations were complete, and walls were beginning to rise. It was starting to look like a real house, at last, he thought. The front door would be just here –

134

was it large enough? Sufficiently imposing? Castello frowned. Not his usual expression, and it crunched his face up uncomfortably. But no, it had all been measured, and re-measured. It would look as imposing as you like, once the walls were tall enough. A run of fine weather had meant the work had continued uninterrupted, and the Captain was pleased with progress, really. He turned and looked out across the harbour. There was a mist on the water, and the stillness was almost palpable.

Something stirred in the mist, far out, and was gone. What was that? A moment later, there it was again. A red sail. It vanished again, leaving Castello on the alert. But then he relaxed. Of course, it was the *Brothers Three*. Ligo must have been becalmed out there. And the Captain watched the sail appear and disappear for a while.

"A boat becalmed, Captain?" said Ligo, in his ear.

"Yes, it's... Oh!" said Castello, turning. If Ligo were standing here beside him, what boat was that out in the harbour?

Ligo answered the question himself. "I believe that is the *Honest Trader* come back to us, Captain."

Castello was so horrified, he stood rooted to the spot. And sure enough, a little while later the mists parted, and there she was. It was undoubtedly the *Honest Trader*. And she was indeed becalmed.

Word spread very quickly. Master Salticus is back! Within the hour, there was a small crowd on the quayside, all talking at once. The mist had cleared, and a little breeze had sprung up. The great red sail was filling, lazily, and the ship began to move. But she didn't head in for the quay. She circled, making Castello think of the shiny ships of the previous year. It stirred a memory, somewhere deep down. "She circles like a shark," said the Captain to himself. How did he know what a shark was? They never appeared off Larus. But somehow he knew how it felt to be in the water with those slicing fins circling, waiting for the attack. Was it a real memory, or a story someone had told him? He didn't know. Salticus had told him he had been a seagoing man. At least, he thought, if it is a real memory, I survived the experience. But will I survive this one, he thought, watching the *Honest Trader*.

"She is waiting for the high tide!" somebody said. "She must have something aboard that cannot be brought up the ladder."

Like my ancient mother, thought Castello, growing cold. Or possibly my ancient wife.

They didn't have long to wait to find out. It was true that any vessel tying up at the quay at a low point of the tide could only be reached by the ladder, making it difficult to unload anything large or unwieldy. As the tide came in, so did the *Honest Trader*. Standing in the prow was Salticus. People muttered excitedly. He is wearing an entirely new suit of clothes! Where is his turban? The turban, in point of fact, had been lost in a card game, and Salticus now affected a large broad-brimmed silk hat with an immense white feather. He waved, regally, as the ship came in to the quay, and leapt ashore. The Reverend Pontius had collected Rissa and brought her down to the quay as soon as he had heard of the ship's return, and they stood with Castello, forming what they hoped would appear to be a united front, rather than a guard of honour. Salticus swaggered up and bowed extravagantly. The three inclined their heads civilly.

"Aha," said Salticus. "The Captain, his lady, and the good Reverend. Good day to you all, my dears." *My dears*? thought Pontius. The barefaced cheek of the villain.

"Have a care, there!" Salticus shouted to his crew, who were putting in place a large gangplank. Castello could hardly bear to look. Was he about to be publicly humiliated? In front of his wife, in front of his friend, in front of just about everybody?

"Don't look so worried, Hugh, my old shipmate," said

Salticus, quietly.

Not everyone heard this, but Rissa certainly did. The snake had called her husband by his first name. A thunderous look came over her face, but before she could act on it, there was a communal gasp from the crowd.

The unloading of the *Honest Trader* had begun. People stared in amazement. Look, look. They were magnificent. They were beautiful. They were horses. One after another, the three jog-trotted across the gangplank and onto the quay, where they stood swishing their tails with highbred finickiness. They were creatures built and bred for speed – a big, classy-looking brown, a flashy piebald and a small, close-coupled sorrel.

"Lo and behold, good people," said Salticus gesturing to the horses. "May I present my friends Bruno, Presto and Rufus."

The Reverend Pontius was outraged. "You are calling that beast *Rufus*?" he said sharply.

"Indeed. It is the animal's name, as my crew will tell you. No disrespect intended to your esteemed colleague on the east cliff, naturally. Pure coincidence."

Pontius wasn't sure whether to believe this or not. He glanced across at Castello for support, but the Captain avoided his gaze, staring firmly at the ground. Ah, thought the Reverend, so that's how the land lies. Salticus returns, and the Captain turns away from me. And from his wife, too, I expect. He didn't know whether to be sad or furious first. But sadness got the better of him, and he said nothing more.

The majority of the islanders had never set eyes on any sort of horse, other than Ferro's old grey mare, and these three were an object of wonder. They were certainly not working horses of any variety.

"But what are they for?" somebody asked at last.

"Excellent question, sir," said Salticus. "And I shall be answering it very soon. I shall shortly be announcing a great event, here on Larus, for the delight of you all."

Ferro's forge was smack in the middle of the island, making it convenient for everyone, whatever point of the compass they lived at. Being the topmost point of the place, he could see the sea from all sides here, when there was no mist. "All of Larus looks up to me!" he would say, jovially. It didn't take much to make Ferro laugh.

It was certainly a commanding place, and he was aware that Captain Castello had cast envious eyes on it, once or twice. But the forge had been there since time immemorial, and there it was going to stay. It was a squat, chunky building, encroached on over time by persistent ivy that defied all attempts to dislodge it.

In the winter pigeons came and ate the ivy berries, their heavy bodies bending the boughs. Ferro noted their comings and goings, but as an islander, did not bother to count the years. He was very content – content with his life, content with his wind-battered, ivy-green forge, and content with his family. He was specially content with his son, Young Ferro, a youth of such startling good looks that all the island girls had their eyes out on stalks whenever he passed. He had his father's jovial temperament, too, which made him even more appealing. He was learning the skills of the blacksmith from his father, and was, as everyone said, wonderful with animals. Practically talked to them, he did.

There wasn't a huge amount of work for a blacksmith, and even less for a farrier, so Ferro had his finger in a number of pies to make a living. He owned a small fishing boat, which he leased out, and acted as resident doctor to the island animals, and sometimes people, too. His tooth pulling was legendary. He kept a mixed flock of hardy sheep and goats, which ate practically anything, and did deals with the local families who made cheese from their milk.

Ferro had no disagreement with Salticus. On the contrary, he fancied himself as a businessman, and recognised a fellow-creature in the trader. They had done a small deal or two during the *Honest Trader's* previous sojourn at Larus. Ferro had assisted Ligo with the ironwork and rigging of his innovative new red sail for the *Brothers Three*, and had plans to make more of them, if it proved a success, so he was hoping to buy further red sails from Salticus or, better still, learn how to make red sails for himself. Either way, he was anxious to stay on good terms with Salticus, so when the opportunity arose to house and care for the new horses, he was only too happy to oblige.

So it wasn't long before a makeshift stable had been built near the forge, and a little paddock roped off. Had he been more of a businessman, Ferro could have charged a small fee to all the people who came to see the horses in their glory. As it was, he simply stood and admired them with everyone else. Young Ferro had quickly taken on the horse-care duties. He was an absolute natural with them, according to Salticus, as Ferro proudly told all the visitors. The lad was besotted with them, and they took equally well to him. Soon he was riding them to exercise on the cliff tops too, flying along bareback on one with the other two running alongside. Where Young Ferro went, the three horses followed, and he slept in the stable with them. He was a natural and fearless rider. Not bad, as his father said, for one whose only horse experience came from the old grey mare. And she has just two paces, you know – slow, and very slow indeed.

Captain Castello had tried, he really had, not to let his life be too much affected by the return of Salticus. He had been hugely relieved that the big surprise had been the horses, and not the arrival of his other wife and family. Salticus had said nothing at all on the subject, though they spent a good deal of time together. There was a new cargo of powder and shot aboard the *Honest Trader*, and a bargain needed to be struck. It had been agreed among the islanders that payment for these supplies should consist partly of a batch of salt fish barrels, and partly of silver from the treasure chest. The gun crews had now settled into a comfortable weekly training session, and everyone agreed that, for safety's sake, this should become a permanent arrangement. So the deal was done. There was no denying that Salticus charged a very honest and reasonable price. A little on the cheap side, in fact. But who was going to argue with that, people said.

The Captain took special care to cover the treasure chest when Salticus visited him. He would find out about it eventually, of course, from the islanders, but there was no need to dangle it under his nose. Castello was glad he had asked Ferro to fix the chest, and see to all the locks. It was all about as secure as he could make it. Rissa, unsurprisingly, had refused to come anywhere near the quay or the fort since the day of Salticus' arrival. She had a little chatelaine of keys, which she sadly handed back to her husband, and retreated to the southern end of the island 'to keep out of the way of that *rogue*'.

Castello gave the keys to Limanda, now promoted to full household manager in Rissa's absence. She had proved herself a trustworthy girl. She would not let the Captain down, she said, she would guard the keys with her very life.

"No need for that," said Castello, kindly. "Just don't leave them lying around."

The Reverend Pontius found, as he had feared, that his leisure hours were his own again. Captain Castello had drawn away from him, as before, once Salticus was back on the island. The Reverend had turned to his books once more, and decided it was time to go and see what he could learn from Mother Culver. He had put off the visit, many times. The old woman made him intensely uncomfortable, not least because he knew part of his purpose was to steal her stories. It weighed on his conscience, and he had consulted the Spirit of the Sky about it many times. The spirit hadn't exactly given him its blessing. But neither had he been struck by a bolt of lightning.

The spirit had shown no sign of disapproval, and that would just have to do.

The return of Salticus had made it urgent to hear any further prophecies, given their previous alarming accuracy, and Pontius trudged off to see her.

"You've been a long time, Reverend. I've been expecting you," said Mother Culver. She and Rufus were as bad as each other, thought Pontius, crossly. They both spoke to him as if he were a naughty five-year-old, late for his tea. He did his best to ignore it, and kept his questions as dignified as possible.

"Is there more to hear, Mother, of the prophecy? The one about the thief?"

"There is," she said, and went straight into her trance.

Upon the day they come, avengers three
They turn to put the evil all to rout
Swift they are, from far across the sea
And come to stamp the wicked spider out

Not soon enough for me, thought Pontius, whatever they are.

A maid betrayed will answer questions all
She brings a tale of greed and theft by stealth.
But then – two rains of silver brightly fall
And shall restore the island's rightful wealth.

He had it all committed to memory instantly, whatever it might mean, and was able to sit and bandy words with Mother Culver for a while. It looked much less suspicious, thought the Reverend, if he didn't rush off immediately. He should have felt that this little deceit was shameful. But he didn't. Actually, this time, he rather enjoyed it. He'd have enjoyed it far less if he'd heard Mother Culver's quiet remark to his retreating back.

"Ah Reverend," she said to herself. "You'd not look so smug if you'd heard the other prophecy. But you shan't hear it. Oh, dear no. Not yet, anyhow."

Having carefully written out the verses into the *Book of the Archive*, Pontius sat late into the night trying to puzzle it all out. The three avengers – could they be the three horses, perhaps? They were certainly swift, and they did come from far across the sea. Could it be that Salticus was fated to be trampled underfoot by his own horses? The Reverend really was ashamed at the pleasure he gained from this thought. But not before he had permitted a satisfied smirk to spread across his features. The 'maid betrayed' was more worrying. This could predict real harm to an islander. Unless, of course, thought Pontius, it was an oblique reference to Rissa. Not a maid, exactly, of course. But she *had* been betrayed by Salticus, duped into taking part in the bet – by answering questions about the weather. It was possible this explained the reference to answering questions, wasn't it? The rains of silver had him completely stumped. Did this refer to the treasure hoard? Or what else? All in all, though, Pontius was reassured. It sounded as if it all turned out right in the end. But he would have dearly loved to know exactly how. He put the book away and went off to bed.

Chapter Six
The Stupendous Event

Captain Castello's housekeeper, Limanda, was greatly impressed with Salticus. She had met him several times when he had come to see the Captain and, on occasion, had hung around longer than was strictly necessary when a meeting was likely, just to enjoy the compliments the trader showered on her. What a man, she thought. Such wealth, such clothing, such jewels, such presence, such a beard! Why had she made herself miserable over that namby-pamby Ralham, when there were men of substance like Salticus in the world? He had his own beautiful ship, with ruby-red sails! He owned three magnificent horses! And he had bowed to her, actually bowed. Kissed her hand. Paid her such pretty compliments. Her eyes were like jewels. Her hair like spun gold.

None of the island boys behaved like that, least of all Ralham. He is an honest enough soul, she thought, but not exciting enough for me. Indeed, he had done her a great favour in his reluctance to marry her. She wondered, at first idly, if Salticus were married, and then determined to find out. There would be many benefits in becoming the wife of such a man, would there not?

The opportunity was not long in arriving. Limanda, lingering, as prettily as possible, on the quay was spotted by Salticus who strode across. "Why," he said, bowing over her hand. "'Tis Miss Manda! You brighten my day with your presence, my dear."

143

Miss Manda fluttered her eyelashes. "Master Salticus," she simpered, "I wonder if there might be, among your goods for sale, some especially pretty ribbons? For me?" And she took out of her pocket one of the silver coins from the treasure chest, which had been paid to her for her housekeeping duties. Why should she not spend some money on some nice things for herself?

Salticus glanced at the coin. Bowed again. Told her not to move from the spot. He would be back in a moment with the finest ribbons in the world. Within minutes, he returned with a box full of ribbons, buttons, brooches and lace trims, and waited patiently while Limanda looked through it all, wide-eyed, her silver coin held between finger and thumb.

At length, she made her choices and held out the coin. Salticus took it and looked at it quizzically. "May I ask how you come by such riches, Miss Manda?"

Limanda told him. She was not a mere serving girl, you know. She was housekeeper to Captain Castello, no less. It was a responsible position. She would be housekeeper – no, house *manager* – when the Captain's new house was complete, and would help in the receiving of visiting dignitaries. The Isle of Larus was wealthy now, since the finding of the treasure hoard, and could afford to pay someone of her calibre to perform these duties. She was a woman of means.

"Ah," said Salticus. "I have heard of this hoard. I hope it is kept safe?"

"Of course. The Captain has care of it. I polish the treasure chest myself."

"Then it is in the most beautiful of hands," said Salticus, seriously. "And I beg you will accept these ribbons free of charge." He handed the coin back to her. "I hope I may see you wear them very soon."

It was the opportunity Limanda had looked for.

"Oh, sir," she said, artfully, or so she thought. "What would Mrs Salticus say?"

"Ah," said Salticus, with a mournful look. "Do not concern yourself. I have no wife, alas." And with a final bow, he walked away. Both parties were very satisfied with this exchange. Limanda was left wondering if such a splendid catch could be hooked, while Salticus was thinking how easy it would now be to set up the profitable scheme he had in mind with no more cost to himself than the price of a few cheap ribbons, and an hour or two paying compliments to a passably attractive girl.

It wasn't long before the gambling began again. The Reverend Pontius would have given you long odds against it taking more than a week for this to happen, if he had been a betting man, which he wasn't. So, here we go again, he thought.

Salticus soon had everyone playing a simple betting game with a pack of cards, and this time he took part himself. The strange thing was, at least to the Reverend, that Salticus lost, and lost again, and again. He gambled with the silver coins that had formed part of the payment for the powder and shot, and soon they were circulating freely. Pockets and purses all over Larus were jingling with little silver coins. How could an experienced trickster like Salticus be losing so often? And when he did win, which was rarely, he was simply regaining his own money. How could it profit him? And, more to the point, how could the Reverend preach effectively against the evils of gambling when everyone in the congregation had benefited from it? It was a big, worrying puzzle.

It wasn't long, too, before people began to speak very knowledgeably about the best way to calculate the odds on or against something happening. Silver coins were laid down and odds offered on anything and everything. It was worse than the outbreak of gambling during Salticus' previous visit, because everyone had so many more coins to bet with.

Pontius felt very much alone in the face of all this. Rissa, although scandalised, refused to have anything to do with any of it, and went into a silent retreat at home, coming out only to make her weather forecasts or stand alone on the great rock watching for ships. And Castello. Well, he was no help at all. Although he in no way involved himself in the gambling, he said nothing at all against it, to anyone. And certainly not to the Reverend Pontius, who was righteously annoyed. There are four guardians on this isle, he told himself, and I am left to deal with this alone. It is entirely outrageous.

But he did his best, anyway. On the next Sunday, he returned to his former anti-gambling, pulpit-walloping style of sermon with gusto. Everyone listened politely, but every time they moved or fidgeted, their purses and pockets jingled with silver, making everything he said seem more than a little comical.

"Beware, you will lose everything to this evil!" Jingle. "Your children will be left destitute!" Jingle, chink. "Larus will be ruined!" Jingle, jingle, stifled giggle. Pontius gave up the unequal struggle, and was about to dismiss them, when the door flew open and Salticus strode confidently in. The Reverend was caught off balance. The trader had never come into the chapel before.

"Please excuse the interruption, your Reverence," said Salticus. "And good day, all. I had understood the time after you finish prayers is traditionally used for announcements."

This was true. There were murmurs and nods. "Then, by your leave, I have an announcement to make," said Salticus. He had everyone's undivided attention. "I should like to announce, a great, a stupendous event. We will be holding our Grand Horse Race, between my three beautiful racing horses, a fortnight today." And with that, he bowed and swept out, leaving everyone talking and the Reverend Pontius fuming. How dare he, how dare he, how dare he use the chapel, use *my* chapel, as an advertising board for his unspeakable underhand schemes?

Very soon the local gossip changed from talk of the likely

146

odds on pretty much anything, to talk of odds on something very particular indeed: the outcome of the race. Or the Great Race, as everyone referred to it, to Pontius' annoyance. And suddenly everyone was an expert on racing horses. There were wise remarks upon one or other of the horses having *gone well on the gallops*, looking *well in their coats*, or carrying a *little too much condition*. Where are they getting all this jargon from, wondered Pontius. But the answer was obvious, really. Salticus' nightly card schools were full of talk about the horses. Within a short time the horses were no longer merely being exercised on the cliff top, they were *in training*.

Two young crewmen from the *Honest Trader* were drafted in as jockeys with Young Ferro aboard the third horse, and regular training sessions were held, all well-attended by the islanders. It was no secret at all that money was beginning to change hands. Specifically, it was moving out of the islanders' hands, and into those of Salticus. He had set himself up as bookmaker, the Reverend Pontius heard. Had actually set up a table at training sessions, with a proper book to write all the wagers in, and a big bag to hold the stake money. When it was not in use, the bag was held at the forge by Ferro, who was only too happy to oblige. The islanders knew the blacksmith could be trusted not to interfere with it, and of course, Salticus was a wealthy man who could easily cover any losses. And he had been losing so much, betting at cards, lately, hadn't he? All you needed to do was choose the winning horse. And that was only three to one against, wasn't it, whichever way you looked at it.

The word was that the race would be held over a measured mile-and-a-half circular course. It had been carefully chosen to provide lots of convenient viewpoints for the race goers. In the interests of not favouring one horse over another, the course covered a variety of surfaces, beginning on the grassy cliff top, then cutting across east on the old cinder track, and back to the beginning along the main road, which was relatively stony.

A true test of a horse that copes with any sort of going. The start and finish were the same point, to be clearly marked out, just outside the chapel. In effect, the islanders could walk straight out of the chapel after Sunday prayers and straight onto the racecourse. Pontius was convinced this was probably sacrilegious, but sadly the Spirit of the Sky had never provided him with a list of things that thou shalt not do on a Sunday, and it was normally regarded as a general day off.

As the race drew nearer all sorts of horse-related gossip proliferated. Ah, people said, with shrewd looks, the little sorrel, Rufus, is unbeatable over the mile. Runs like the wind, he does, but he will not stay the extra four furlongs. Simply will not stay the course, you know. And as for the piebald, Presto. Well, now, that nag pulls his jockey's arms out, every time, and he will exhaust himself within the first half mile fighting for his head. Trust me. It's true. The real good bet is Bruno, the brown. Has a very amiable temperament indeed, that one. Doesn't pull at all. A horse with stamina. Will stay the course, Reverend. You should have a bet yourself.

The Reverend, of course, had no intention of engaging in gambling activities, and he faintly hoped his good example might rub off on the islanders. But it was a faint hope.

"Where is all this information about the horses' capabilities coming from?" he asked Ferro.

"The form?" said Ferro. "From Master Salticus himself, of course. Who knows the horses better than he does?"

Hearing that from Ferro, who was generally considered to be one of the cannier islanders, Pontius knew he had no chance of convincing anyone that they might be about to be swindled. He looked into Ferro's big ingenuous face. Our good honest blacksmith, he thought, you are as gullible as any of them. And where the devil are they getting all this silver from, to gamble with?

It also came to the Reverend's notice that people were surreptitiously visiting Rufus for betting tips. Would the Spirit of the Sea have any idea of the likely result of the race, people were asking? Not even for an extra-special offering? Rufus had uncharacteristically lost his temper and sent them packing, apparently. Had told them the Old Man would be deeply displeased with such enquiries, and they'd better watch out – their boats might be swamped in retribution, come the next big storm. Most people had scuttled off and called Rufus rude names behind his back. And it had not prevented the book of bets growing ever larger.

Captain Castello had done his best to keep out of the whole thing. He had continued to work on his house, often alone, which suited him perfectly. Since the race had been announced, Salticus had spent his time out and about on the island, making arrangements, inspecting the horses at exercise with everyone else, and taking bets, so Castello had seen little of him. This suited him perfectly, too. Rissa had made it very clear that normal service of any variety would not be resumed while Salticus remained on Larus, so the Captain had scarcely seen her either. Regretfully, this also suited him for the time being. Or as long it took to get rid of Salticus. Castello hoped the trader would grow bored after the race and move on. Hoped so very fervently. He was standing in his new doorway fervently hoping when his gun captain Ralham appeared. Ralham was obviously very upset indeed. "Why, Master Ralham," said Castello in surprise. "Whatever is the matter?"

"It's Alvan. Limanda's father. He… he says… he says I have…" Ralham ground to a halt, looking equally hurt and indignant.

"Says you have what?" asked Castello, puzzled. Ralham was normally on the best of terms with absolutely everybody.

"He says I have… he says Limanda is with child!"

"What?" said Castello, completely taken by surprise. "Limanda? But you called the wedding off last year. Surely you haven't…?"

"No I have not!" said Ralham hotly. "I told her fair and square I'd decided not to marry, as you know. She wasn't best pleased, but she accepted it, Captain. And then she got the job as your housekeeper. She was happy with that. Delighted. Even told me she was glad we hadn't wed. But her father, he thinks this is down to me, and that I'm trying to get away with it. Is threatening all sorts of things if I don't marry her." He looked hopelessly out to sea, at all the adventures he could feel slipping away from him. "I need your help, Captain, to speak to Alvan for me. You know I'd never treat a girl like that, any girl. No man would. It's not our way on Larus."

No. It wasn't their way on Larus. A horrible thought was occurring to the Captain. "Ask Alvan to come and visit with me," he told Ralham. "And I'll see what I can do."

It had been a difficult interview with Alvan. He had been understandably indignant. Had Limanda specifically accused Ralham of being the father of her child? She had not. But it stood to reason, didn't it, Captain? They had been sweethearts. Engaged to wed. Well, unofficially. The Captain said he would speak to Limanda. Try to establish the truth of the matter. Alvan was content. Or more content, at least.

Castello was seriously concerned. If it were accepted that Ralham was not the father of the child, Alvan might conclude that Castello himself, as the girl's employer, might have had the opportunity to approach her. The last thing the Captain needed was another accusation of fatherhood. It was potentially disastrous, and he called Limanda in immediately.

The girl arrived, dishevelled and tearful. Castello's heart sank. It was so hard to deal with a weeping woman. At least Rissa never wept. She just yelled and threw things.

"Calm down, Limanda," he said, as kindly as he could. "Now tell me dear… Your father says you are…" he faltered in acute discomfort, and then pulled himself together. "Listen now. Are you quite sure you are with child?" Limanda nodded, chewing her handkerchief.

"Your father thinks Master Ralham is responsible."

She shook her head and began to wail. Oh lord, thought Castello. If only Rissa were here. She'd know what to say.

"So it isn't Master Ralham?" said Castello, squirming with embarrassment. "Then... who?"

"Oh, Captain!" she howled. "He said such pretty things. Such compliments. I thought... I thought he would marry me, when I told him about the child. Really I did. But he laughed at me. Said not on your life."

This was just as the Captain had feared. It had to be one of the crew of the *Honest Trader*.

"He said... he said if I did as he asked... he said he would give me a locket with a great ruby. A silk dress... wonderful things..." she trailed off.

Castello got the picture. He wasn't sure how to sort it out, but he felt he could now exonerate poor Ralham, at least, even if he couldn't explain it in full. And he told Limanda to dry her eyes and go home. He would speak to her father for her.

Meanwhile, the Reverend Pontius was finding history writing a little more challenging that he had expected. It was easy enough to list events and set them in order, but it became more complex as soon as he tried to explain them in detail. His own likes and dislikes, approvals and disapprovals, and, dare he admit it, prejudices, kept barging in and skewing the story, however neutral he tried to be in the telling. In the end, he decided to tell the bare bones of each tale, as simply as possible, and then allow himself free rein to comment in any way he saw fit. The commentaries were sometimes for public consumption, and sometimes they were asides to himself. Either way, he labelled them carefully with his initials, PP, so that any future reader could distinguish opinion from fact. He felt this was a fair compromise – it was a reasonably honest way to go about it and it made him feel like a real scholar, too. Since the return of the *Honest Trader*, the Reverend had had more time to devote to his writings, and he had made considerable progress. He was just in the process of putting his books away one afternoon when, to his surprise, Salticus walked into the chapel and came swiftly up to the pulpit.

"Ha!" said Salticus. "A very nifty place to keep your secret treasures, Reverend."

It *was*, Pontius thought. But now he would have to find a new one, and he didn't at all fancy the idea of Salticus knowing he had something to hide. This was a minor disaster. He had carelessly left the *Book of Larus* open and Salticus glanced at it curiously.

"Well, well," said Salticus, with a friendly wink. "Writing is it? Something racy, Reverend?"

"Certainly not!" said Pontius, indignantly. How much had the trader seen, he wondered. Could he even read?

"P.P. Is that you, Reverend? What does the first 'P' stand for, then?" Apparently, he could.

"Never mind that," said Pontius, thoroughly rattled. "Can I help you at all?"

"Ah, yes, indeed you can," said Salticus, more politely. "You are the most respected personage on the island, Reverend. I would like to invite you to declare the winner of my Great Race. The people will trust you to see fair play."

Pontius didn't know whether to be flattered or outraged. He was just working himself up to an apoplectic outburst, when he paused to think it through, and took on a puzzled expression. Salticus, a practised observer of faces, saw the change, and looked away, politely waiting in silence. Over all, thought Pontius, was it not safer for him to declare the winner in the event of a close finish, rather than risk Salticus doing it himself? The bookmaker could not be allowed to declare the result of the race, and if the result were disputed, there could be serious trouble. Better to do it himself. Besides, he was one of the few people on the island who hadn't made any wagers on the outcome. Rissa and Castello would surely have nothing to do with it. And Rufus never left the east cliff. No, it was safer to attend to it himself. The Spirit of the Sky would understand.

In no time at all everyone knew and happily accepted the Reverend Pontius as the judge of the Great Race. Rissa's eyebrow shot up almost into her hairline when she heard. After all the fuss that prissy old fool made about my settling a bet for a silver sixpence, she thought. Goodness knows how much money is riding on this race, and there he is, right in the middle of it all.

Captain Castello had thought long and hard about the Limanda problem. It would be very difficult to challenge Salticus about his crewman's behaviour. Very difficult. And Alvan would be expecting some sort of answer. The Captain had been sitting a long time in his chair beside the treasure chest nursing a glass of brandy, but not actually drinking it. He put the brandy glass down on the chest and sighed. All very difficult. Something on the floor glinted and caught his eye. He reached out for it. It was a silver coin – part of the treasure, for sure. How did it come to be there? He had not opened the chest for a quite a while, not since Salticus had been paid for the powder and shot. It had been kept closed and covered, for safety. Limanda had been in to polish it occasionally... Castello felt a rising panic. He tore the cloth cover off, knocking over the brandy glass, fumbled for the key, and opened the chest. He stared inside, breathing hard. The silver was still there, everything was just as it should be, except... there was a gap between the coins. He plunged his hand into the chest. Under the top layer of coins it was full of sand.

First thing the following morning, Limanda arrived to carry out her cleaning duties, as usual, and Castello was waiting. He hardly knew which problem to attack first. He stood in the middle of the room with his hands behind his back, trying to look businesslike, and only succeeding in looking deeply embarrassed and unhappy.

"Limanda – now don't cry, dear, please, I'm trying to help you. It, um, seems to me from what you say, that the father of your, er, infant must be a member of the crew of the *Honest Trader*. Is that right?"

Limanda stared at the toes of her shoes, snivelling, and slowly nodded.

"Yes. Forgive me, dear – here, have my handkerchief – but the ship has only been here a few weeks. Are you quite sure? I mean, after such a short time…" He was mentally counting weeks, trying to work it out. Dash it all, women knew about this sort of thing. If only Rissa…

"I'm quite sure, Captain, I…"

"All right, all right," said Castello, hastily. He certainly didn't want the full details. "So long as you are sure."

She nodded again. Things were steadily looking worse.

"And…" he struggled for the right words. "And did he ask you to take money from the treasure chest?"

Limanda burst into fresh floods of tears. It was as the Captain had feared.

"He said… we would go away together if I took some of the silver. Only my fair share. Nothing more. I did take some. Only a little. Just a little, Captain. The lady warden gave me all her keys, didn't she? He said he would give it all back to us. That it shouldn't be kept in the chest. That everyone should have a share – that he would share it out among us. That I should have my share, too. But then I realised, I found… And he said he wouldn't marry me unless I took more and more. And then it was all gone. Nearly all." She faltered to a halt.

"Limanda, would you still wish to marry him? Never mind about the silver, dear. Don't cry. Would you wish to marry him? We can insist that he do the proper thing, you know."

"Marry Master Salticus?" said Limanda with sudden resolution. "Never, Captain. He is a bad, bad man!"

Master Salticus himself might have felt his ears burn at this remark, had he not been fully occupied at the time making the final preparations for the Great Race. Everything was in hand. The course was properly marked out. The horses prepared. A little grandstand set up at the finish – paying guests only, of course. And there was lots and lots of money riding on the result. Perfect. That silly, silly girl had brought out the silver from the hoard, and he had carefully lost it, coin by coin, game by game, to the islanders. And now, thanks to the information he had spread about, practically all of them had used it to bet on the brown horse, Bruno. Of course, he had no intention at all of allowing the brown to win. A loosened horseshoe, just before the race, would do the trick. Oh yes. The horse would run well, even on three shoes, so long as it was on the grass or the cinder track. But when they reached the stony road... Salticus chuckled in anticipation. The horse would go lame long before the finish, and all those bets would be lost. A cast shoe – it could happen at any time could it not? Sheer bad luck. Dear me. All bets are lost. He would be able to walk off the island with the treasure openly in his possession. And all above board. The islanders had given it to him themselves. Their names were all in the book with the wagers. Simple daylight robbery. Neither that fool Castello, nor that dozy girl would dare challenge him. By the time the islanders found out everything that had happened, the *Honest Trader* would be long gone. He might even buy himself an island with the proceeds, Salticus thought, idly.

He had made the magnanimous gesture of offering Young Ferro the opportunity to ride Bruno in the race. The favourite to be ridden by their own splendid jockey! There had been a considerable flurry of late betting on Bruno to win, after that. They simply fell over themselves to make the wagers. And, of course, when the horse lost, they would have Young Ferro to blame. Salticus smiled to himself at the neatness of it all. It really was the best scheme he had ever thought of.

The Reverend Pontius was bent over a book frowning, writing intently when Captain Castello arrived at the chapel that evening. The Captain took a seat and tried to decide what to say. Pontius was so delighted to see him, that he said nothing, closed his book, folded his hands and waited. After a few moments of silence, he gave a little encouraging smile.

Castello hesitated. It had been so difficult to decide what to do. Decision-making was not easy for him at the best of times, and the whole unravelling mess of Limanda, the missing treasure and his probably bigamous marriage had him feeling he was a ship about to be cast helplessly onto a lee shore. It was all going to come out soon whether he did anything or not, and he found he preferred action of some kind to waiting it out alone. And on reflection he found the only person he could turn to was his friend the Reverend Pontius. The worst that could happen was that Pontius would refuse to speak to him, and he had walked up to the chapel in a state of acute anxiety. But no. Here was his friend, sitting patiently before him, smiling his gentle little smile. Castello took a deep breath.

"There is evil abroad today, Reverend," he began.

"Too right," said Pontius, evenly. "Gambling and chicanery, it is."

"It's worse than that, colleague," said the Captain, sadly.

Pontius looked up and caught the expression on his friend's face.

"Why, friend Castello, what is the matter?"

"Salticus is the matter, the scoundrel, the scallywag!"

This was quite strong language, for the Captain, and although the Reverend was in complete agreement with this assessment of the man's character, he was becoming concerned at what Castello might be about to reveal. "What has he done?" asked the Reverend, fearfully.

"He has… tricked me," said Castello, and buried his face in his hands.

My heroic friend, thought Pontius, affectionately, is that all?

"He has tricked us all, friend," he said, consolingly, and patted the Captain on the back.

"No, you don't understand. It isn't just the gambling, the horse race. There is worse, much worse."

And he poured out the story of Limanda, the treasure, and her unborn child, and how he now knew Salticus was responsible for it all, and how unlikely he thought it that the rascal would do the honourable thing and marry the girl, according to island tradition. And the island's money – it had been in his care and he had lost it all! Castello paused for breath while the Reverend took all this in. Ha! thought Pontius. A maid betrayed! Telling a tale of theft by stealth! This is the prophecy coming true. But he kept this thought to himself.

"This is very serious," he said at last, frowning deeply. "He must marry the girl or make proper reparation. He must give us back our commonwealth! You must challenge the fellow publicly."

"I cannot," said Castello, becoming tearful, to the Reverend's alarm. "He... he has a hold on me."

"A hold on you?" said Pontius, in astonishment. "What sort of hold? He has never lured you into gambling debts, has he?" Pontius thought for a moment that he understood it all. The Captain could be easily led at times. Had he got into difficulties gambling? Was that why he had drawn away from his friends?

"No," said Castello, puncturing the Reverend's certainty. "Not gambling. He says I have a wife and family – *another* wife and family, from my old life, before Larus. He says I am a bigamist, Reverend. And he says he won't tell anyone, if I do what he wants. I am compromised – I cannot continue as a guardian of the isle." There, it was out.

The Captain broke down completely. Pontius was so busy

being scandalised by Salticus' behaviour he completely forgot to be scandalised by the possibly bigamous marriage he had performed. "The blackmailing swine!" he burst out, before he could stop himself.

"My children, Reverend," moaned Castello. "They will be called... terrible names. And my dearest Rissa... if she should hear of it..." He broke down again.

"My dear Captain," said Pontius, genuinely moved, "This Salticus is a snake, a swindler and a thief. There may be nothing to this story. Tell me, did he know of your marriage to the lady warden *before* he told you this tale of your old life?"

The Captain looked up. He stared for a moment, wiping his nose on his sleeve. "Why, yes. Rissa was at the quay with the children when he arrived. I *introduced* them," he said bitterly.

"And did you tell him how little you remember of your former life?"

"I did. He called me by name, by my first name – he must have known me – and I told him I had few memories of my life before Larus."

"Well, there you are," said the Reverend encouragingly. "Salticus is sly. An opportunist. You handed him everything he needed to know in a single conversation. Whatever he knew of you before, he saw you are now a person of importance on the isle, and he saw that you loved your wife and family. Twas a gift to a rogue."

"What you say is true, Reverend," said Castello. "But how can I prove it? If he spreads these terrible stories, how can I gainsay them? I do not know for sure myself if they are true or not."

If only he had told me before, thought Pontius, when the Captain had gone, perhaps I could have thought of a way to help. He is such a fool sometimes; did he not believe his friends would stand by him? It was all such a tangle, and very worrying. A fatherless child, the loss of the island's commonwealth, and a guardian compromised. Not to mention all this mania for gambling. How much more damage could that rat Salticus do?

The Reverend dropped to his knees to consult the Spirit of the Sky. The spirit was, in general, a deity of few words, unlike the Spirit of the Sea who seemed to have an awful lot to say through that grubby hermit. Pontius regretted the thought immediately. It was clear to anyone that Rufus was ailing. Even dying, perhaps. It was a terrible thought that an island guardian could die, and Pontius concentrated on having a word with his own spirit, in the uncertain hope that it might send a word or two of support back to him. He knelt a long time, concentrating on the various problems and trying to ignore the nagging pain in his back and knees. But nothing came to him, at all. At last, as he was about to get up, a gentle, breathy voice sounded in his ear. It said, 'Rely on the three avengers'.

This was so unusual that poor Pontius nearly jumped out of his skin. He thought for a moment that someone had come into the chapel unseen. But he was quite alone, he saw. The spirit had spoken to him, and not only that, it had referred to Mother Culver's prophecy. Surely not, he thought. That old crone, dishing out prophecies like mutton stew, surely the Spirit of the Sky could not approve of her? He didn't know whether to be scandalised, worried or intrigued, and settled for a combination of all three. However, he did go back to his *Book of the Archive* to double-check what exactly Mother Culver had told him.

Chapter Seven
The Avengers

The day of the Great Race was to be a festival. The islanders had jointly decided that the race itself would be followed by a celebration and feast. It was, without doubt, the biggest event ever to take place on the Isle of Larus, and everyone came to Sunday prayers dressed in their finest. Even Rissa appeared in a scarlet gown that was definitely not of the workaday variety. The Reverend Pontius was slightly shocked at this. But then he remembered the lady warden was a person of note on the island and would not wish to be overshadowed by anyone. She's putting on a brave face, he thought, that's all.

The congregation was fidgety. It was a warm, muggy day, and very close in the chapel, so the Reverend kept his sermon short and simple. They were clearly anxious to get out and find a good vantage point before the race began, too. He gave them the blessing of the Spirit of the Sky with all sincerity, and dismissed them.

Outside, Salticus had set up his table to take any last minute bets. While everyone had been in the chapel, he had completed his preparations. The grandstand was decked with bunting made of scraps of red and white sailcloth. The whole circuit of the course was marked with little flags on sticks. The *Honest Trader* had been quietly prepared to go to sea, so that they could leave as soon as possible after the race. And one of Bruno's shoes had been loosened to the point where it would undoubtedly fall off when the horse began to gallop in earnest.

160

People came out and milled around at the starting line. Hot, wasn't it, people said. Shouldn't be surprised if we have a bit of thunder later.

Castello appeared, bowed to Rissa, and stood silently and unhappily at her side. The Reverend Pontius, in his capacity as judge, took his place on the grandstand. Salticus strode into the middle of the crowd and lifted his hands for silence. The excited babble fell quiet.

"Good people of Larus!" he cried. "Friends! Respected dignitaries!" with a particularly ingratiating bow to the three guardians, who remained stony-faced. "It is with great delight that I present to you..." he paused for effect. "The runners and riders!" And the three horses, which had been kept out of sight behind the chapel, paraded forward. There were gasps of astonishment. Out came Presto, Bruno and Rufus, all wearing scarlet leather saddles and bridles with golden trimmings. The three jockeys wore matching scarlet shirts. Young Ferro, on Bruno, was clearly bursting with pride. But then, of course, he didn't know about the loose horseshoe. The other two jockeys, crewmen from the *Honest Trader* did know about this, however. They also knew that Salticus had promised a bonus to whichever of them won the race when the brown horse went lame. Just to make the finish look nice and genuine.

Everyone said how magnificent all the horses looked. How good a rider Young Ferro was. He had been far too modest to say for certain that he would win the race, oh yes. Such an excellent young man. But his father says the brown horse is a certainty, my dears. An absolute, copper-bottomed, racing certainty. The three runners lined up, jig-jogging in anticipation, tossing their heads. The little sorrel, Rufus, was a bundle of sweating nervous energy, itching to run. Presto the piebald was already pulling, testing his rider's strength. Good grief, thought Pontius, watching from the sidelines, that man will have arms like an ape if this goes on. Bruno was the very picture of contained horsepower.

Salticus turned to Rissa and asked if the lady warden would care to give the signal for the race to begin. Rissa said she most certainly would not. "Very well," said Salticus. "Then I shall do the honours myself." And he took off his silk hat with the great feather, held it aloft. "At the drop of my hat, let the race begin." And he swept the hat down. There was a great roaring cheer, and the runners were off, followed by a whooping crowd of children, who were convinced they could keep up.

One or two of the older lads had climbed the chapel bell tower, careless of life and limb. They had ascertained in advance that they could see the whole course from here, and began shouting down a fractured commentary. The horses were running side by side, going a cracking pace. No, wait a minute, Presto and Rufus were pulling ahead! Break-neck speed! You never saw anything like it! The leaders were running very close to the cliff edge – Rufus was on the brink – he's going over – no, he's recovered. Cries from below of, "How goes Bruno, how goes the favourite?" A pause. "He goes steady – he follows the other two. He is letting them wear each other out!"

For goodness' sake, thought the Reverend Pontius, let them be done with the section by the cliff top, before someone has a terrible accident. He looked down the finishing straight. There was a big crowd on each side of the road. Ferro the blacksmith had come up on his old grey mare, partly to get a view from a movable platform, and partly to show off by being the only audience member on horseback at such a horsy event. He waved his hat to the Reverend, who lifted his hand in reply.

The running commentary continued. The horses had reached the cinder track. "Presto is showing signs of slowing! The piebald is tiring." Loud cheers. People nodded sagely. This was just as predicted. "Rufus pulls ahead! But wait… Bruno goes with him. The brown is full of running. Rufus is falling back. They are turning onto the road, and Bruno is ahead!" Ferro Senior threw his hat in the air, lost his balance, and nearly fell off the old grey mare in his excitement. "Come on Bruno!" Everyone was shouting, jumping up and down and anticipating a very nice win indeed.

"Bruno! Bruno is drawing away from them...but wait... what's happening? Bruno is pulling up. Pulling up! Bruno is stopping! Presto and Rufus have caught him, passed him... Young Ferro has dismounted. Bruno is lame!" Everyone craned their necks to see what was going on. It was true, the sorrel and the piebald were galloping towards the finish, neck and neck, and the brown was nowhere to be seen.

The cheers subsided into a disbelieving silence. Ferro Senior looked thunderstruck. As the two runners approached, the old grey mare suddenly whinnied and kicked up her heels. Ferro really did fall off her this time, flattening a group of bystanders as he fell. The mare whinnied again and careered off at the gallop. "Well, blow me down! I didn't know she could gallop," said Ferro in amazement.

But no one else was looking at her. Presto and Rufus stopped dead in their tracks as she passed, and wheeled round as one to follow her. Their jockeys, taken by surprise, were catapulted sideways into a gorse bush. The horses clattered off down the road past a tearful Young Ferro who was just diagnosing a lost shoe and a badly bruised foot for Bruno, and the three ran off across the fields whinnying loudly and disappeared through a little hedge.

People ran in all directions. Some went to help extract the jockeys from the gorse bush. Others turned towards the finish line. What would happen? Would the race have to be re-run now? None of the horses had crossed the finish line. Some people tried to persuade Young Ferro to remount and complete the course. But he wouldn't hear of it. Bruno was lame. He needed care and attention, and could not be ridden. No way.

Salticus was beside himself. This was not at all the outcome he had expected. He picked up the heavy bag of silver and clasped it possessively to his chest. Rissa saw the movement, and stared pointedly at him to let him know he had been seen. He thought for a moment, then, with a look of steely determination, called one of his crewmen over and spoke to him quietly. The *Honest Trader* was to be prepared for sea this minute, did he understand? Yes, now, immediately. No, never mind about the horses. Pick up as many of the crew as possible on the way to the quay. Leave the men who fell in the bush. They didn't deserve to escape. The sailor dashed off. Salticus started to sidle away, the bag of money in a vice-like grip, when he noticed a peculiar hissing noise. He looked up, and saw everyone else was staring out to sea. The water heaved in an oily swell. And over it, at a fair rate of knots, came three monstrous waterspouts, one after another, heading straight towards the island.

"Not so rare, then," muttered Salticus to himself. "And not a bet running on them!"

People were turning, starting to run. The Reverend Pontius was already at the chapel door, panting, and calling people inside. Salticus was nearly run over. "Don't be so foolish, they won't come ashore," he yelled. "Water spouts aren't dangerous…" Moments later he was sucked bodily off his feet by the first waterspout, money bag and all and carried off inland, yelping. He was deposited in the same gorse bush recently vacated by the jockeys, with a resounding yell. He struggled to his feet. The second waterspout was upon him. He was slurped up again, spun until he was breathless and dizzy, and deposited painfully on the stony road. Staggering up, he took to his heels and legged it down the road with the third waterspout in hot pursuit.

The braver souls, including the Reverend, came out of the chapel to watch, and were promptly pelted first with silver coins and then with little fish falling out of the sky.

The Reverend Pontius looked and thought for a moment. "It's the two rains of silver," he said to himself, taking a handful of coins and a pilchard out of his hat. "Gather up these coins, people of Larus," he yelled. "They are our commonwealth. Pick them up. Don't lose them. And fetch a bucket for these fish. They are a gift from the Spirit of the Sky."

Castello appeared beside him, shaking his head in wonderment. Rissa came out of the chapel, rather dishevelled.

"Lady warden," said Pontius. "Is it safe? Will the waterspouts come back?"

"Unlikely, Reverend," said Rissa with conviction. "They'll quickly blow themselves out now. Remarkable, was it not, the way they chased that thief Salticus?" She was trying to look dignified, but couldn't suppress a giggle.

"The Spirit of the Sky works in mysterious ways," said Pontius, and felt like a bit of a giggle himself.

Captain Castello called Ralham over. He felt this was a good moment to confide in his gun captain, at least in the matter of Salticus being the father of Limanda's child. And when the outburst of righteous indignation had calmed a little, the Captain said, "Not only that, friend, but he talked her into stealing the silver for him. Do not mind the Reverend – he knows all about it." Pontius had come up, having cautiously sent Rissa off to check for any more marauding waterspouts.

"Yes," said Pontius. "And it's my guess he used it to gamble with. Deliberately lost it. Did you not think it odd that there should be so much silver in circulation?"

Ralham was puzzled. "But why would he lose it, Reverend? Why not just run off with it?"

Pontius thought for a moment. "Because the good Captain, and you yourself, would have put a cannonball through his ship before he could get out of the harbour, had the theft been discovered." This was undeniably true. The gunnery at Fort Resolute had improved dramatically with practice.

165

"As it was, you were all distracted by the race. The bets all seemed to be above board, didn't they? Everyone followed the advice to bet on the brown horse. Everyone. And the brown horse goes lame as the race is run. Most convenient. All bets are lost. And the scoundrel goes off with our money and our blessing. All won fair and square." Pontius wasn't absolutely certain that this was all true – but he thought it was close enough, and congratulated himself on his skills of detection.

Ralham was thinking how right he had been not to marry Limanda. The girl was a fool. And was about to say so, when he remembered the sizeable bet he had put on Bruno. With money won oh-so-easily from Salticus. He had been a fool, too. They had all been fools. He thought he had better change the subject. "Captain, your Reverence – shall I organise a proper work party to pick up all the coins and fish? They seem to have fallen over a small area."

The Captain and his Reverence thought this an excellent idea, and Ralham hurried off to take charge.

"Well, now," said Pontius. "I suppose we should go and see what has befallen poor Master Salticus."

They set off down the road, but had not gone far when they met a group of people who knew just what had befallen the trader. The waterspout had pursued him all the way to Ferro's forge. All the way, your Reverendness! Touched nothing else. Seemed to be, well, chasing him. Reached the forge, he did. Ran inside and slammed the door. And then – you'd never credit this, your Reverence – the waterspout stopped. Seemed to think. Yes – ridiculous – but it did. Then it lifted its great foot off the ground and – well – it *stamped* on the roof of the forge. Only word for it. Roof disintegrated, of course. Master Ferro was furious when he saw the state of it. Stamped his foot too.

"Wait, wait," said Pontius. "What of Master Salticus? Does he live?"

"Oh, yes, your honour, he lives. You'd better come and see."

Salticus had indeed taken refuge in the forge. Pontius and Castello were shocked to see the roof was entirely gone. According to eyewitnesses, the waterspout had collapsed the roof downwards, and then sucked it up again with a great slurp, before wandering off a little way and disappearing up its own vortex. "He is inside," someone said to Pontius' unspoken question. And so he was, crouched in a corner, scared and dishevelled. The ragged remains of his hat, feather and all, was hooked on the chimney stack.

"Ha!" said Pontius. "The honest trader himself, I see. How goes it with you, sir?"

Salticus eyed Pontius and Castello as if they were a couple more waterspouts come to stamp on him. The three avengers, Pontius thought, had done a pretty thorough job.

"Come sir," said Pontius after a long pause. "Are you hurt?"

Salticus began to gibber in reply, between frequent fearful glances upwards. He was completely incoherent.

Pontius patted Castello on the shoulder. "I think your other secret is perfectly safe, Captain, true or not," he said, quietly. "It will take him a long time to recover his wits, I think. And he will never dare return to Larus." Castello gave a hopeful smile.

"And," went on Pontius, "we will retrieve most of the silver, I think. If we confiscate the horses their value will go far towards paying the upkeep of the child he leaves behind." The Reverend was quietly pleased with this neat solution to their problems. He ought to be a magistrate, really. Castello had had the same thought. The Reverend had latched on to what was happening far sooner than anyone else. He would indeed make a very good magistrate. But in the meantime, there was Salticus to deal with. Pontius and Castello hauled him to his feet, and he was half carried, half dragged out of the forge. The sooner he was put on his beastly ship and sent away the better.

Outside, a group of islanders came to take Salticus off their hands. "Now, now, Reverend, we'll take him, before you do yourself a mischief, what with your back, and all." Pontius really wished they wouldn't go on about his back like that, but he had to admit that he could barely restrain Salticus, who seemed to have developed about eight legs, the way he was kicking. Ralham had spread the word of what the trader had done at high speed, and no one questioned the need to take him to his ship immediately, so he was hustled off, shouting nonsense all the way.

The message had clearly got through to the crew of the *Honest Trader*, too, and they had wasted no time in retreating to the ship. Indeed, they had tried to leave without Salticus, and been actively prevented from doing this by the islanders.

Everyone gathered at the quay to see fair play done. The crowd parted for the little procession with Salticus in the middle, still kicking and babbling to himself, to come through. He was unceremoniously bundled aboard his ship.

Castello came forward. "See that he doesn't return," he said to the ship's crew, who nodded agreement, apart from the pair who had fallen in the gorse bush, as they were fully occupied having prickles removed.

The crew hastened to take the ship to sea, and soon the ruby-red sail was drawing. Rissa came quietly up and slipped her hand into Castello's. He smiled tenderly down at her. There was no need for words, at all.

The Reverend Pontius had an idea. "Captain, how about a little gunnery practice? Not to injure the ship, you understand, just to, um, *see her on her way.*"

"Excellent thought, Reverend," said Castello, leaping into action. "Ralham!"

And within a few minutes they had sent a perfectly-aimed cannonball into the *Honest Trader*'s wake. She picked up speed quite visibly after that.

"How about another one for luck?" called the Reverend, with an uncharacteristically evil grin.

Chapter Eight
The Last Word and the First Name

The following day, the Reverend Pontius was just updating the *Book of Larus* with all these exciting events when Captain Castello walked into the chapel looking very chipper indeed. Pontius was about to put the book away in haste. But then he hesitated. Why should he not confide in his friend? A history of the isle was not such a bad thing to admit to. The *Book of the Archive*, on the other hand, was probably best kept a secret.

The history was thus left open, and Castello cast a curious eye over it.

"Well," he said, "I never did! A history. This is something we should certainly have here."

He had come over, he said, to give the Reverend all the latest news. The silver had been carefully gathered up and counted. There was indeed some of it missing. But that was only to be expected under the circumstances. It would probably turn up somewhere. But the bulk of the island's commonwealth was safely back in its chest. Some of the difference had been made up by the sheer quantity of fish that had been dropped by the waterspout. The Spirit of the Sky had been most generous, had he not? Young Ferro was attending to Bruno's injured leg. The horse would do very well, apparently. No permanent damage. The other two racing horses were still at large, but they would be rounded up, all in good time. And Ferro Senior's old grey mare had trotted back to the forge with a very smug look on her face, by all accounts.

169

And everyone agreed that Limanda had had a lucky escape from that thief, and that she and her child would be taken care of at public expense.

Pontius said this was all excellent good news.

The Captain looked again at the *Book of Larus* with great interest. "You have done us a great service with this wonderful book. All done properly and with notes, too. You are a true scholar sir! Tell me, who is PP? Is that you Reverend? I never thought of you having a first name. Can I ask what it is?"

"I have no wife here to call me by my first name, alas," said Pontius, evasively. He wasn't about to tell the Captain, or anyone else, that his devout parents had named him Patience. Patience! A name most usually given to girls. It had been a torment to him in his childhood, but as his father had said, with a name like Patience, you will soon begin to develop that quality, will you not. Actually, he had not, and his frequent impatient outbursts made the name even more comical, at least to everyone else. So upon arriving at Larus, the Reverend had abandoned the hated name, along with his old life. And he was not about to take it back again. But he couldn't tell a lie, so he shut his mouth firmly for a few moments, closed the book and briskly changed the subject.

AND WHAT *OUR* WORLD MADE OF IT ALL...

From *The Western Clarion:*

Rain of silver falls on ship

A mysterious rain of silver coins has fallen on the deck of a freighter at sea in the English Channel. The ship was passing through the same sea area, now being hailed as the British Bermuda Triangle, where a number of strange events took place last year during the world sailing championships. An eyewitness stated that three waterspouts were seen approaching at speed – unusual in itself – and on reaching the ship, dropped a shower of small fish and silver coins onto the deck. Experts say it is not unusual for waterspouts to suck up fish and sometimes other objects, but the presence of the coins is inexplicable.

No one was injured and the ship was undamaged. A sample of the coins is being examined at the British Museum. A spokesman stated they are of a design never encountered before. "They have us baffled," he said, "No one has any idea of their origin, much less how they came to fall out of a waterspout at sea. I've heard of it raining cats and dogs, but this is ridiculous."

172

Part Three
'The Isle of Silver...'

174

Chapter One
The Namesakes

"Quick, quick! Oh, come, your Reverendness, come now. Something terrible has happened at the east cliff!"

The Reverend Pontius and his friend Captain Castello, having had their pleasant conversation so rudely interrupted, stared at each other in consternation. They had just been discussing the Captain's latest improvement to the plans for his half-built house at Fort Resolute. An oriel window, to be set above the main door. A really imposing new feature. No one could fail to be impressed, could they? And it would gain them a little more light and space upstairs.

"What? What is it?" said the Reverend, getting to his feet. "Hoy, there! Come back in here."

The messenger was one of Rissa's runners, red-faced and almost apoplectic, despite his youth. He dodged back inside the door. "It's Rufus, your honour. Oh, it's awful. Please, please come." And he legged it out of the chapel.

Rufus? Did he mean the hermit or the horse?

"Come, Reverend," said Castello, "we must see what's to be done. I can get there faster – don't rush. Take your time, friend. I'll take charge until you arrive." And he, too, dashed out of the chapel. Before Pontius could even reach the door there was an angry shout outside. Castello had run headlong into his wife, who was just coming in.

The Reverend decided discretion was the better part of valour where the lady warden in a temper was concerned, and

175

made himself busy looking for his hat while Rissa shouted at her husband. Eventually, she came in the chapel door, brushing herself down.

"Clumsy oaf!" she said. "Never does look where he's going."

"Lady," said Pontius, "have you heard this alarum from the east cliff? Do you know what's amiss?"

"No idea," said Rissa, but she looked worried.

"We'd better go and see, then," said Pontius.

She took his arm and they made their way out at a more sedate pace.

It soon became clear that everybody else was heading to the east cliff, too, and it was very crowded on the narrow path. "Make way there! We are guardians. Have a care... that's my foot!" yelled Pontius, at top volume. The islanders were used to ignoring the sound of his voice in chapel – could happily sleep through it – so they took no notice.

Rissa elbowed him out of the way. She drew herself up to her full height, and took an enormous breath. "LET... ME... PASS!" she bellowed, with a commanding tone and volume the Reverend Pontius could not in his wildest dreams hope to attain. He stood aside for her meekly. So did everyone else, in respectful silence, and she sailed off along the path muttering bad-temperedly.

At the cliff top, the rock on which the hermit usually held court was empty, and the silence was ominous. Castello, already there, was white-faced, and tried to prevent Rissa from coming to the cliff edge by barring her way.

"I am a guardian of this isle, husband," she said loudly, "and I need to know what is happening." So she stamped on his foot and pushed past.

Far down below, at the base of the cliff, two bodies lay side by side on the shingle, being gently washed and ruffled by the incoming tide. One was Rufus the Hermit. The other Rufus the sorrel stallion. However they had got there, their end must have been unpleasant. The Reverend Pontius, having

176

finally caught up, joined Rissa and Castello on the cliff top. The three guardians stared in horror at the scene below, and then at each other. There was a very long silence, punctuated only by the breathing sound of the sea on the pebbles. The island itself seemed to be holding its breath. Then Rissa fell to her knees and began to keen for the violent loss of an islander. The rest of the crowd took up the dreadful sound, and the air was full of howling. Pontius and Castello, offcomers both, stood transfixed. They had never heard this before, for the excellent reason that sudden death of this kind was extremely rare on Larus. Castello was about to try to comfort his wife, and looking desperate, too, when Pontius caught him by the arm.

"Friend Castello, I need your help. Don't lose your head, man."

The Reverend looked around desperately, and saw Mother Culver standing quietly nearby. Not keening, nor wringing her hands. She was Rissa's friend, he knew. "Mother," he called, over the racket, "will you tend to the lady warden? She is in distress." Mother Culver came silently over and gave a curt nod.

"See, the good Mother will take care of your wife," he said to Castello. "Now, there is much to be done. We must retrieve the bodies before the tide carries them off. Where are your gun captains?"

"They are islanders," said Castello. "They are mourning with the others."

"They are military men! You trained them yourself. Now command them!"

The Captain looked affronted for a moment, then his expression changed from doubt to certainty. He straightened himself, and looked round for Ralham.

"Master Ralham! Find your gun crew and get down to the cove, there."

Ralham's automatic salute broke the spell of the keening,

177

and he rushed off, shouting, "Yes, Captain," over his shoulder.

"Come, Reverend, we must go down too, to supervise and see that all is done properly. I will assist you down the path. Mind the bramble." And they stumbled down the steep track to the cove.

At the bottom of the path it was very quiet in Rufus' Cove. It usually was quiet down here. The keening from the top of the cliff didn't penetrate this far. Rufus' Cove. Where else would the hermit wish to meet his end? But this was so violent, so sudden. The Reverend Pontius, when he had retrieved his breath and wits, realised he was shaking. His knees quivered and threatened to give way, and rather than cause a scene by a sudden collapse, Pontius chose to sit on a boulder, mopping his brow.

"Stay there and rest a moment, Reverend," said Castello. "I… I will go and look." He crunched across the pebbles to the tide line and peered fearfully about. Meanwhile Ralham and his gun crew came racing down the path, nearly knocking the Reverend off his boulder.

"Where have you been?" said Pontius, testily, "run and assist the Captain, now. Before the gulls get to them. There'll be nothing left to bury." He had just noticed the gulls. They were gathering on the cliff ledges in silence.

Presently, the Captain strode back across the beach. Pontius looked up, questioningly. Castello shook his head sadly. Nothing to be done. "Would you… I mean… could you perhaps give him the last rites? Or something?" said Castello.

The Reverend got to his feet. "I, er, can say something over our colleague," he said. Come on, Pontius, he told himself. This is your job. Think of something to say. "Take my arm, Captain, and help me over these dratted pebbles before I break my neck, too."

When Pontius woke up, he simply couldn't fathom where he was for a moment. "Where in the world am I?" he said, dozily.

Castello's face appeared before him. "You fainted, Reverend. It's all right. I don't think you have harmed yourself."

"I'll be the judge of that," said Pontius, raising himself on an elbow. It was a very uncomfortable bed. No – it was shingle. He was still on the beach. Memory came back to him in a rush. Ralham had brought a blanket to cover the body. They had pulled it back from Rufus' face. The mouth had moved. Was he still alive? But no, it had been a crab. A crab scavenging in Rufus' mouth.

"Get that vile thing off him!" Pontius had heard his own voice cry. And then his knees had finally given way, and he collapsed into Castello's arms. Two guardians laid out side by side. And another howling hysterically on the cliff top. It was ludicrous. It was improper. It was very bad for morale. "Help me up," he said urgently. It was suddenly very important that he get to his feet.

They assisted him back to his boulder, and he sat collecting his thoughts, while everyone discussed what to do next. There was nothing to be gained, they decided, in trying to carry the body of the horse back up the cliff. It was a logistical nightmare. There was a patch of sand behind the pebbles, and it seemed logical to bury the animal there and then. One or two of the young lads had come down the cliff by now, curiosity being stronger than fear at that age, and one was sent back up to fetch shovels and something more suitable to cover the late guardian.

Reinforcements arrived with tools and an embroidered cloth, and within the hour, the russet-coloured coat of the horse had vanished beneath the sands, and the guardian's body was decently swaddled and covered and lashed to a makeshift stretcher. They were ready to take Rufus the Hermit on his final journey.

It was a very solemn procession that made its way, slowly

and painfully, back up to the top of the cliff. The entire population of the island was waiting, gathered on the cliff top and along the path. They had fallen silent now. Rissa had got to her feet and composed herself, and she stood stock still, the signs of deep distress settled on her face. Island guardians were not supposed to die under suspicious circumstances like this. She had checked with Mother Culver, to see if there were any histories recording such a thing. There were not. It was absolutely unheard of.

Castello had the Reverend Pontius by the elbow. They both looked very shaken. All eyes swivelled to the Reverend. People had seen him collapse beside the body of Rufus. There had been a deep groan and gasp. Two of their guardians fallen, and a third beside herself with shock and grief. It was one of the most terrible moments ever known on the Isle of Larus. There had been a complete, helpless silence for the minute or so it had taken Pontius to get to his feet. And then a relieved whisper, "He is getting up! See, the Reverend is getting up. We have not lost him. The Captain is helping him." This was not lost on Rissa. Sometimes, she thought to herself, we forget how important the guardians are to the people here. And from that moment she was herself again. She had her part to play, too.

Pontius had recovered himself, and begun to think of practicalities. He would get them to carry Rufus to the chapel, for the time being, until proper arrangements could be made for an interment. Out of the corner of his eye, he saw Mother Culver with a look on her face that could only be described as triumphant. Was she just gloating over the very final accident to Rufus? Or was she somehow involved? Pontius really didn't want to think about it, not now, thanks all the same. Let us deal with one crisis at a time.

Chapter Two
A Feisty Female

There had been considerable debate about the last resting place of Rufus the Hermit. The graveyard near the chapel was the province of the Spirit of the Sky, people said, and not really suitable for one who had communed so readily with the Spirit of the Sea. Some people said the hermit should be buried at sea, returned to the spirit. A few said he should never have been brought out of the cove. The Reverend Pontius said this was nonsense. They couldn't possibly have left the body of a guardian just lying about on the beach. It was unthinkable. But he was inclined to agree that the graveyard was the wrong place for the interment.

While they argued, the elder island women tended the body. Trimmed his white hair and beard, what there was of it, as they occasionally had done for him in life, and gently washed away the sand.

In the end, they took Rufus, now looking more respectable than he ever had in life, back to his cliff top. It just seemed logical to return him to the place he had lived so long. The part of the cliff he lived on was solid rock, and could not be dug out, but a little to the south there was a grassy outcrop, halfway down the cliff face and reached by a precipitous path. And there they buried him, all alone, as he had lived, with nothing but the sound of the sea, the wind and the gulls, the island's natural voice, for company.

Small details can be very comforting in times of loss, and so can small kindnesses. The three remaining guardians supported each other carefully, and went out of their way to present a united front. They brought each other small gifts, took time to talk quietly. Rissa gave up shouting at Castello, if only temporarily, and he responded by taking care not to walk mud over her clean kitchen floor. Pontius came and sat with her when she was distressed, as she was frequently in the days after the death of Rufus. The friendship between Castello and Pontius deepened. The three were intensely united in adversity.

Nonetheless, they all knew there was an important question to be answered: who would replace Rufus? There was no doubt that he would have to be replaced. But by whom? How would it be decided? They agreed that the best approach would be to discuss it with everyone after Sunday prayers.

The islanders made it very clear that Rufus must certainly be replaced. It was of paramount importance that someone should commune with the Spirit of the Sea. Absolutely vital. Pontius made a face at this, but was ignored. The eastern quarter could not be left unguarded indefinitely.

"But how do we select such a person, where do we find them?" asked Pontius.

"Guardians just come when we need one," somebody said, with an air of stating the blindingly obvious. Everyone nodded and murmured assent. This was true. They did. Had not the Reverend himself arrived just when they were in need of a western guardian? Had not the Captain been sent by the Spirit of the Sea to be their northern guardian?

"But what are the qualifications for the job?" asked Pontius, feeling that he was straying into very murky territory. This was apparently blindingly obvious, too. They needed someone with a mystical turn of mind. Someone who had the ear of the Spirit of the Sea. Someone prepared to live on the east cliff for ever and ever.

The Reverend was touched by the islanders' simple certainty that the perfect person would appear, but he found

182

he couldn't share it. Neither could Captain Castello. Rissa was greatly disturbed by the manner of Rufus' passing, but, as an islander, she had no doubt that a replacement would appear all in good time.

But, as ever on Larus, the whole incident slipped gently into the past, and life returned to normal. The thing that most surprised the Reverend Pontius about it was that no one really asked exactly what had happened to Rufus. How had he and the stallion come to be in the cove? Had they fallen off the cliff together? Or had there been two unrelated accidents? The Reverend always fancied himself as a detective. He had, or so he thought, just the right turn of mind for this sort of thing. Incisive. Penetrating. Wit beyond measure. And a terrier-like grip on the problem in hand. Not that he would have said as much aloud, of course. Goodness, no. Heaven forefend. But in his idle moments it was good to have something to work on, something to occupy his mind. Use it or lose it, thought the Reverend. And so he went to see Mother Culver.

At the back of the Reverend's mind was the look on the old woman's face on the cliff top that dreadful day. She had looked *fulfilled*, there was no other word for it. Had she been expecting something to happen? Was there a prophecy? Surely, thought Pontius, surely she would not have kept it to herself? Would she?

"Here comes that nosy parson again," said Mother Culver softly to herself as he approached. "Come to steal my archive, he is. Thinks I don't know it. But I have his measure, never fear." She had known he was on his way long before he appeared at the end of her path. Useful information of that kind just popped into her head from time to time. He wouldn't come indoors. She knew that, too. So she went outside.

Pontius came straight to the point. "Can you shed any light on how Rufus and the red horse came to be on the beach, Mother? Such an event as that – was it not prophesied?"

She decided this was as good a time as any to come clean, and began to sing:

Two namesakes then shall share a common doom
Swift they run, and swifter shall they fly.
Together shall they find a watery tomb;
Each leaves a feisty female standing by

"Why didn't you tell me this before?" he yelled in exasperation.

"You didn't ask," said Mother Culver, sullenly.

"How could I ask about it, if I didn't know about it, you silly old…" Pontius stopped, took a deep breath, closed his eyes and regained his decorum a little. Shouting wouldn't bring Rufus back. Nor the valuable horse, for that matter.

She stared at him defiantly.

"Well," said Pontius, "I suppose it's beyond help now. Perhaps he could not have been saved, whatever we did."

"It was his time. As foretold," she said, nodding. "I told *him* about it, as the person most concerned. Not best pleased. But he knew his time had come."

The two namesakes were clearly the hermit and the red horse, thought the Reverend. But if I *had* heard this before the event, would I have identified them? It could just as well have referred to Ferro and Young Ferro, couldn't it? Or Castello's son Petrus and the child's late grandfather. Pontius sighed. Perhaps it was just as well he hadn't heard it, all things considered. And, even now, he couldn't imagine the hermit as a swift runner. Unless he had been on the horse's back. That would explain quite a few things. They would certainly have flown swiftly off the cliff. But how would a blind old man have caught a runaway horse? How could he have got onto its back? Blast and damn these prophecies, thought the Reverend irritably, as he walked back to the chapel, they always throw

184

up as many questions as they answer. And he refused to even think about the two feisty females, though he suspected one of them might be Mother Culver herself. Was that it? Was she waiting in the wings to take over from Rufus? The hermit had certainly seemed depressed, ill, even frightened, these last weeks. Had the old woman frightened him half to death with a prophecy?

This was such a dramatic and unsettling thought, that the Reverend went so far as to call an urgent meeting of the three remaining guardians. Rissa and Castello appeared at the chapel, without demur, and very promptly. They were both clearly prepared to listen.

"I have visited Mother Culver today," began Pontius, "and she chose to share a prophecy with me – one that has already come to pass," he added hastily, seeing a look of fright on Rissa's face. She took a breath, and settled again. The Reverend then recited the verse – or the Song of Rufus, as he now thought of it. Rissa and Castello looked at each other. Had the Reverend memorised all the prophecies he had heard, then? Actually, he had them written in copperplate handwriting in his *Book of the Archive*. But he wasn't about to divulge that, or not yet, anyway.

Rissa and Castello listened as Pontius outlined his thoughts on how Rufus and the red horse might have met their deaths together, the hermit on the horse's back.

"That animal nearly galloped over the cliff during the race," said Castello, thoughtfully. "It had a reckless streak, for sure. But how could our colleague…"

The unanswered question hung in the air. Pontius hesitated, wondering if he should share his suspicion that Mother Culver had had a part in making sure the prophecy came true, might even have been somehow responsible for the whole terrible event.

"Mother Culver," he began, and then changed his mind. "I, um, believe she might have her eye on the job as eastern

185

guardian."

Castello looked shocked. "That old woman?"

Rissa looked up sharply and spoke for the first time. "She speaks with the Spirit of the Sea. She is a Seer. She makes true prophecies. She has the island histories. Very well qualified for the post, if you ask me. And she has already gone to the east cliff, by the way."

Captain Castello was still slightly bemused at his wife's vehement support for Mother Culver's takeover bid on the east cliff. He was aware of the prophecies, the island archive. He knew the Reverend Pontius gave them credence, but they were just so obscure, thought the Captain. His practical mind dealt with straightforward and measurable things, rather than all this mystical mumbo-jumbo. Straightforward things like the rebuilding of Ferro's forge, for instance, which was where he was heading. It was a fortnight and more since the waterspout had destroyed the forge roof, and the autumn gales would be upon them soon. The death of Rufus had distracted them all from the practicalities here, and poor Ferro had been left to camp out in the wreckage of his own house as best he could. It was high time that something was sorted out, so the Captain shrugged off the whole Mother Culver business, and thought out what he would say to Ferro. The forge occupied the highest point on the island – ideal for a lookout post, and, if Ferro was willing, Castello wanted to build one close by, in exchange for assistance with the re-roofing.

Ferro's usual good humour had taken a considerable knock with the destruction of the forge. He couldn't help feeling aggrieved that Salticus' comeuppance should also have been visited upon himself in this way. He had been able to rescue quite a few of his possessions and household goods and tools, but nonetheless a missing roof was a missing roof. He and his son had rigged up a tarpaulin as a temporary measure to keep the weather out and restore some sort of household normality, but this couldn't possibly last out the winter. And then there was his wife to deal with. Ah yes. She took the stern view that it was entirely her husband's fault for doing all those deals with that bad man. Red sails, indeed! Such a fortune they had been going to make, selling sails like Ligo's. And what had it cost them? The very roof over their heads. Mrs Ferro had chased after the waterspout shouting, "Give me back my roof this minute!" and then chased back in the opposite direction when it obliged and started raining roof tiles on her head. Most of the tiles had shattered on hitting the ground and were not easily replaced, thereby creating the problem. The righteous nagging had continued solidly from the moment she had recovered from the shock of seeing a waterspout stamp on her home, and Ferro was beginning to crack under the strain. So he was very glad to see Captain Castello approaching with a determined look on his face.

The Captain spoke courteously to Mrs Ferro, and she was more than slightly overawed at having a guardian in her parlour, roof or no roof. Indeed, she was so quiet that Ferro thought he had gone deaf, for a moment. She made to leave the men to their talk, but Castello called her back, saying that the repair of the house was very much her business, too, and that she should stay to hear what he proposed. Secretly he was thinking that anything that pleased Mrs Ferro was likely to please her husband too, circumstances being as they were. The Captain usually wasn't very good at this kind of manipulation, but in this case it worked like a charm. Materials would be found – taken from those earmarked for the building of his own unfinished house, if necessary – and he would ask his gun crews to donate some time to help rebuild the roof, so that all should be snug and secure before winter.

Mrs Ferro's gratitude knew no bounds. She was all smiles – the first she had cracked for quite a while, Castello suspected. The Captain was a hero, she said, a true guardian, a great gentleman. Such kindness! Such consideration! Castello glanced at Ferro, and it was clear his gratitude knew no bounds, either. So it was an easy matter to bring up the subject of the lookout post. A future project, of course. When timber became available. Next time there was a wreck, perhaps. A great benefit to all the island. Dual purpose. Weather-watching. National security. What did Ferro think?

Ferro thought, of course, that any arrangement that put a smile on his wife's face was a rattling good idea. He slapped Castello so hard on the back that he was thrown into the fireplace and slightly singed.

"Not to worry," he said quickly, inspecting the smoking burn mark on his jacket, "I shall go directly to Fort Resolute and begin making arrangements. We can start work right away."

And with that he left, before Ferro's gratitude did any further sartorial damage.

The Reverend Pontius had concluded that, once installed on the east cliff, Mother Culver would be very difficult indeed to dislodge. More difficult to dislodge than Rufus himself had been, indeed. And the Reverend had been entirely right. To his irritation, the islanders accepted her straight away, no questions asked. Everyone said the Old Man would not permit an impostor. The fact that she was still there a couple of weeks later spoke for itself. Within a short time, Pontius was astounded to hear people beginning to refer to her as 'Mother Rufus'. There had been no love lost between Rufus and the Reverend, but all the same, it was outrageous. In the end, he thought, resignedly, the people must have the guardians they want, and I must make the best of it.

And so Mother Culver moved pretty smoothly into Rufus' place. Literally and metaphorically. On arrival at his old hovel, she cleaned it out and added a little more in the way of home comforts, but not very much. She was very pleased indeed at her promotion to eastern guardian of the isle. And, of course,

188

as people said, she was double value for money, being keeper of stories, too.

Pontius put it off for a while, but eventually decided an official visit of sorts could not be further delayed. Rissa had wanted to go and officially greet the Good Mother as new guardian, but the Reverend had resisted the idea. "Let us wait a little," he had said, "and see how she settles to it, before we call it anything official." He had rather hoped she would prove to be a dead loss at sea communing. But not so, and here he was, this chilly morning, making the familiar trek to the cliff. He much preferred to make the visit alone, as it gave him the opportunity to ask privately for another verse or two of the archive. Mother Culver's archive of stories and prophecies, all mixed up and disorganised, were firmly encased in her head. And it was the Reverend's unwavering intention to prise them all out of her thick skull, sort them into order and write them down for the benefit of all. At least, that's what he told himself.

Mother Culver, on the other hand, prized her wonderful, and alarmingly accurate, prophecies very highly, and was reluctant to part with them. She tended to let them out on a slow drip feed. Very slow, sometimes. In his darker moments, the Reverend suspected her of witchcraft, which was an uneasy thought relating to a fellow guardian. But then, she was an islander, and he was an offcomer, and they were never going to properly understand each other. But he had, he simply *had* to know more of the archive.

Could she really commune with the Spirit of the Sea, or did she just make it all up, Pontius wondered as he trudged along.

The wind, thinking it was already winter, and not just late September, tried to make off with his hat and made his ears burn red with the cold, so he was thoroughly cross by the time he approached the old woman's hovel. There would be no warmth or comfort there, he knew, and he longed for his cosy room under the bell tower. As a matter of fact, he preferred to sit outdoors when he visited Mother Culver. The thought of being enclosed within four walls with her made him profoundly uneasy, and he hoped she would come outside to speak to him.

"Good morning to you, Mother," said Pontius, his numb fingers feeling in his top pocket for the little brandy flask he had brought for her. He liked to think of it as a gift, but it was actually a bribe. Payment in kind for a verse or two of the archive. She snatched it out of his hand before he could offer it, and secreted it in some hidey-hole inside her shawl.

The old baggage had no manners at all, thought Pontius. She was insufferable. Irritating. But she did have the prophecies, and they had all come true, so far. So he said nothing.

"You'll be wanting a history, Reverend," said Mother Culver, knowing perfectly well this wasn't the case. She just enjoyed baiting him.

"I'll be wanting a useful prophecy, Mother. Something that hasn't already happened, this time, if you please," said Pontius, firmly. He wasn't going to be messed about again by this old crone, guardian or no guardian.

She didn't reply, but went straight into the trance-like state that she seemed able to call up at will. Pontius waited, poised to memorise whatever she sang. He was getting quite good at it these days.

Come the strangers, seekers of the key,
Every ship and heart they mean to break;
Beware the hornèd poppy of the sea,
The future of the island is at stake.

Mother Culver stopped. Was that it, then, wondered Pontius. The exchange rate of one verse of prophecy to one flask of brandy these days was pretty steep, he thought. Still, there was plenty of food for thought in this one. The old woman waited, daring him to demand more, but the Reverend was already on the case.

Now this key, thought Pontius, fancying himself as an interpretative expert on the archive, is it a real object, or merely a symbol of understanding? Mother Culver watched him beadily as the thought ran across his face. He tended to wonder if she was reading his mind, but in point of fact his expression was always completely transparent.

"It's a real key, Reverend," she said at last. "Golden. Long lost."

I really wish she wouldn't do that, Pontius thought. They're so damned deep, these islanders. There's no working out what goes on in their heads. But he didn't think it for very long. His attention was deep in the scrap of prophecy. The part about ships and hearts was clear enough, wasn't it, if a bit disturbing. But what was all this nonsense about hornèd poppies? How could a flower threaten the freedom of the island? He turned and walked away without a word, engrossed in these juicy new mysteries.

"How rude," muttered Mother Culver to herself. "No manners at all, even for a parson. And, as usual, he has stamped off without waiting to hear the rest of it."

But the Reverend Pontius was gone, both in person and in attention. "I shall solve this conundrum for the sake of the island!" he said, gallantly. But deep down in an unacknowledged, shadowy corner of his soul, he knew that he would do it to satisfy his compulsion to *know what it all meant*. He stopped, realising he had walked away without making the official visit he had intended. The damned archive was becoming an obsession. He turned and walked back to make his little speech.

"Listen, Mother," he said, "we cannot be at loggerheads like this if we are to be colleagues – and I'm not saying we will be, mind – but if we are, we must learn to work together. To, um, trust each other a little more. For the sake of the island, you understand."

Mother Culver drew herself up, flicking her thick white hair out of her eyes. She understood perfectly.

Chapter Three
The Seekers of the Key

It was the day of the equinox, calm enough for now, but a big swell was crashing into the cliffs, and roaring past the southern tip of the island. Rissa had sent her runners round with the news that there was likely to be a lot of weather in the next few days, and to make boats and buildings secure. Generally speaking, everything on Larus was pretty well nailed down, but works in progress, such as Captain Castello's house, needed to be checked for weak spots, and this was just what he was doing when his gun captain Ralham ran down, breathless with excitement.

"There is a ship, Captain! Mother Rufus says it's racing for the harbour, down the east side, hell for leather."

"Mother Rufus?" said Castello.

"Yes, yes," said Ralham, breathlessly, and as impatiently as he dared. "Mother Rufus. Mother Culver, as was."

"Ah," said the Captain. "A ship, you say? In trouble?"

"Not yet," said Ralham. "But it's only a matter of time, I reckon."

They looked at each other, sharing the same thought. A wrecked ship meant timber. Timber meant they could start work on the new lookout post at Ferro's forge. The Captain caught himself wishing it might be a big ship and that it might run aground somewhere fairly convenient, if it was going to. And then suppressed this unworthy thought.

"Keep a careful watch on it, Master Ralham. They may need assistance, there's a storm coming."

Among the many things that had been bought and bartered from the capacious hull of the *Honest Trader* was a beautiful brass telescope. It was Ligo's new pride and joy, and as soon as news of the unknown ship filtered through, he appeared with it on the quayside. Everyone wanted to have a look through it, but only Captain Castello was permitted to touch such a perfect and precious object. He peered through the eyepiece, and soon saw the ship in question, trying to find a way into the harbour. It was a large boat – scarcely a ship, really – and was being handled with spectacular incompetence. He handed the glass back to Ligo. Say what you will about Salticus, he thought, he and his crew could certainly handle a ship.

"If I didn't know better, Captain," said Ligo, raising the telescope, "I'd say that boat came from Arjento Rock."

Castello was perplexed. What was Ligo talking about?

"Arjento Rock?" he said.

"Yes," said Ligo. "Our nearest neighbour. Surely you've heard of it, Captain?"

The Captain had not. How could he not have been aware of a neighbouring isle, after all these years on Larus? He decided to admit his ignorance.

"I never heard tell of it, Ligo. Is it far away?"

"Far enough. Over the horizon to the south. Out of sight to us on Larus."

"And why should that boat not come from there?"

"Because they're not seagoing folks, Captain," said Ligo, as if teaching a child.

"Is it not an island?"

"Oh, yes, sir, it is. But they have other ways of earning a living. They have precious metals in the rock. They are miners. People come to them for the metal, to trade for it, so they rarely need to go anywhere. They like the solid ground under their feet in those parts. They have a boat or two, I suppose, but they rarely put to sea."

Even seen from the quay, it was clear the boat was careering about, more or less out of control.

"See," said Ligo, "she tries to take the channel by the Grassy Islet. They'll run her aground like that... no she still floats. More by luck than judgement, I'd say." He winced, hating to see a boat being steered to her doom. "What is that fool doing at the tiller? Left hand down a bit... not that way, friend, mind the sandbank... Oh, Captain!"

"What has happened?" said Castello, squinting out across the harbour. But it was clear to anyone. The boat had run pell-mell into one of the islets. It stopped dead in its tracks and mast and sails fell forward with an audible crack, even at this distance.

"She has run aground on Shingly Islet!" He handed the glass to the Captain. There was the boat, firm aground, and there were signs of people struggling out from under the fallen sail, waving their arms about helplessly and obviously yelling at each other.

It was a ludicrous situation. But it was also a dangerous one, and Castello snapped out his orders.

"The tide is ebbing – they'll not refloat her before the storm comes. Get the *Brothers Three* or the *Mergoose* – whichever is most ready, and rescue them before they're all swept away."

Ligo saluted. He just loved this sort of thing. Soon a crew was assembled, and they were preparing the *Mergoose*, since she was moored in the deeper water, and could get underway soonest.

"They won't want to leave their boat – bring back any cargo you can carry, but get them off that islet," bellowed Castello. "Don't take no for an answer, Ligo." Another salute, and the *Mergoose* began to move off.

There was nothing to do now, but wait, for those on the quay. The Captain bit his lip. Would there be any timbers left after the storm? Would there be any people left on Shingly Islet by the time the *Mergoose* reached it? Rissa appeared, rather red in the face, having rushed all the way down the hill.

"How long," Castello asked her urgently, "before the storm?"

The crunch of swell and surf on the west cliff could be clearly heard, now. Rissa looked at the sky. "Long enough, husband," she said. "What boat is that, on the islet?"

"Ligo thinks it's from Arjento Rock. I never heard of it."

Rissa said nothing. She had certainly heard of Arjento Rock.

Out in the harbour, the *Mergoose,* with her crew of four, was making good progress with the wind and the ebbing tide in her favour. "Getting there will be easy enough. Getting back might be a different matter," said Ligo, to his brother Lineus, glancing uneasily at the sky. There was a huge, heavy, dark grey cloudbank advancing from the west. Ligo brought out the telescope and looked ahead to Shingly Islet. There were six or seven people ashore, some of them unloading things from the grounded boat. As he watched, one figure aimed a hefty smack at the ear of another. Within moments a brawl had broken out, with everyone else joining in. Ligo couldn't believe his eyes. He lowered the telescope, looked at it, lifted it again, looked again.

"What are they doing?" asked Lineus. They were fighting, that's what! The biggest storm of the year approaching at the gallop, and they were fighting. And what's more, the figure in the middle of the whole punch-up was clearly a blond-haired woman. She was busy thumping someone over the head with what appeared to be a chair leg. Ligo shook his head. Who were these lunatics?

Still, practical matters had to be dealt with. They anchored the *Mergoose* as close to the islet as they dared. It was of paramount importance not to run her aground, too. They had brought a small boat, with oars, and they lowered it over the side. Ligo and Lineus climbed into it and pushed off, taking an oar each and pulling with practised synchronicity across to the islet. They ran the boat onto the shingle beach, and pulled its forefoot clear of the water. The fight was still very much in progress, so much so indeed that none of the participants seemed to have noticed the arrival of the *Mergoose*. Ligo and Lineus looked at each other and shrugged.

"We need to put a stop to this, brother," said Lineus, "if we're to get them to listen to us." And with that, they waded into the battle. Most of the combatants were on the short side, so it was easy enough for the lanky brothers not to get punched on the nose, although Ligo received a nasty kick in the shin, enough to cause even someone as even-tempered as he usually was to lose patience. Lineus had his hands full already, with a fellow grasped by the scruff of the neck on each side. It was clearly a struggle to keep them apart. Ligo was about to go and assist when he was hit squarely in the ear by a solid object, and fell to the shingle.

"Hey," said a voice. "This un's not one of ours."

"Nor this un."

Ligo sat up, painfully, nursing his ear, which had gone strangely numb, and listening attentively to the ringing noises in his head. Lineus was flat on his back nearby, apparently unconscious. "What have you done to my brother, you idiots?" said Ligo, grateful to find he could still talk.

"Talks strange, don' 'e?"

"They are long men, eh? They come to steal our stuff, I reckon."

Ligo pulled himself together. "We come... that is, we've come to rescue you. There's a storm coming. Look." He pointed at the advancing cloudbank. "You can't stay here on the islet. It's too dangerous."

The blond-haired woman swam into Ligo's view. "You come to rescue us, zur?" she said. "And thanking you kindly for it, but we must get our boat back a-floating."

"You don't understand," said Ligo. He wasn't sure that he understood, either, not just at that moment. "You can't get the boat back afloat before the storm comes. Because of the tide."

Blank looks all round. "We will help you salvage your goods and take you to safety."

"Zalvage, zur? Never 'eard tell of. But we sees the storm, zur." Ligo stared at her. She was plump, pretty, an angelic vision. Had this pretty angel felled him with the chair leg? He struggled to his feet, clutching his head.

"Decide what you want to bring. Hurry. Hurry up! Lineus, are you all right? Help my brother, somebody."

"Do as 'e say!" bellowed the blonde woman, with surprising force. "Get the boxes. Move y'selves!"

Soon the first cargo of boxes and crates was in the boat, with Lineus. The shipwrecked group, still suspicious, refused to let Ligo leave, and substituted one of their number at the oars. His rowing wasn't up to much, and it took a while to reach the *Mergoose*, unload, and come back for the next lot. Ligo was anxious. The wind was increasing alarmingly, and a surf was beginning to break on the shingle beach. Soon it would be too rough to land on the islet. He insisted on everyone going aboard the *Mergoose* as soon as possible. When the blonde woman objected, he lifted her up bodily and threw her into the boat. He and Lineus came back to the beach once more and brought out as much of the cargo as they could. After that, he judged it too dangerous, and they hauled the boat aboard and set sail for Larus once more.

It was a pretty bumpy ride, with quite a sea getting up, this far out in the harbour. The shipwrecked party sat miserably in the bilges, wailing in fright when spray broke over the bows, and being sick. Ligo, at the tiller, shook his head. "Not seagoing folks at all," he said to Lineus. "Stopped fighting, though, at least."

It was a long wait for everyone on the quay. The detail of what was happening on Shingly Islet was lost on Captain Castello, since Ligo had taken the telescope with him. "We should have one of those for Fort Resolute," Castello murmured to himself. "Don't know why I didn't think of it before. And another for the new lookout, too."

"One of what, friend?" said the Reverend Pontius, who had just heard the news and come down from the chapel.

"One of those telescopic glasses. Very useful, Reverend."

"Ah. How is the rescue going?"

"The *Mergoose* is on her way back. Let us hope they managed to save all the people. It'll be a while before they get here, Reverend, sailing against such a wind. Would you care to come inside and wait?"

The Reverend would indeed care to come inside and wait. He was chilled to the bone, and he happily followed Castello indoors, where Rissa was already busy with refreshments.

At length, Ralham put his head round the door to say that if their honours pleased, the *Mergoose* was coming in, and the three guardians went out to greet their visitors.

A bedraggled group was being helped ashore. Most of them collapsed on the quay, one or two kissing the cobbles in gratitude for their return to dry land. The blond-haired woman alone, though distinctly unsteady on her feet, stood still and calm as Castello came forward to greet them all.

"I am Captain Castello, commander of Fort Resolute, and northern guardian of the Isle of Larus."

"I know you are, zur," she said cryptically. Castello was a little thrown by this unexpected reply, but quickly pulled himself together.

"Er, I hope you and your party are not harmed, ma'am?"

"Not so's you'd notice, Cap'n, no. My name is Zostra, and very pleased to be meeting you, zur. But not as pleased as I am to be ashore and out o' that infernal boat-contraption."

"Yes, indeed," said Castello. "Um, may I present my colleagues? The Reverend Pontius, western guardian of the isle, and my wife Rissa, ship warden and southern guardian."

Zostra inclined her head to the Reverend and fixed her eye curiously on Rissa. "How goes it with you, sister?" she asked.

Rissa merely nodded.

A bit familiar, thought Castello, but the poor woman has just had a nasty fright. Any further thoughts he might have had were cut off by a sudden drenching downpour as the black cloud finally burst, and everyone scattered. Rissa excused herself saying she needed to be on ship-watch in such weather, and Castello and Pontius were left to take the castaways indoors to dry off and recover.

A hot drink and half an hour or so with their feet on solid ground saw them all in better spirits, and the Captain thought it reasonable to ask a few questions. Zostra seemed to be very much in charge, so he addressed her first.

"Tell me, Mistress Zostra, where have you come from, and where were you hoping to arrive when you had your, er, accident on Shingly Islet?"

"Shingly Islet, is it? Is that what we bumped into? Confounded stupid place to put an island," said Zostra. "You should keep your seagoing water-roads clear of such obstacles, Cap'n."

"My apologies, ma'am, for leaving an island in your way," said Castello, politely.

"Ah, zur, you are kind. The fault is ours. We on Arjento Rock is not seagoing folks. Never at all."

Ah, thought Castello, to himself, so they do come from this Arjento Rock. Ligo was right.

"And as to where we go, zur, why it is here! The blessed Larus Isle. And very nice and solid under the feet it is too, zur, if I may make so bold."

"We find it pretty steady, ma'am," said Castello. "And now you are here, may I ask the purpose of your visit?"

"Oh, yes, zur. I am come to see my mother, if she still lives, and I think she does. My voices says she does."

Before Castello could reply to this interesting statement, Zostra's crewmembers all leapt to their feet at once and began energetically punching each other in the eye. "Hey…" he said,

200

faintly. "I beg you, leave the furniture alone…"

Zostra strode forward, pushing the Reverend Pontius, who had been listening keenly, firmly out of harm's way. "Never you mind about them, Cap'n dear. I shall be dealing with… STOP THAT. Or I'll 'ave the lot of you put back in that boat-thing. This minute." The fighting stopped instantaneously. Zostra glared at them fiercely. "Now be'ave y'selves."

Castello realised for the first time just how short they all were. Zostra herself was easily the tallest, and she only came up to his shoulder. Not only short, he thought to himself, but short-tempered. He would have stopped to savour this little *bon mot*, if he'd had time, but Zostra was speaking again.

"Now, where was I? Before we was interrupted with such rudenesses?" One of her crew looked mutinous, and she paused briefly to cuff him in the ear. "Ah yes, I was about to tell you of my sainted old mother."

It had been a very rough night indeed, one of the roughest anyone could remember. Captain Castello was just thinking how fortunate it was that they had completed the new roof up at Ferro's forge before such weather blew in. Had they still been depending on a tarpaulin up there to keep it all out, poor Ferro would have been in very serious trouble with his wife, and very wet and windblown, too, in all likelihood. He certainly owes me my lookout post, thought the Captain, but will I have anything to build it with, now? It had howled and rained until dawn, but now, at mid-morning, things were calming down. None of the fishermen had thought it safe to take their boats out that morning, and most were gathered on the quay. Castello called Ligo over and asked if he would bring his telescope. There was no sign at all of Zostra's boat on Shingly Islet, so far as he could see, and he hoped the glass might reveal some useful wreckage.

"Ah," he said, squinting through the telescope. "Yes, the boat is destroyed – but there are objects – timbers, perhaps, still ashore on the islet. Can we get a boat out there, Ligo, to see what can be saved?"

Ligo said he could be ready shortly, since the wind was dropping, and would the Captain care to come along.

"Yes, indeed," said the Captain. "Ah, Mistress Zostra. Well-rested, I hope?"

Zostra, having taken emergency accommodation at Ralham's neighbour's house, had come out to assess the state of her boat and baggage. "The Spirit of the Rock protect us! It is all gone!" she clapped her hand over her mouth.

"Come, ma'am," said Castello, kindly, "there may be all sorts still there, that can be rescued. Your boat is gone, as you say. But, see, Master Ligo is preparing his boat again, to go and look."

"Master Ligo, is it?" she said, turning her bright blue eyes on that gentleman, who blushed to the roots of his hat.

"Yes, ma'am, and I shall accompany him to see that all is properly done. If any of your goods are intact, we shall bring them back to you." Castello thought it best not to mention the timbers he hoped to acquire for the lookout.

Zostra was appeased. "You are kind, zur, and I thank you." There was something in her expression, as she said it, which put the Captain in mind of someone he knew, but try as he might he couldn't pin the likeness down.

"Excellent," said Castello, recovering himself. "And perhaps while you are waiting, ma'am, you would like to pay a visit to your mother? My gun captain Ralham will escort you. Ralham!"

The *Brothers Three* was approaching Shingly Islet after an uneventful journey, and the crew were preparing to drop anchor. They had brought the larger boat in order to carry, or even tow, back any sizeable timbers they might find. She also accommodated a larger crew to help with the work. Castello peered over at the shingle beach and was gratified to see a mixed collection of timber and boxes. "Some for Mistress Zostra, and some for me," he muttered.

Some of the boxes proved to contain foodstuffs, and had been damaged by the storm, so Castello ordered the crew to empty out the spoiled food and keep the boxes. Any sort of wood was useful. The wrecked boat's anchor was found, along with a good part of its mainmast, and there were timbers everywhere. The Captain was delighted, and rolled up his sleeves to help gather the precious planking. He and Ligo fell to discussing their visitors from Arjento Rock.

"They like to fight, for sure," said Ligo. "Lineus has a lump the size of an egg on his head where one of them hit him. And another on his elbow. Thinks one of them ran into him headfirst. Straight into his elbow, Captain. Master Ralham says they have extra-thick skulls in those parts. Comes from cracking their heads on the roofs of the mines all the time."

"Yes," said Castello. "They fell to fighting among themselves when we took them indoors last night."

"Fighting? In your house, Captain?" Ligo was scandalised.

"Yes, indeed. A proper scrap. I feared for the furnishings. But Mistress Zostra put a stop to it immediately. She is a remarkable lady."

"Mistress Zostra… did she happen to mention… did she say… is she a married woman, at all, Captain, do you know?" Ligo was clearly having difficulty getting the question out, and he blushed in confusion.

"I believe she is a widowed lady," said Castello, carelessly, noting the small hopeful smile that lit up Ligo's face. "But who would have thought she was Larus-born, with all that fair colouring? Not like a native of the isle at all."

Ligo thought she was nothing less than an angel sent from the sea, and would have said so, had he not thought better of it. Such a pretty compliment would we utterly wasted on the Captain, and he would do better to bestow it upon the lady herself, should the opportunity ever arise.

By the end of the afternoon, a considerable proportion of the remains of Zostra's boat was neatly stowed in the *Brothers Three* with whatever intact boxes they had found, and they set off on their return journey. Progress was slow, the ship being so heavily laden, and it was another long wait for those on the quay.

Zostra, long back from her visit, was talking to Ralham.

"Tell me, Master Ralham, is that great sea-carriage out there a boat or a ship, as you might say? I would wish to learn the proper word." She pronounced his name Ral-ham, instead of the more contracted version usual on the island, and Ralham couldn't decide whether he was charmed or irritated by it.

"The *Brothers Three*, Mistress?" said Ralham. "'Tis difficult to define. They say a ship can carry a boat, but a boat can't carry a ship, don't they. And since what's left of your boat is being carried by the *Brothers Three*, I guess that makes her a ship, ma'am!" And he chuckled wholeheartedly.

"Thank you, zur, for shedding the light on the matter," said Zostra, looking as if no light had been shed on it at all.

When the *Brothers Three* finally came in, everyone rushed to assist with the unloading. Castello came ashore and was just explaining to Zostra that they had managed to retrieve some of her goods, and that they would be restored to her directly, when shouting broke out. A fight had begun between Zostra's crew and the islanders. The Captain closed his eyes for a moment. Give me patience, he thought, what is it this time? Zostra was way ahead of him.

"Master Broad!" she bellowed. "Leave that Larus-man be!" The Larus-man in question was Ralham who was hanging doggedly on to a splintered piece of timber from the shipwreck. Master Broad, who lived up to his name in all directions, was hanging on equally doggedly to the other end. Master Broad let go obediently, and Ralham staggered back and fell over the side of the quay straight into the hold of the *Brothers Three* with a startled yelp and a great crash.

"This timber, it is ourn, Mistress," said Broad, defiantly. "It is a bit of our boat, that's what. These men is a-thieving of it."

Zostra stood her ground and proceeded to give the fellow a most impressive ear bashing, with an occasional wallop for emphasis. Captain Castello, who had rushed over to ensure that Ralham had not come to any serious harm, couldn't help but admire her. She could certainly tear someone off a strip, and he was deeply grateful not to be on the receiving end.

"Mistress," he said, when she paused for breath, "I beg you, be still. You are not seagoing folks on Arjento Rock, you said so yourself. Perhaps you do not know it is traditional that the remains of a wrecked ship become public property here? My gun captain – you are not too much injured, Ralham, I hope – was merely following the tradition. We have recovered some of the timbers, but I assure you, ma'am, it is less than a whole boat. We cannot put it back together again. But we will be happy to provide a boat of ours to carry you home whenever you wish it."

"Why, bless you, Cap'n, dear," said Zostra, her furious frown replaced instantly with an engaging smile. "Most kind, indeed. But if enough of my boxes and supplies are rescued and unbroke, I shall be wishing to stay here on Larus. I has it in mind, zur, with your gracious permissions, to open up an alehouse.'

"An alehouse! Have we not had enough bother this year with gambling and horseracing, without someone setting up an alehouse in our midst?" The Reverend Pontius was just working himself up to full steam of indignant rage. The word had got back to him very quickly indeed. He had not yet consulted Rissa and Castello on the matter – he was quite sure they would both disapprove – and had rushed off as fast as his stout old legs would carry him to see Mother Culver, or Mother Rufus, as he was now beginning to think of her. Surely, if all four guardians disapproved of this dangerous new initiative, it could be nipped in the bud. "There will be drunkenness, fighting – there is already fighting – and untoward behaviour of all kinds. Do you not agree, Mother?" Mother Culver had listened calmly to a rant of considerable length, and this was the first time Pontius had properly paused for breath.

"Well," she said, "I can't say that I do. I'm partial to a drop of ale myself. And you, Reverend, you take a little brandy, now and then. A glass of ale would do you more good, I'd say."

"But, Mother," spluttered Pontius, "you cannot possibly approve! This Mistress Zostra – she is not a proper person, at all, she is in charge of a band of ruffians, she hits people with chair legs, she uses immoderate language, she is no lady!"

"She is my daughter," said Mother Culver, matter-of-factly.

"Your daughter?" said Pontius, after a long, astounded moment. "Your *daughter*?" The Reverend was probably the only person on Larus who hadn't yet heard this news.

"You hadn't heard, Reverend?" said Mother Culver. "Oh, yes. Her father came from Arjento Rock. Stayed with us here on Larus a year or two. And when he went away, he took her with him. Took my little Zostra." She stared sadly out to sea, with a very Rufus-like sigh. "Said I wasn't a fit mother for her, Reverend, can you believe that?"

Pontius, recovering himself a little, could all too easily believe it.

"He was your husband, Mother?" he said.

"Oh, I thought he might have been, Reverend. But… there were complications, you see. And he left. And took my girl with him, back to Arjento Rock."

To Pontius' alarm, tears began to leak from Mother Culver's eyes.

"Well, then, you must be very glad to have her back," he said lamely, patting her on the shoulder, and handing her his handkerchief. The old woman would never oppose the alehouse, and that was that.

Chapter Four
The New Inn

Mistress Zostra was, if nothing else, a woman who knew exactly what she wanted and had no hesitation at all in making her wishes known, thought Captain Castello. He had also been pretty surprised to discover she was Mother Culver's daughter. It was quite hard to imagine their eastern guardian ever having been young enough to produce offspring. Zostra was not obviously like her mother in any way, except in terms of a certain unbendable determination to get her own way.

The Captain had barely had a chance to get over the surprise of her plan for an alehouse before she was back with a full-blown plan. There was an old deserted building on the north-western corner of the island behind a little shingle beach. It had not been used or inhabited in living memory, and no one had any particular claim on it. Zostra and her crew would like to be a-fixing up of it, if he didn't mind, Cap'n dear. Castello said that he would need to consult his fellow guardians, but on the whole it seemed a good idea to make use of a building rather than let it collapse in ruins.

Within a day or two it was a done deal. The Reverend Pontius had looked defeated, and said on your own head be it, when the Captain had spoken to him on the subject, and Rissa had shrugged and taken no interest at all.

Zostra was anxious to get to work immediately and appeared on the little shingle beach in front of the building wearing a hessian apron with capacious pockets, and a red and white spotted scarf wound around her head.

The prospective alehouse was an old stone building and it was full of pebbles, absolutely full. In lively weather, the sea hurled the shingle through its empty windows and door frame. The building had long ago lost its roof and the sea hurled pebbles through that, too. Zostra said that they had their work cut out all right, with this one. But it could be done. She strode into the gaping doorway and filled her apron pockets with pebbles, and then hauled the whole lot out onto the beach and tipped them out. And so she carried on all day. Her crew were busy creating temporary quarters behind the building, out of the wind, with some timber and tarpaulins recovered from the wreck.

Castello begged her to come back to her former lodging at Alvan's house at the end of the day, but she insisted on camping out under the tarpaulin. The islanders brought her gifts of food, and offers to help with the work. They were, for the most part, quite taken with the idea of having their own alehouse. The sooner the building was fit to use, the sooner the first brew of ale would be on its way, Zostra told them, and a regular working-party, enthusiastically led by Old Billy, was soon in operation.

All this had an unfortunate effect on the work on Captain Castello's new house. In fact it stopped completely. Not only that, but building materials prepared and set aside for the house at Fort Resolute began to vanish mysteriously. Castello turned a blind eye to this to begin with. People were entitled to give their free time to whatever project they chose. But when the timbers earmarked for his new roof disappeared he decided enough was enough. It had been galling, for sure, when the wind was in the right direction, to have to listen to the sound of hammering and sawing coming from Zostra's, when no progress was being made on his own house – but to be unwittingly supplying the materials too, was the giddy limit. "Where are my gun captains? Ralham!" bellowed the Captain, striding down onto the quay. No reply. Where was

Ralham?

"Ligo? Lineus?" Not a sound. Were they at sea? No. The *Brothers Three* and the *Mergoose* were tied up at the quay. The sorry truth dawned on the Captain. The whole kit and caboodle of them must be helping out at Mistress Zostra's. "And with my timber, too!" said Castello, to no one in particular. "We'll see about that!" And with that he went indoors to fetch his sword. Not that he intended to hurt anyone with it, but he felt it would show that he meant business.

Down at Zostra's, Ralham, Ligo and Lineus were indeed assisting with the rebuilding work. Most of the pebbles had been cleared out, and they were about to haul up the first of the timbers for the new roof. They had been a bit sheepish about the 'borrowing' of the Captain's timber, but, as Ligo pointed out, "An alehouse is to the benefit of us all. But especially to us, lads." It also gave him the opportunity to spend a good deal of time in Zostra's company.

Mistress Zostra herself had been delighted with the response to her prospective new business, and even more delighted when a trapdoor in the floor had been found under the pebbles and proved to be the entrance to a stone-lined cellar. Perfect for the ale keeping, my dears. So she was considerably surprised to see Captain Castello rushing towards her with a furious scowl on his face and brandishing his sword. "Mercy on us, Cap'n dear," she cried, clasping her hand to her heart, "what goes on? Are there pirate-men a-rampaging?"

"Pirate-men indeed, madam," said Castello, thinking that if there were any rampaging to be done, he would do it himself. "Out! Out you timber thieves! You know who you are. And so do I."

Ralham, perched on the gable end, gave a worried look to Ligo and Lineus below, and then scrambled down to face his Captain. The three lined up and took off their hats.

"I have given my permission and blessing for this alehouse," Castello said loftily, "doubtful enterprise though it is. And how do you repay me?"

Ralham went cross-eyed as the tip of the Captain's sword was thrust within an inch of his nose.

"You repay me by stealing my timbers. The very roof from over my head."

Ligo considered pointing out that the roof hadn't actually been over the Captain's head, yet, but thought better of it.

"My own gun captains. My most trusted men. Nothing but a bunch of sneak thieves! What do you have to say for yourselves?"

Ligo came forward. "Captain, sir, your honour, we thought you'd not want to leave Mistress Zostra without a roof, sir, and the winter coming on so soon, too."

Castello thought Mistress Zostra could live in an upturned beer barrel for all he cared at that moment. But he could hardly say so.

"It's not the timber, Ligo," he said. "It's the deceit." And he sheathed his sword and stalked off, leaving his three gun captains looking stricken.

Zostra tried to run after him, but was hampered by her apron pockets being full of pebbles. "Cap'n, dear, oh Cap'n, zur," she called. "I beg you wait." Castello paused and glared at her. "Zur, I shall be sure all your timber-pieces is returned to you. I am truly sorry."

"Never let it be said I left a woman without a roof over her head," said Castello, looking down his nose. "You may keep them, madam."

"She's a formidable woman, Reverend," said Castello, later that day, "I'll say that much for her. She keeps that rabble of a crew in surprisingly good order, most of the time. But all the same – encouraging my own gun crew to make off with my roof timbers…"

"You're quite entitled to be annoyed, brother," said Pontius. "Oh, quite entitled. It's next-door to mutiny. And all for this wretched alehouse. I said no good would come of it."

The two were sitting in the Reverend's comfortable little room under the bell tower. The Captain's anger was dissipating under the combined influence of a sympathetic ear and a little nip of brandy.

"This might be a good moment to plan ahead," mused the Reverend. "Once the building work is finished down there, what do you think will become of Mistress Zostra's crew? Would it not be wise to offer them a boat back to Arjento Rock before the winter sets in? They are argumentative by nature, and if they fall into idleness they will be picking fights with all and sundry. And with ale in them, too. We shall not have a moment's peace."

Castello thought this an excellent idea. "But how shall we suggest this to them, Reverend, without making them feel unwelcome and stirring up bad feeling?"

"As to that, I have the solution," said Pontius, smiling. "Your gun captain, Ralham. He works on the alehouse, does he not?" Castello nodded. "And he is a man in need of a little adventure, I think. Well, brother, you must make your peace with him, and put this idea in his head: when the alehouse is finished, he shall act as escort to Mistress Zostra's crew. Go back to Arjento Rock with them, and bring our boat back afterwards. He will be beside himself with eagerness to make the trip, to see foreign shores. Let him persuade them to leave."

"Reverend, you are a genius, sir," said Castello, visibly relaxing. "I shall do exactly as you say. Let us hope Mistress Zostra will think it all acceptable." He sat back, nursing the brandy glass. "Have you ever thought, Reverend, that is, have you noticed…"

Spit it out, man, thought Pontius.

"Mistress Zostra – there is something in her manner that

seems familiar. I don't mean a similarity to Mother Rufus, daughter or not. I mean she puts me in mind of someone else, and I can't pin it down at all."

Rissa had become exceptionally ill tempered, even by her own standards, as the autumn wore on. Castello put it down to the fact that the twins were teething and keeping her awake with their relentless grizzling. He took his life in his hands each time he went to visit, he thought, and begged her many times to come and stay at his room at the fort. She had steadfastly refused, saying it was inconvenient for her weather forecasting and ship-watching duties, but after a solid week of particularly tiresome and unremitting new-tooth-induced howling, she caved in and agreed to come down, just for a night or two.

When Castello arrived to escort her, the babies were in full cry and he felt a twinge of guilt at leaving the nursemaid to deal with it all. But the sight of his wife with great indigo-blue circles beneath her eyes, distractedly trying to pack herself a little bag to bring, convinced him that this was not an indulgence, but an absolute necessity. He was genuinely concerned for her health. Rissa wandered about the house in a daze, muttering, picking things up and putting them down again. She was clearly exhausted.

"Dearest – give me the bag. Do you need this? And this?" Castello followed her, packing random clothes and objects into the bag, as the din continued upstairs. His idea of suitable overnight necessities for a woman was a little hazy. He simply wanted to get her away from the noise before she collapsed. In the end he threw her cloak around her shoulders and bundled her out of the door, saying they would send a runner if she had left anything essential behind. She allowed herself to be led by the hand as far as Ferro's forge, where she sat down on a rock and went to sleep.

Castello called Mrs Ferro to bring a blanket for her, and

asked Young Ferro, who happened to be at home, if he would harness the old grey mare to the cart, and carry Rissa down to the fort that way.

Young Ferro took the reins and was affably talkative all the way down the hill. Castello remarked that the old grey mare was looking rather well padded. "She is, too," said Young Ferro. "I believe she is in foal, Captain. No wonder she kicked up her heels so during the horse race. She was in season, I think. And she ran off with our two stallions, you remember. I wonder which of them caught her?"

Castello shrugged. He wasn't about to discuss the breeding habits of horses in front of his wife, even if she was fast asleep.

When they reached the fort, he carried her in and set her in a chair before the fire, and there she slept until the following evening.

Fort Resolute's loss was undoubtedly Mistress Zostra's gain. The roof was complete, and the lady of the house celebrated by preparing to brew her first batch of ale. Before long, the beguiling smell of the brew-house began to waft about. Old Billy took careful note of the wind direction, day by day, and placed himself wherever he could get the best benefit of the fumes. It seemed he was forming a queue all by himself against the happy moment when the ale would finally be ready. Zostra regularly found him asleep outside her front door in the mornings.

"Tell me, Master Ralham," she said one day, "do the Larus-folk read? Do they have their letters?"

"They do," said Ralham. "The Reverend has seen to it that everyone reads. We are a literate isle, Mistress."

"Good," said Zostra, thoughtfully. "I have it in mind to do some advertising-writing." Ralham thought the smell of brewing beer was probably advertising enough, but humoured her, and found some suitable pieces of wood for what she had in mind.

Two days later there was an advertising hoarding in place by the main track near the quay, where everyone, sooner or later, was sure to pass by. It read:

'Best Ale on Larus Isle
At the Sign of the Sea Poppy
Mrs Zostra, proprietor
Grand Opening Sunday Next'

The Reverend Pontius had stopped and was standing stock-still. Despite his best efforts, he could feel the colour draining from his face.

"Why, Reverend," said Captain Castello, who was walking alongside him at the time, "Whatever is the matter? You look…" he groped for the right word. "Ghastly."

"Oh, er, nothing, brother," said Pontius. But he continued to stare fixedly at Zostra's roadside sign. At the sign of the sea poppy, it said.

Beware the hornèd poppy of the sea,
The future of the island is at stake.

The prophecy came back to him, and he remembered his thoughts at the time he had heard it: how could a flower threaten the island? Unlikely that it could, of course, but this wasn't a flower. It was an alehouse, a building, named after a flower. He was seized with the certainty that this was the answer to the riddle, though he still couldn't see quite what the threat might be, apart from universal drunkenness. Eventually Pontius realised he had been staring at the sign for far too long, and Captain Castello was giving him a very concerned look. Castello knew, of course, that his friend greatly disapproved of the whole alehouse plan. Was the Reverend upset because Zostra was planning to open for business on a Sunday? Or because of the blatant advertising? He was just wondering whether to politely ask Zostra to take the sign down, when her second-in-command, Master Broad, came galumphing round the corner.

"Free mugs of ale," he grunted, obviously repeating a much-practiced speech, "for you, Mister Captain, zur, and you, your Parsonage. Sunday-after-prayers. All of Larus isle will be there, for certain-sure. At the Sea Poppy Inn. There, I has it right!" He gave a great gurgling laugh of satisfaction, and went on his way. In passing he slapped them both on the back, as high as he could reach, so hard, that Pontius fell into the sign and found himself nose-to-petal with the large yellow sea poppy Zostra had painted on it. Broad was full of apologies, and tried to assist, but the Captain sent him on his way, not unkindly, and said he would take care of the Reverend, thanks all the same.

"I shall be glad when that fellow goes back to Arjento Rock, where he belongs," said Pontius, when the Captain had picked him up, brushed him off and retrieved his hat for him. "Has Master Ralham made any progress in persuading them to leave?"

"I think he has," said Castello. "Or some of them, anyway. You were right about Ralham, though, Reverend, he certainly wants to go. I suggest we leave it to him."

"Yes, indeed," said Pontius, glaring at the pestilent sign. "I suppose we had all better go down on Sunday. Just to keep an eye on things, you understand. Will the lady warden come, do you think?"

"She will if I ask her to," said Castello, sounding far more confident than he felt, and changed the subject as they continued their walk.

"Did you know, Reverend, that Ferro's old grey mare is in foal?" It was such a sudden change, that Pontius stared at Castello in surprise for quite a few moments before replying.

"In foal…?"

"Yes. She ran off with the two stallions during the horse race, disappeared behind the hedge…"

215

"Yes, yes," said Pontius, testily. "I understand. There's no need to tell me every detail."

"No," said Castello, hastily. "Of course not. But I suppose it's a good thing for Larus. An extra horse or two will be useful. We could build another cart…"

"Yes," said Pontius, "there is that aspect."

"I wonder if the foal will favour the piebald, or the red horse," said Castello, reflectively.

For the second time, the Reverend Pontius stopped and stood stock-still. The words of the other prophecy, the Song of Rufus, came back to him. The two namesakes, Rufus the hermit, Rufus the horse. *Each leaves a feisty female standing by.* Mother Culver was the first feisty female. Was the old grey mare the other one? "If I were a betting man, which I'm not," said Pontius, "I'd wager the foal will favour the red horse." And he stomped off down the hill.

Castello stared after him in surprise, about to ask what had made him say such a thing, but the Reverend wasn't about to stop and answer questions.

"There are altogether too many feisty females on this island for its own good," muttered Pontius.

Chapter Five
A Night to Remember

As it turned out, all four guardians attended the grand opening of the Sea Poppy Inn. Mother Culver had come over rather snooty when she heard about it, said she was a guardian of the isle, and such things were beneath her these days. And, besides, she didn't frequent pubs. In the end, Zostra herself had bustled up to see her mother. "Do you say, Mama, that you will not be a-coming off this draughty cliff-place to drink my health and success-to-come?"

Mother Culver regarded her loftily. "Free ale, is it?"

"Free ale, it is."

"Then come I shall, Daughter. Just for a while, mind. I have important duties, nowadays."

This conversation had been reported all round the island. The Reverend Pontius said the old baggage was getting ideas far above her station. And the sheer quantity of brandy he had given to her in exchange for her archive! Well, anyone who could put away that amount of alcohol was scarcely in a position to be sniffy about frequenting pubs, he thought. But he kept the thought to himself. Both he and Castello had been expecting some acid remarks on the subject from Rissa, but she had said nothing. In fact, she had said nothing much about anything since Zostra's arrival.

For all that, she turned out in her best scarlet gown and cloak, and paraded down to the inn on Castello's arm, with the Reverend Pontius bringing up the rear. It was a dull, still day, with a gentle swell rolling under the oil-thick surface of the sea and breaking on the shingle with a soft hushing. Not that you could hear it, for the racket the inhabitants of the island were making outside the pub. The drinking was well under way, and had been for some time, to judge by the state of Old Billy, who was collapsed on the shingle, waving his empty mug and querulously requesting a drop more ale.

There was a considerable crowd, far too many to fit inside the inn, and people had spread themselves about outside, sitting on benches, upturned buckets or the ground. There was a discordant din of music. An uneasy duet was in progress, with a fiddle and drum on one side of the pub, and a rival orchestra of two flutes on the other. They were playing entirely different tunes and trying to drown one another out. People were trying to dance, following the rhythm of one band or the other, depending on which was loudest. Dancing, on a Sunday, forsooth, thought the Reverend Pontius, and was about to administer a stern ticking-off when Zostra came out of the inn to greet her distinguished visitors. She was wearing a gown as yellow as the sea poppy on her painted inn sign, with a dark green spotted sash and matching shawl. The whole ensemble was topped off with a forget-me-not blue tricorne hat that perfectly matched her eyes, Castello couldn't help noticing.

"Painted trollop," muttered Rissa.

Zostra seemed not to have heard. "Shut that racket!" she bellowed, silencing the music and chatter. "Master Broad, bring ale for our respected guardian-folk."

As the ale was handed out, Mother Culver scuttled out of the pub and took her place beside Rissa, clearly thinking she was entitled to be welcomed as a guardian, too.

Captain Castello stepped forward, and raised his tankard. "On behalf of my esteemed colleagues, may I wish you every success with your venture, ma'am," he said formally. "Let us drink a toast: to Mistress Zostra, landlady of the Sea Poppy

Inn."

All four guardians drank to the success of the inn, but with very varied amounts of enthusiasm. Mother Culver said, "Hear, hear!" and drained her tankard in a very unladylike fashion. Rissa sniffed the ale and took a polite sip. Castello and the Reverend also took polite sips, but, to their obvious surprise, found it was rather good ale and both took a much more hearty draught, and emerged smiling.

Zostra watched carefully, saying, "Thank you, Cap'n dear, thank you for your kindly thoughts. Master Broad, more ale for our guardians. And go find some apple-wine for Mistress Rissa. I think it will agree with your gizzards better, sister."

Rissa nodded gratefully, and put her nearly-full tankard into the nearest outstretched hand, which was Mother Culver's. "You won't be wanting that, now, will you, colleague?" said the old woman, who apparently considered the formal greetings over with, and made off with the ale. The lopsided music and dancing started up again, and lively chatter broke out.

When the Captain's tankard had been refilled, and Rissa supplied with a dainty wineglass, the two strolled away from the worst of the noise. "I could wish that ale-wife were not so familiar with you, Hugh," said Rissa, very deliberately.

"Familiar?" said Castello, puzzled.

"Yes. She called you 'Cap'n dear' did she not?"

"Oh. Perhaps she did. But I think it is just their way of speaking on Arjento Rock." He didn't add that she *always* called him 'Cap'n dear' and that he rather enjoyed it. Rissa's eyebrow had lifted in a distinctly dangerous fashion, and he had no wish to antagonise her, particularly when she was carrying a wineglass. A very nasty weapon in the hands of a furious woman. He struggled to change the subject. "I don't think she means any disrespect, dearest. In any case, I have twice heard her refer to you as 'sister'. Is that not a little over-familiar? I am sure it is just her way of speaking."

Rissa looked out to sea. "No," she said. "It isn't over-familiar, and it isn't her way of speaking. It's because I *am* her sister." She sipped her wine while Castello reeled at this sudden revelation.

"You are… but how can that be? She is Mother Culver's daughter." The obvious, alarming thought occurred to him. "You don't mean that Mother Culver is your…?"

"No, of course not," snapped Rissa. "We had different mothers, but the same father. We are half-sisters." Castello was struggling with the various permutations of possible parentage.

"So your father Petrus was Zostra's father, too? I thought her father was a visitor from Arjento Rock."

"Yes," said Rissa, unhelpfully. And, after a pause, "I mean that her father *did* come from Arjento Rock. He was my father, too."

Castello was so astounded, he took a steadying gulp from the tankard, splashing the ale down the front of his uniform. "But… but, why did you never mention it… we named our son after your father…" The questions were welling up at considerable speed, and so were the tears in Rissa's eyes.

"It was a family scandal! Of course I did not speak of it. I was ashamed. I had hoped it would all be forgotten, after so long. And so it was, until that Zostra and her drunken rabble showed up," she said bitterly, and began to cry in earnest.

Castello almost launched into the tale of his possible other wife and family, as told by the hated Salticus. Almost, but not quite. He pulled himself up in time, handed Rissa his somewhat beer-sodden handkerchief, and took another swig from the tankard. "Good, strong ale," he muttered.

Rissa ignored him, and went on, sniffing. "That swine – I will not call him my father – left two women in distress. He spent a year or so with Mother Culver, and, after Zostra was born, he took up with my poor, stupid, trusting mother. I was a babe in arms when he left us, but he took Zostra with him. They say Mother Culver keened for her child a whole year.

That is when she began to have visions and make prophecies."

Castello nodded. "And your mother…?"

"She was left behind. My father Petrus – I think of him as my real father – married her, and took me, too. My mother died in childbirth. It's rare, but it happens," she added seeing Castello's shocked expression. "My father Petrus brought me up and taught me the weather-lore. I owe him everything. But I have spoken of this before." She had, indeed, spoken of Petrus many times. She had simply omitted to add that he was not her real father.

"Well," said Castello. "Well. Now I know all about it. You may tell me more another day, if you wish. When you are more composed. In the meantime, if Zostra or anyone else has anything to say on the subject, we will deal with it together, dear wife." And he offered her his arm.

Meanwhile, outside the Sea Poppy Inn, the Reverend Pontius was having a deep and meaningful conversation with the landlady. The ale was certainly very good, but Pontius had drunk sparingly. He wanted to keep his wits about him, and do a bit of snooping if possible.

"Tell me, ma'am," he said, "what made you choose the name of Sea Poppy for your inn?"

"Why, Mr Reverend, zur," said Zostra, "wasn't it the first sane and steady thing I saw, after our boat collided with that Shingly Islet, drat the place, and begging your pardon. I got down on my knees on that shifty shingle, to give thanks for dry land at last. And there was the yellow sea poppy, zur, a-growing in the pebbles. It was the most welcome thing I ever did see."

"And – if I may enquire, ma'am – what made you take ship for Larus at all, since you so dislike the sea?"

"Ah, zur," said Zostra, nudging him in the ribs. "I is my mother's daughter!"

"Ah," said Pontius, thinking this was a statement of the

221

blindingly obvious. "Um, so you are, madam, but…?"

"My mother has the Sight, your holiness, and so do I. I foresaw the death of old Rufus the Hermit. Indeed I did. Him and that red horse-creature. Saw them flying off the cliff together, on a great windy gust, I did. And my Mama left to take over the job. Thought it time for a visit. Daughterly support, like."

"Very commendable," said Pontius, mildly, though his mind was whirring. "And you brought all the equipment for your alehouse just by chance?"

"Well, zur," said Zostra, "I thought to make it a long visit. So I brought the means to earn my living, zur, you understand."

"Indeed," said Pontius, spotting an opportunity. "But surely, ma'am, having lost a good deal of your goods in the shipwreck, you must be in need of further supplies, if you are to continue brewing?"

"This is all true-said, zur, but that Master Ralham says the Larus-folks will lend one of their ship-contraptions to take my crew home to Arjento Rock. And when it comes back it will bring the brewing-necessaries. I has sheds-full of supplies at home."

"That will be a happy outcome for us all, ma'am," said Pontius, and he bowed politely, said he mustn't keep her from her other guests, and moved on. She had given him much to consider. His little plan to rid the island of the quarrelsome Arjentans, or most of them anyway, was coming to fruition nicely. But, all that stuff about having the Sight, having seen Rufus and the red horse flying off the cliff, was there any truth in it, at all? Or was it pure evasion to stop him asking awkward questions? There had been plenty of time for Zostra to hear all about the death of Rufus, after all, and to consult with her untrustworthy mother. Nonetheless, the Reverend thought, she could have come up with a rather more plausible excuse.

The autumn day was wearing on, and the light was beginning to fade, but the party showed no signs of coming to an end. On the contrary, it was becoming ever more lively. Lights had been brought outside, and the music and dancing, such as it was, continued. And so did the drinking. Especially the drinking. Even Captain Castello was looking, shall we say, a little the worse for wear.

As a matter of fact, the Reverend Pontius observed, as he looked over the merry scene, there was no one at all inside the inn. It was the opportunity he been hoping for, and he slipped inside the door. There was nothing but a candle or two to light the room, and not much furniture, since most had been taken outside.

Feeling quite the detective, Pontius moved around the room, staying in the shadows. Still, there was nothing to see, and he was about to step out again when his foot collided with something solid on the wooden floor. He stooped and peered at it. It was a rusty iron ring. "Why, there is a trapdoor," said Pontius quietly. He looked around guiltily, and then bent and took hold of the ring. The trapdoor lifted easily and surprisingly quietly. The hinges had been well oiled. Underneath was a flight of stairs. Of course. This must lead to the cellar. The Reverend had heard there was a cellar. He absolutely couldn't resist having a look, and took one of the candles. A warm, beery, waft came up the stairs to meet him.

It was a large cellar – probably as large as the whole footprint of the inn. It was scattered with little ale barrels. Pontius knew that Ferro the blacksmith had been helping to make them up. He naturally disapproved, though Ferro himself was undoubtedly out on the beach at this moment enjoying the fruits of his labours. There was a messy collection of clothes and personal belongings in the cellar too, and a number of makeshift beds. Zostra's crew were clearly using this as an accommodation block. All very interesting, but no great surprise.

"Hm," said Pontius to himself. "There is nothing to see here." And he turned to make his way back up the stairs, when the light from his candle fell upon the far wall of the cellar. The Reverend stared. There was a door. A very heavy oak door, surely containing the timbers from many a shipwreck. Pontius stumbled forward, barking his shins on a discarded barrel. "It's a door!" he said to himself. "And such a door." It had clearly been designed to keep something very safely in. Or something very alarming out.

Pontius ran his hand wonderingly over its cobwebby timbers. It was wide, very wide. But not particularly high. But then it wasn't a very high cellar. The rusty iron hinges looked as if they hadn't been opened for many years. And there was a blackened brass lock. No key. No key... But where could such a door lead? What could its purpose possibly be? Was there another chamber behind it? Pontius was just considering all this, when he suddenly had the most uncomfortable feeling that someone was standing on the other side of the door, holding their breath. He felt compelled to put his eye to the keyhole, and was just bending down to it when a shout came from the staircase.

"Oy! You sneak-thieving rapscallion! What is you a doin'-of, down here below?" It was Master Broad.

"I... I was, er, looking for a refill," said Pontius, playing for time and trying to find a means of escape. He considered the great door, for a moment. But, no. No key. No way out but the stairs. "I, um, lost my way," he added, lamely. Master Broad came down with surprising speed and soon had the Reverend's arm in a strong grip. Pontius tried to shake him off, with no success at all, and was bundled off up the stairs and out of the front door.

"Mrs Zostra!" yelled Broad. "I have found this here sneaky-thief parson-person a-foraging in your understairs ale-room. Permission to smack him, Mistress?" he added, hopefully.

"No! No smacking," said Zostra, hurrying forward. "Thank

you, Master Broad. Leave him go, now."

But Broad was not to be stopped so easily. "Abusing of the 'ospitality, it is. Found 'im pokin' around our inn, I did." He had let Pontius go, as instructed, but shook his fist menacingly.

Somebody yelled: "*Your* inn? This place is Larus-owned. And get you back to Arjento Rock if you don't like it, you thick-skulled mining monkey!"

"Who are you calling a monkey, you over-lanky fish-face?" And within seconds a huge fight had broken out. Every one of Zostra's crew was immediately involved in a scrap with one or more of the locals. Even so, there were definitely not enough Arjentans to go round, so the remaining Larus-men fought among themselves, not wishing to be left out. It was a complete riot.

"Stop, stop it!" yelled the Reverend Pontius. He looked round to Zostra for support. But, no, she was fully engaged whacking Ligo with an empty tankard, after he had misguidedly tried to escort her to safety. "I can fight my own battles, you great lollop," she yelled, and looked around for a more substantial form of weapon. Ligo sensibly retreated before she found one.

Rissa had been sitting talking to Mother Culver, and not getting very much sense out of her, truth to tell, when the fight broke out. She leapt to her feet and strode determinedly around the outer edge of the scrum, dodging flying fists and feet. Where was Zostra? Why was she not controlling her rabble? Where was Castello, for that matter? Why had he not called on his gun captains to restore order? The answer to the second question quickly became clear. The good Captain was fast asleep on a bench, his head resting on Rissa's folded cloak, blissfully unaware of the chaos. His wife bypassed him, snorting with disgust. She spotted Ligo, and shouted "Master Ligo, what are you doing, there?"

Pontius had been trying to battle his way through to Ligo's

side. "Make way… I am a man of the cloth… put that down at once… don't you threaten me, sir, whoever you are, I am a guardian of the isle… Oh, where is my shoe?" The Reverend had lost a shoe in the crush, and he bent and scrabbled about to find it. Unfortunately, he picked the moment that Master Broad, not to be deprived of a smacking opportunity, charged headlong at Ligo, just as he was distracted by Rissa's call, knocking him backwards off his feet. The pair of them landed on the Reverend, who was sent flying by the onslaught, and all three fell in a heap.

"Oh, Reverend!" cried Rissa, clapping her hand to her mouth.

Zostra appeared beside her. "We must stop this, sister," she said. "Mr Reverend, he is an old man, he will be injured and harmed." The sisters stood side-by-side and yelled, "STOP!" The combined volume was considerable. And effective. The battle stopped, obediently, as if frozen in time.

"That's better," said Rissa. People were picking themselves up and backing away. The Reverend Pontius was face down on the ground. "Are you hurt at all, colleague?"

Pontius slowly sat up, nursing his head. Something – a fist, somebody's elbow, he knew not what – had collided with his head, and he was aware that his right eye was closing up.

"Oh, Mr Parson!" said Zostra. "You has the makings of a proper shiner, there. Is all your bones in one piece, zur?"

"I think so," said Pontius, slowly. "But I think I will sit here a while and just make sure."

"Stay still, colleague, and recover yourself," said Rissa. "I shall go and deal with my husband." And she stalked off.

Zostra ran after her calling, "Do not be too hard on him, sister. He is not used to the strong ale."

Rissa ignored her. Castello was still on the bench, snoring peacefully. But not for long. With a single swipe, Rissa whipped her cloak from under his head, and he jerked awake. "Uh? What… what is it?"

"Get up, you drunken fool. We're going home." Rissa shook out her best scarlet cloak. It smelt horribly of stale beer, but she put it around her shoulders anyway. Castello got to his feet, and stood swaying, staring uncomprehendingly at his wife and Zostra, standing side by side before him, a blurred vision of scarlet and yellow in the torchlight. A crowd was beginning to gather round the bench. The lady warden in a temper was always good entertainment value, and the presence of the lively Zostra was an extra wild-card.

"I pray you, dearest," said Castello, unsteadily, "do not stand next to Mistress Zostra. The colours of your costumes, side by side, are making my head swim." And he sat back down on the bench with a thump.

"Why, Cap'n, dear, I believe you are a little tipsy-like," said Zostra, affectionately. Altogether too affectionately for Rissa's liking.

"How dare you speak to my husband in that familiar way?"

Zostra squared up to her. "I'll speak to 'im any way I likes, and who's to stop me? You, Mistress Hoity-toity?"

There was a nasty silence between them, broken only by the muttering of people starting to take bets on the outcome of this confrontation. The lady warden and the ale-wife – an evenly matched contest. What a day it had been: free ale, a punch-up, the parson with a black eye, the Captain drunk as a skunk, and now a catfight. This really was the best party ever.

Castello looked up woozily, and wagged a finger at Zostra. "Oh, Mistress, do not pick a fight with my wife. She's ver' fierce."

"Shut up, you nincompoop," snapped Rissa.

"See?" said Castello. "Dear wife... says I'm a poocomnimp."

"Don't you call him a nincompoop!" said Zostra, patting Castello on the shoulder consolingly. "He's a dear, sweet man."

"I'm his wife and I'm entitled to call him a nincompoop. And he's not a dear, sweet man, he's my husband. And I'll thank you to keep your mucky paws off him."

"Mucky paws, is it?" said Zostra turning to face her.

Castello's head swivelled from one sister to the other. The look of determined fury on their faces was identical. "Not mucky," he said stupidly. "Ver'pretty. Most becoming." He attempted to bow and nearly fell off the bench.

Rissa turned on him, "Shut up, you great ninny. And take that moon-struck smirk off your face before I knock it off for you!"

"Leave 'im be," said Zostra. "Poor lamb." And she clasped Castello's head to her bosom.

Rissa turned to her sister again. "This is all your fault. You brought all this alcohol and ale. And look what we have – fighting and drunkenness. It's a disgrace. You and your rabble should be packed off back to Arjento Rock first thing tomorrow."

Zostra let go the Captain and stood her ground. "Everyone was dancing-happy til you poked your great nose in, sister. Whatever did the poor Cap'n-dear do to earn a wife so shrewish?"

"The people here depend on me to act responsibly," said Rissa, slowly and dangerously, "I am southern guardian of the Isle of Larus, ship warden and wise woman of the weather. And don't you forget it."

"There's hoity-toity, with your fancy Larus job-names," spat Zostra. "But, sister, you is half Arjentan, same as me. And don't you forget that, neither. Our daddy, he took me back to Arjento Rock with him. And he left *you* behind. So there."

Rissa turned as if to walk away, then stepped back suddenly, fist clenched, and punched Zostra forcefully on the chin. The ale-wife collapsed in a flurry of yellow skirts and lay still.

"Oooh," said Castello. "Fell over."

Bets were immediately settled. The lady warden was the winner by a knockout, no doubt about it.

Rissa's temper drained away. This was awful. She felt like crying, but that would do nothing to sort out this mess. She looked around for support. Mother Culver had vanished. The Reverend Pontius was on the ground nursing a stupendous black eye and looking around for his missing shoe. And Castello was sitting on the bench staring stupidly into space. I must deal with all this myself, she thought. She closed her eyes for a second to marshal her thoughts and then felt in the deep pocket of her gown and found her smelling salts.

Zostra was out cold on the shingle, with Ligo kneeling on one side and Master Broad on the other. Each of them was patting one of her hands, and glaring at each other.

"Ligo," said Rissa, "take this. Let her breathe over it – she is breathing, isn't she? It will bring her round. And no fighting!" Ligo and Broad were showing signs of squabbling over the right to administer the smelling salts. They stopped, and glared at each other again. "See," said Rissa, "she is waking. Take her indoors and make her comfortable. And then come back out here, Ligo. I have need of you. The Captain has need of you. Master Broad will take care of her."

Rissa turned and peered into the darkness beyond the torchlight. "Master Ralham – are you here?"

Ralham appeared from nowhere. "Aye, Lady."

She was relieved to see that he wasn't drunk. "Is Lineus here? In a fit state?"

"Aye, Lady." Lineus appeared, and saluted smartly. As a matter of fact, the three gun captains had agreed it would not be wise to become inebriated in the presence of all four guardians, and had taken very little ale at all.

"Good. Excellent," said Rissa. "Master Lineus, would you go and find Mother Rufus, and escort her home. She is here somewhere. Pick her up and carry her if necessary." Lineus bowed politely, and rushed off.

Young Ferro came out of the crowd, fresh as a daisy, and stood before her. "I would like to help you, too, Lady, if I can."

"Certainly you can help," said Rissa. "Go and assist the Reverend. Find his shoe for him and bring him down here." Young Ferro saluted, a tad self-consciously, and trotted off to do as he was bid.

"Master Ralham, take care of the Captain. See he doesn't fall and hurt himself." She was becoming aware of a big, bruised pain in her knuckles. "And the rest of you – find your friends and see them home. Some of them have drunk too deep, for sure. I want no one left on this beach all night. It is mortal cold and damping." She shivered and drew her cloak tightly around her.

The party quietly dispersed.

Winter would be coming soon, and everyone would feel it, sure enough. But it wasn't always very visible, not on Larus. Autumn shows its presence most clearly in a woodland setting, and that was distinctly lacking. It wasn't totally true to say there were no trees on the isle. There were certainly some. But they tended to be stunted things, almost to the ground sometimes. Or bent flat-topped and crooked by the gales. There were even a couple of little, walled orchards over near the chapel. But the fruit trees were neatly sliced off at top-of-wall height. Every spring they poked their noses up above the wall, and every autumn the gales burned the twigs completely black, and they never got any taller. Any autumnal colour which did manage to show through would be lucky to last out the day before being torn off and hurled into the sea.

The Reverend Pontius sighed. He could feel the advancing season in his bones, loud and clear. As Zostra had predicted, he found himself the reluctant owner of a magnificent black eye. None of the four guardians had emerged unscathed from the riotous party at the Sea Poppy Inn. Nor with their dignity intact, neither.

Pontius had kept quietly to the chapel for a few days while

his bruises faded from purple to green to grubby yellow. Nonetheless, word had filtered through to him regarding the condition of the other three guardians. Mother Culver – I suppose I must call her Mother Rufus now, thought Pontius – had been carried back to the east cliff under Lineus' arm, cursing him loudly in outrageous language all the way.

Castello had been helped home with some difficulty by Ligo and Ralham. His wife had put him to bed, berating him for making such a scene. That was very rich, coming from her, thought Pontius. It wasn't the Captain who had indulged in a very public shouting match. Nor had he knocked anyone unconscious in a bare-knuckle fistfight. Indeed, thought the Reverend, did I not hear the bets being made on the outcome with my own ears? Scandalous, all of it. Still, it had to be said in Rissa's favour that she had taken charge and dealt with a volatile situation very efficiently.

As for the Reverend, he was thoroughly ashamed of himself. How could he have been so careless as to let himself be caught while investigating the cellar? That Master Broad was too cute by half. And then to be the unwitting cause of a brawl, and to end it with a black eye and his best silk stockings in ruins. It was all too bad. Nonetheless, he *had* seen the door. There had been plenty of time to think about it, while he stayed at home recovering. And there had been plenty of time, too, to remember Mother Culver's prophecy:

Come the strangers, seekers of the key
Every ship and heart they mean to break...

Well, the strangers had come, all the way from Arjento Rock, and now he had seen this mysterious door, a door with a lock but no key. It all tied up neatly. And had there really been someone standing behind the door? If he had managed to put his eye to the keyhole, would he have seen another eye staring back?

Under normal circumstances, the Reverend would have visited Rufus the Hermit for clarification. But Rufus was gone, and in his place, Mother Culver. Mother Culver, whose own daughter was the leader of the strangers. How can I trust her, Pontius thought, to put the interests of Larus first? And as for Rissa, she had been revealed as Zostra's half-sister – what a surprise that had been – and half-Argentan to boot. The Reverend didn't think the lady warden would ever betray the island, but still, the doubt remained.

And Castello – why Zostra was his sister-in-law, no less, and he seemed mildly smitten with her. Pontius felt that the whole balance of the guardians' loyalty to the Isle of Larus had been shifted. On the whole, though, he felt his friend Castello was his best hope of assistance, and decided to put the whole story to him. If the strangers were indeed seeking the key to that great door, it was imperative that he should find it before they did, and ships and hearts began to be broken. And he knew that he couldn't do it alone.

As it turned out, though, all of this would have to wait. The Reverend was about to adjust his hat so that the remains of his black eye was as inconspicuous as possible, when Ralham burst through the chapel door his eyes blazing with excitement. "Reverend, oh, Reverend, sir, they are packing up. They are leaving. And I am to go with them!"

"What?" said Pontius, taken by surprise. "Oh, Master Ralham, do stop and take a breath. You will give yourself a seizure."

Ralham paused and steadied himself. "Mistress Zostra's crew, sir, they are to leave for Arjento Rock on the next tide. Today, sir. All except for Master Broad. He is staying to help at the inn. We are all going in the *Mergoose*, sir, with Lineus. And I am to be head of security for the voyage! If only, if only we still had the Captain's musket," he added regretfully.

The Reverend's only regret was that an excellent opportunity to get shot of Master Broad had been missed.

Still, the rest of the rabble would be gone. It meant that only Zostra and Broad remained to search for the key and guard the door. Ralham was hopping from foot to foot as if afraid the boat would leave without him if he let it out of his sight.

"Captain Castello has been at the inn, sir, and he asks if you would like to come down?"

"Is he still there?" asked Pontius, getting ready to leave.

"No, sir, he is at the quay. Or the inn. Well, he is at one or the other, Reverend. Shall I run ahead and find him for you?"

"Yes. Tell him I am on my way down." Ralham was already halfway out of the chapel door. "Oh, and Master Ralham – *bon voyage*!" Ralham flashed a delighted grin, and was gone.

As he turned onto the track leading down to the harbour, Pontius saw the unmistakable figure of Rissa heading towards him from the direction of her house. He stood and waited for her. Her left hand was heavily bandaged, and she saw him glance at it.

"I fear the spirits have punished me for losing my temper, Reverend," she said ruefully. "I think I have broken something in my hand. It is a great nuisance. I cannot climb the great rock, or pick the children up. How is your eye, now?"

"Improving, thank you, colleague," said Pontius, with a little smile. "I trust you will not be incapacitated too long. Come, take my arm and we will walk down together. Oh, not with that hand," he added quickly. "On the other side, perhaps."

And so they walked quietly down the hill, deeply unsure of each other, but hoping they presented a united front. Neither much wanted to visit the inn, as the scene of the recent debacle, so they headed for the quay. Castello would catch up with them sooner or later, they knew.

In due course, the *Mergoose* set sail for Arjento Rock, the Arjentans pale and terrified at the prospect of the sea voyage, and Ralham beside himself with delight. "I don't think they will cause Lineus any trouble," said Captain Castello as the boat departed, "apart from being sick all over the place."

Castello had given his two gun captains strict instructions not to linger on Arjento Rock; to see to the loading of Zostra's brewing supplies, and return as soon as weather and tide permitted. It was a great relief to him to see the back of the quarrelsome Arjentans. Master Broad, on his own, was enough of a handful. But at least there was only one of him, and he would be well-occupied helping out at the inn. The Captain had regained both the use of his brains and his decorum since recovering from the party. Rissa had made him swear never to touch ale of any kind ever again, and had then magnanimously forgiven him. He had resisted the temptation to ask her to swear to refrain from indulging in fisticuffs.

Later, Castello and Pontius sat warming themselves by the fire. "Perhaps," said Castello, "there will be some chance of work re-starting on my house now."

"Indeed," said Pontius, "I hope so. But speaking of houses, brother, I must consult with you urgently on something I saw at the Sea Poppy inn."

And he poured out the whole story of Mother Culver's prophecy, the cellar, the great door and the missing golden key. Pontius was quietly thrilled with the mystery of it all, and greatly relished the telling of the tale and the prospect of finding the solution.

Castello, on the other hand, looked distinctly unimpressed.

"Is there no end to our trammels and troubles?" he said with a sigh. "Life used to be so quiet and simple here, Reverend. I polished my guns, marched up and down the old castle, kept a lookout. Slept easy at night. Nothing more worrying than the occasional shipwreck. It was all as comfortable as could be. But this last year or so – everything has become chaotic. One thing after another. What have we had? Shiny ships appearing and disappearing, if you please;

that pirate Salticus; horse races, gambling, alehouses, fighting. Every possible evil. The poor hermit dying like that. No end of pestilential prophecies, that we never had before. And now we are presented with doors that have no business to be where they are and lost golden keys that affect the island's future." He sighed again and rested his chin wearily in his hand.

Pontius was mildly shocked. He had expected Castello to find it all as interesting as he did himself. But then again, the Captain had weathered rather more trials then everyone else. There was all the worry he had endured as a result of Salticus' threats. He had a family to consider these days. And, goodness knows, his family life seemed to become ever more complicated. The Reverend was thankful for bachelorhood at the thought of it all. He looked thoughtfully at his friend and realised for the first time that Castello was mortally tired. The straitlaced, but relatively carefree man he had been two summers ago was gone. The new Castello was weighted down with many cares, and it showed on his face and in his bearing. No wonder he had overindulged in the strong ale.

"Be easy, brother," said Pontius, soothingly. "The shiny ships are gone, and not likely to return for many a year, as I understand it. You have achieved so much. Your new fort, the training of your gun captains. You have secured the island against such threats. As for the drinking and gambling – they are nuisances, but we can deal with them together. You are not alone, colleague. And, perhaps, now that our Arjentan visitors have gone home, there will be no more fighting."

"What you say is true," said Castello. But he didn't look very convinced.

"And the prophecies," Pontius went on, gently, "well, I have visited them upon you, with my prying and poking about. I hoped they would help us to be prepared."

"So they did, Reverend," said Castello, with another sigh. "But I could wish there were an end to them."

"I will deal with this one myself," said Pontius. "Do not

concern yourself about it."

Castello roused himself, sat up straight. "No, no, Reverend. I will assist you. If it threatens the future of the island, then it must concern me. Tell it all to me again, so I can have it clearly in mind."

When Pontius had told the story over again – the prophecy, the cellar, the door, the missing key – Castello thought for a moment.

"There are many matters to consider here, Reverend. But let us begin with the key. We do not know, do we, whether it was deliberately hidden, or accidentally lost, if anyone actually wished it to be found again? If it was lost, it could be anywhere, and we are wasting our breath discussing it. But if it was hidden… What would you do with a key if you never wanted it found?"

"I'd fling it into the sea," said Pontius, at once. "But if that is what happened, we have nothing to concern ourselves with, brother, for it is the last place our Arjentan friends would ever look for it, is it not?"

"True. Well then, suppose you wanted it securely hidden?"

Pontius thought. His eye lit on the chest of silver, which was still here in Castello's old room while he awaited the completion of his house. "I suppose… might you not put it in a strongbox?"

They looked at each other. "That is an old, old chest," said Castello, thoughtfully. "It was deeply buried in the ground."

The Reverend was miles ahead of him. "Could that chest have a secret compartment, do you think?"

They set to, immediately, opening the chest and moving all the silver out of it. The Reverend was dropping the coins about in his excitement. "Have a care," said Castello. "I wouldn't wish to lose any more of these." And they piled the silver carefully.

At last the chest lay empty. It did, indeed, have a false bottom, and they prised open the little panel. Pontius was breathless with anticipation. But no, the little compartment was completely empty. They felt around inside the chest for any more hidey-holes, but found nothing. Castello had a disturbing thought: "If the key *had* been in this chest, then Limanda might have found it, when she was taking the silver for Salticus."

Pontius stood up. "You don't think, do you, that Salticus might have got hold of it? That would be grave indeed for the island's security."

Castello jumped up in alarm. "Then I will call Limanda in, this minute, and demand to know if she has seen it."

"Wait, brother, wait," said Pontius. "Let us not be too hasty. Limanda is not a bad girl, at heart, but she is easily led. We cannot trust her to tell the truth. And besides, she is a chatterbox. Anything we say to her will be all over the island in a flash." Castello had to admit this was true.

They began putting the silver back into the chest, thinking it all through as they worked. Castello had another thought: "If Zostra wishes to open the door, why does she not set Master Broad to work with an axe?"

"You haven't seen the door," said Pontius. "It is a vast and solid thing, iron-bound. Besides, perhaps she wishes to close it securely again afterwards."

With the chest locked and covered, they settled back into their chairs.

"One more thing," said Castello. "How do we know they haven't found the key already?"

"They haven't," said Pontius, mysteriously, "I feel it in my bones. Besides, something dramatic would have happened by now."

"So what must we do, Reverend? Keep a close watch on Mistress Zostra?"

"You and I can scarcely spend our evenings sitting about in an alehouse, can we?"

"No," said Castello, thoughtfully, "But I know a man who

can. My gun captain, Ligo. He spends much of his time there, anyway. She would not suspect him."

"But surely he has a… a liking for Mistress Zostra. Where would his loyalties lie, Captain? With her, or with Larus?"

Ralham was rendered speechless by Arjento Rock. Its name suggested it was a small place, but no, not at all. It was a big island, much bigger than Larus, he thought, and so utterly different. It was a considerable shock to a young man who had never been away from home. He simply couldn't get over the scale of it, and walked about gaping like a codfish.

It had been an easy voyage from Larus, apart from the Arjentans moaning and calling on the mercy of any spirit they could think of to deliver them safely from this purgatory.

There was a surprisingly well-built quay and dock area, with a trading ship or two tied up, and the *Mergoose* slid into port almost unnoticed. The Arjentans scrambled unsteadily and gratefully ashore at the first opportunity, saying they would send the brewing supplies down directly. Leaving a crewman or two on board, Lineus and Ralham went ashore for a look around. They soon attracted curious glances from the locals, both being at least a head taller than anyone else. The mining operations were clearly very large and complex, and there were carts and barrels and boxes everywhere. It was, thought Lineus, a very prosperous place, very prosperous indeed. But, as the senior officer of his ship, he tried not to stare open-mouthed, and attempted a partially successful look of blasé indifference. He nudged Ralham in the ribs. "Shut your mouth, Master Ralham. Do you want them to think we have never seen anything like this before? You are a gun captain of Larus. Stop behaving like a tourist."

"We never *have* seen anything like this before," said Ralham, still staring. "And I *am* a tourist."

They strolled on, taking everything in. "I wonder," mused Lineus, "why we have never set up trading arrangements with this place? They have much to offer – but so do we. They do not fish. We do. And Larus is their nearest neighbour. It could be profitable for us both." He was imagining the *Mergoose* as the flagship of a whole fishing fleet. Bigger, better boats. A more organised undertaking altogether. "I shall put it to our guardians when we return."

Ralham nodded in keen agreement: "Yes, oh yes. Especially since Mistress Zostra has set up in business on Larus. We already have a foot in the door, trade-wise." He was imagining himself promoted to Ambassador to Arjento Rock. They would both have been horrified if they had heard the conversation the Reverend Pontius was having at that very moment with Mother Rufus on the east cliff.

"You are a guardian of the Isle of Larus, colleague," the Reverend was saying, sternly. "Your first duty must lie with us here."

Mother Rufus glared at him in mutinous silence. Pontius had been deeply reluctant to consult her, but in the end conceded that she was the only person who could provide him with more information.

He tried again: "You must, you *must* tell me what we can expect. Are we to be overrun with Arjentans? You must let us prepare, if that is to happen." She still said nothing.

"Mother, if you will not assist us you must stand down as eastern guardian. I understand your loyalties may be divided."

She spoke at last. "And the warden? Are her loyalties divided, too, Reverend? Have you asked her to stand down?"

Pontius took a steadying breath. "In all the years I have known the lady warden, she has never for a single moment given me cause to doubt her loyalty to the Isle. I trust her implicitly."

"Then will you not trust me, Reverend?"

"You are new as a guardian, Mother, and you must prove your loyalty. Will you not give us another prophecy?"

"No," said Mother Rufus, to Pontius' dismay. "But I will give you a history. It may help." And she began to sing:

The evil men of Larus cross the sea
To take by force the precious thing they lack,
Such pirating well-punishèd must be;
The Isle of Silver wants its treasure back!

Pontius memorised the verse, as usual, and then stopped, confused. "The evil men of *Larus*…? Surely, Mother, you have misremembered it?"

"It is an old, old history, Reverend. But it is quite correct. I have not gone gaga, you know."

"But… but…," spluttered Pontius, "it presumes… it suggests…" He simply couldn't get the words out.

"That the Larus-men of old were nothing but a gang of thieves and pirates? Yes, just so."

Pontius looked both astounded and affronted. "The Isle of Larus, a nest of pirates?" Mother Rufus nodded, patiently, while he took it all in.

"And the Isle of Silver refers to…"

"Arjento Rock, yes." She stared sadly out to sea, with a very Rufus-like sigh.

"So… let me understand this properly, Mother… at one time, long in the past, the men of Larus went pirating, raided Arjento Rock, stole their silver?"

"That, Reverend, is the long and the short of it."

"And the Arjentans want it back?" Pontius sighed. "Not altogether unreasonable, I suppose. But why did you not tell me this before?"

"You would not have wished to hear it, Reverend. You love the island and its people. You would have defended them, denied it."

Pontius had to admit this was all too true. That is exactly what he would have done, only a short time ago. But now his need to understand what was happening to them all had rendered him less resistant to such unpleasing truths.

"And… might this history relate to the chest of silver we found buried at Captain Castello's?"

"Aye, it might," she said mysteriously.

Pontius thought it all through for a moment or two, and then asked, "But why does no one speak of this, Mother? If it truly happened, then why do we not already know of it?"

"Ah," said Mother Rufus, "the people of this isle have a great failing, Reverend. They forget the past. They let it slip away, and do not learn from it, and so they are never prepared for the future. Are they?" It was true. Pontius had seen evidence of this time and again, and, if he were entirely honest, he was sometimes swept up in this deliberate, live-in-the-moment, forgetfulness himself.

"Thank you, colleague," Pontius said sincerely. "I shall see what I can do to set all this to rights."

In the absence of Ralham and Lineus with the *Mergoose*, Captain Castello had called in his third gun captain, Ligo. This summons had been, ostensibly, to discuss the possible selection and training of a fourth gun captain, as back-up. Would Ligo care to take this on? Ligo would, and gladly. Young Ferro had shown a keen interest, and was just the fellow to learn quickly and keenly, Ligo said. Was he not just a little *too* young for such responsibility, wondered the Captain? Not at all, Ligo had said, stoutly. He was the ideal lad for the job, and, after all, he would only be called upon in emergencies. There should be plenty of time for him to learn. Very well, the Captain had said, you may begin the training as soon as you wish. Ligo was content.

However, he was far less content when he heard the Captain's other matter for discussion. Castello had been gentle and discrete, but Ligo soon realised he was being asked to spy on Zostra and Broad at the inn.

"This is a difficult thing you ask of me," said Ligo. Castello nodded, and examined the toes of his boots.

"You should know, Captain, that I have it in mind to ask Mistress Zostra to be my wife, all in good time, and if she is willing."

"And do you think she will be willing?"

"Yes, Captain, I think she will. But not if I betray her with prying about at the inn."

"We are not speaking of betrayal, Ligo," said Castello, uncomfortably. "Not really. All I would ask you to do is warn me if there are any sudden, unexpected goings-on at the Sea Poppy. There will be nothing to report unless she and Master Broad are up to something they shouldn't be." Ligo looked very doubtful.

"The future of the island is at stake," said Castello, unconsciously quoting the prophecy, "and it could well lie in your hands, Master Ligo. So please keep a careful watch, for the sake of us all."

The Reverend Pontius had been so thoroughly surprised and rattled by the history Mother Rufus had given him that he had once again called a meeting with the other two guardians. Rissa and Castello listened intently while he related what had been said. Rissa nodded, and then said, "I have heard this."

"What?" said Pontius. "You knew of this? And you did not warn us?"

"I had hoped… I thought… you know my parentage, Reverend. I could not countenance a war between Larus and Arjento Rock. My position would be impossible. Speaking of such a conflict could have made it a reality."

"Well, it's the first I've heard of it," said Castello, shooting an annoyed glance at his wife. "Do you mean to say that this whole business is the fault of the Larus-men of the past? They robbed Arjento Rock? And that our cache of silver – our Common-wealth – in truth belongs to them?" Pontius nodded ruefully.

"And the golden key?" asked Castello. "The great door in the cellar? What part do they play in all this?"

Rissa's eyebrow shot into her hairline. "What key? What door? What have you been keeping from me?"

"We have all been keeping things from each other, it seems," said Pontius, and he told her the whole story of the door in the cellar and its missing key, and the prophecy that worried him so.

"What sort of key?" asked Rissa, when the Reverend finally paused for breath.

"Golden, according to Mother Rufus," said Pontius. Despite herself, Rissa smiled to hear the Reverend refer to their eastern guardian as 'Mother Rufus'.

"Such as this one?" She pulled her chatelaine full of keys from her pocket. Among them was a small, perfect, shining golden key.

"But... where did that come from?" Pontius was almost speechless.

"Limanda," said Rissa. "She handed me back my keys after all the trouble with that creature Salticus. I asked about this one, and she said she found it when she was cleaning at the fort. Put it with the others for safekeeping. Why? Do you think it's the key you're looking for?"

Castello and Pontius looked closely at it. "It seems a small key for such a large door," said Pontius, "but perhaps the lock is more intricate than it seems."

Rissa got up. "Where are you going, dearest?" asked Castello.

"To get to the bottom of this. First we will speak to Limanda. And then we'll pay a visit to my sister."

Limanda was terrified. The lady warden had come sailing in at Alvan's house and demanded to speak to the girl. Now, this minute. Captain Castello and the Reverend Pontius had trailed in behind her, the Reverend breathless. As if life were not complicated enough, the poor girl now had three guardians waiting for her, impatient and stony-faced. Her father pushed her into the room, and slammed the door. If she was in any more trouble, he really didn't wish to know about it. She burst into tears.

"Oh pray, do not upset yourself, dear," said Captain Castello, proffering his handkerchief.

"Never mind that, husband," said Rissa, pushing him out of the way. "Now listen, Limanda, about this key…" and she drew the chatelaine out of her pocket. Limanda stared at it.

"It… it's the key I found in the chest of silver. Right down at the bottom. Master Salticus… he asked for the silver. But he didn't say anything about any keys. I thought it must belong to the Captain, so I put it with the other keys."

Castello elbowed his way back in again. "It's all right, Limanda, you did the right thing."

"Bound to happen occasionally, I suppose," said Rissa, sniffily, and she swept out of the house, with the Captain and Pontius following in her wake. "Now," she said over her shoulder, as she set out for the Sea Poppy Inn, "Let us see if the key fits your famous door, Reverend."

"My colleague, the Reverend, says there is an unaccountable door in your cellar. We would wish to see it, if you please."

The three guardians were facing Zostra and Broad outside the inn, and Rissa had stepped forward to speak to her sister.

Master Broad sidled up to Zostra as surreptitiously as possible for a person of his width, with narrowed eyes. "Mistress – permission to smack, for the cheekiness?"

"No smacking," said Zostra, to Broad's obvious disappointment, and turned to the three guardians. "What authority-right do you have for this?"

"We are guardians of the Isle of Larus," said Rissa, simply.

244

"It is our duty to care for the isle and its people. My colleague thinks this door might present a… a hazard to its safety."

"Then look at it you must, sister, for you may be right," Zostra said, and led the way inside. The three guardians shot each other a perplexed look as they went.

"We may be *right*…?" mouthed Pontius, to Castello. But he had no time to elaborate.

"You know the way, I believe, Mr Parson, zur," said Zostra, rather archly. Her eyebrow lifted in a perfect mirror image of Rissa's, which was doing exactly the same. Broad actually growled.

They lit candles, opened the trapdoor and trooped down into the cellar.

Rissa wrinkled her nose. The room still bore traces of occupation by the Arjentan crew, and it smelt stale and beery. Nonetheless, there on the southern wall was the great door, just as the Reverend had reported. The three guardians stared at it. It was even larger and heavier than Pontius remembered. Rissa and Castello could scarcely believe their eyes. What was it doing in such a place? Being well concealed was the only possible answer. And it was highly suspicious that neither Zostra nor her crew had mentioned it at all.

Pontius turned to Zostra. "We have in our possession a key, ma'am, which we think will open this door. Do you have any objection if we try it, now?" Zostra shook her head.

"Very well, we thank you," said Pontius politely, and turned to Rissa. "If you would, Lady." Rissa took the chatelaine out of her pocket, and grasped the golden key.

Master Broad gave a loud guffaw. "You is to open that great door-thing with that little key-scrap?" he spluttered.

Even Rissa, as she looked at the lock, thought it unlikely. She slid in the key. And sure enough, nothing happened. "It is too small," she said. "It does not engage with the lock at all."

Pontius felt a complete fool. All this for nothing. Was it just an old storeroom after all? He had been misled by a prophecy.

A prophecy given by this ale-wife's own mother. He had been taken for a ride, on the grand scale. He hung his head in shame and embarrassment.

Rissa snorted with annoyance and went back up the stairs, followed by the others. She stopped and faced her sister. "I apologise for this intrusion. We have made a mistake. I am truly sorry."

Zostra smiled broadly. "Well of course you have, sister. That there key, pretty-golden though it is, could never open that great door."

"But how could you be so sure, ma'am?" said Pontius, recovering a little. He was grateful for Rissa's apology on behalf of them all.

"Why, zur," said Zostra, "because I found the real-and-proper key myself. Long ago, zur."

Chapter Six
Every Ship and Heart...

The Reverend Pontius was thinking that what he had just heard made no sense at all. Or rather, it made no sense according to what he had been expecting. He had thought that if Zostra had found the key, they would be aware of it – that something would have happened. But she *had* found it, apparently, and nothing much at all had happened. His estimation of himself as a detective was plummeting downwards. So what on earth did it all mean, then? The other two guardians were equally nonplussed.

Rissa recovered first. "Would you care to show it to us, sister?" she asked.

Zostra led them outside and pointed to the stone step outside the front door. "Under the doormat, so to speak, it is. Where else would you put a key? Master Broad, would you open it?" Broad growled again, but nonetheless hauled up the stone step. Underneath there was a bed of dark clay, and pressed into it, a large blackened key.

"But it isn't golden!" burst out Pontius.

"It is a bit dirty-black to be sure," said Zostra, "but 'tis good brass underneath. Would scrub up to a nice yellow-golden if we cleaned it, zur. Come, we will put it in the door-lock." And they all went back down into the cellar. Zostra put the key into the lock and turned it, with some effort. There was a clear click, and the door swung open a little way. Behind it, there was a deep, dark space.

"What is it?" asked Pontius. "What is in there?" He took a candle and peered into the gloom. There were steps leading down through a low tunnel. "Where does this lead?"

"Why, zur, it goes to Arjento Rock, of course," said Zostra, matter-of-factly.

A tunnel to Arjento Rock? The three guardians looked at each other in disbelief. All the way to Arjento Rock, under the sea? Surely it wasn't possible. Such a depth, such a distance. Pontius was fighting down the silly questions that flew into his head. He stopped, and thought of the history Mother Rufus had given him.

"Did the Arjentans build this tunnel, ma'am?" he asked Zostra.

She nodded. "Yes, zur, they did. They are great miners, and extra-persistent, you know. It took a great while, they say. But they would not give it up, zur, not til they had righted the wrong-doing of the Larus-men."

"You mean the silver? The stolen treasure?"

"Yes, zur. The Larus-men came in boat-contraptions, with swords and sharp-knives. They stole the silver-treasure, zur, and brought it back here to this little isle. Our people wanted it back, zur, so they made the tunnel. We Arjento-folks don't like your boat-things. So we burrowed, zur, right under the sea. Better-by-far than over it, we said. Keep our feet on the solid rock, we said, zur."

"But how did they find their way, down there in the dark?"

"Our people is natural miners, zur. They know their direction; 'tis built into their head-skulls."

Rissa said: "This is true. I know the direction of the wind without considering it at all. There is a compass in my head! I had never really thought about it. I must have inherited it from my father."

"How do you know all this?" Pontius asked Zostra.

"Ah, zur, we has a care for our histories on Arjento Rock. Every child knows, from the school-learning, And we sings our stories in ballad-songs, zur, all of us."

"You are more wise than us, ma'am," said Pontius, thoughtfully. "But tell me, what did the Arjentans do when the tunnel was complete?"

"Well, zur, they formed a fighting-army, and broke through the tunnel, and out onto Larus, just here. They had come to see fair justice done, and to take back their silver-treasure. There was a great battle-fight with the Larus-men."

"And who won the battle?"

"Why the Larus-men, of course, zur. They is much better at battle-fighting. My people ran back into their tunnel. And the Larus-men sealed it with this great door-thing."

The Reverend Pontius could hardly believe it all. Zostra had told them the whole story – or at least he hoped it was the whole story. The Arjentans had never forgotten the loss of their treasure, many years ago though it was. Every Arjentan child grew up knowing the *Ballad of the Silver-Treasure* by heart. Nonetheless, most people had given it up as a lost cause long ago. Only the resentment and sense of injustice had remained. The tunnel had been sealed at the Arjentan end, too, just in case the Larus-men should try to come through it and steal more treasure.

But all this changed a few months back when a trading ship arrived at Arjento Rock. Its captain had run mad, completely mad. He had run off the ship and straight into one of the mines, and refused to come out, muttering that there were no water-spouts in a mine shaft. "That was all he would say, zurs," said Zostra. 'No water-spouts in here. No water-spouts in here'. We was all amazed by it."

The three guardians looked at each other. Salticus. It had to be. "Was this ship named the *Honest Trader*, by any chance?" asked Pontius.

"Yes, Mr Parson, it was. And the crewmen told us they had come from Larus Isle, and that there was a great treasure there.

Well, zur, hearing *that*, my people knew their silver-treasure was still in one piece. And they wished to open the tunnel, and come fetch it home."

"Fetch it home?" said Pontius. "You mean, to come through the tunnel, invade the island and fight us for the treasure?" Zostra nodded.

"Yes, zur. And they would burn all the boat-contraptions here, to stop the Larus-men chasing them back to Arjento Rock. That is how the plan was made."

Pontius was beginning to understand. "But they needed the door opened at this end. They needed someone to find the key. And so they sent you…" Zostra nodded again, rather apologetically.

"But… but why… You found the key, some time ago, you said. And you haven't let them in."

"Oh, they is a-hammering on that old door night after night, zur. But I keeps it locked."

Pontius remembered his first sight of the door, on the night of the party, and the strong feeling he'd had that someone was on the other side. The idea that it was a pack of warlike Arjentans was more than a little alarming.

Zostra heaved a sigh and went on. "You must understand, zurs and sister, my father turned me against the Isle of Larus, when I was little-small. I learned as a little kidling, that the Larus-men were bloodthirsty thieves all. My father, he had been there, lived there, and he ought to know. I was shameful at being Larus-born. So when this news comes, of the silver-treasure, I was happy to do my part, zurs, and find the key. We thought an alehouse would be a good disguise. I found this old house, and knew from our histories the door was nearby."

She was becoming tearful, and Pontius spoke gently. "But why did you not open the door for them, Mistress?"

"Why, zur, when I get here, I find my father has not spoken truly. The Larus-folks is kindly. Astounded, I was. You saved our lives, zur, when our boat broke. You took care of us. You helped us with the roofing-beams of the inn. And Master Ligo, zur…"

Ah, thought Pontius. Master Ligo, indeed.

"I have it in mind, zur, to settle with Master Ligo, if the big lug will ask me, and make my home here on Larus Isle. And I hope you will be doing the honours at your chapel-church, when the time is right, zur. So I could not betray my gentle man and his people. Now could I, zur? So I keeps the door firmly shut."

"You may well have saved much injury and suffering for your people and ours," said Pontius. "But will the Arjentans give it up? Or will they grow impatient and put an axe to the door?"

"Oh, zur, they never gives up. Determined, they are. There is muttering, zur. And they grows most impatient. I think I cannot hold them off much longer."

Captain Castello had listened to all this in near silence, with a growing feeling of unease. The whole thing was changing from a tale of uncompleted espionage to a wholly military matter, and he felt it was time to take charge. He stood up and bowed to Zostra. "Have I sent my gun captains, Ralham and Lineus, into danger, ma'am? Will they be attacked on Arjento Rock?" It was a horrible thought.

"No, Cap'n dear," said Zostra, seriously. "I thinks they will be quite safe-secure. My people will not harm them. They wouldn't risk them escaping and raising alarums, zur."

"But they are already overdue," said Castello, looking worried. "I had put it down to the contrary winds. But if what you say is true…"

"There *are* contrary winds," said Rissa, patting his arm. "They will not return for a day or two, husband."

"Dammit," said Castello. "I need them here. I need them now. This is a perilous situation. Mistress Zostra, ma'am, would you kindly ask Master Broad here to go and find Ligo and bring him here. If he is out fishing, leave a message at the quay and ask him to come as soon as he returns. Tell them I said it's urgent. Do you understand?"

Broad looked utterly confused by the Captain's commanding tone, and glanced at Zostra for clarification.

"Do it," she said. "Bring Master Ligo as soon as ever." The little man still hesitated. "NOW!" Broad took to his heels.

Castello turned to them all. "We must secure the island. Put a stopper in this invasion. And the best stopper I know is my bronze cannon."

Ligo was not at sea, in point of fact. He was ashore and working on his nets when Broad came puffing towards him. Zostra's second in command was purple in the face and waving his arms wildly. Ligo frowned. Broad rushed up and collapsed, gasping, on a fish-box.

"Your Cap'n-fella... he wants you... says to bring Master Ligo. Now-immediate... all urgent!"

"Steady on," said Ligo. "Get your breath man, you will have a seizure. Do you mean the Captain wants me to come?" Broad nodded, breathlessly.

"Ar, to the Sea Poppy. Now."

At the mention of the inn, Ligo dropped everything and ran. He was mortally afraid that something might have happened to Zostra. Every possible kind of catastrophe flashed before him as he loped up and over the little hill and down to the shingle beach, Broad toiling along behind him.

When he arrived, Ligo looked around desperately. There was nobody here! Where was the Captain? What had happened? Rissa appeared in the doorway and beckoned him in.

"Lady, what has happened? Has Mistress Zostra been harmed?"

"No, no," said Zostra, appearing out of the back room. "I am quite well, you great lollop. 'Tis the Cap'n dear who wants

252

you. In the cellar, he is."

Ligo rushed forward, grasped her hands, looked torn, and then left her and dashed down into the cellar.

"Ligo! Thank goodness," said Castello, looking flustered. "This great door… it leads to Arjento Rock… a tunnel… we may be invaded. We must secure it." Ligo took all this on board.

"But, Captain – Lineus and Ralham…"

"I think they will be safe. I'll explain later." The Captain sat down on a barrel. "Ligo, I want to bring the bronze cannon from the fort, and lower it down into this cellar. As quickly as ever we can."

Ligo raised an eyebrow. This was a considerable undertaking, especially with Lineus and Ralham absent. Castello was ahead of him. "I know this is difficult. We must call down all the help we can. The lady warden will organise runners to take messages for you. Get Ferro – and Young Ferro, too. And all the gun crews. Everyone you can find. Bring the horses and the cart down, we can use them. And look sharp about it, Ligo. I don't know how much time we have." Ligo said nothing, but saluted smartly, and charged back up the stairs.

The Reverend Pontius, meanwhile, having established that there was nothing practical he could do to help, had gone straight up to the east cliff. Even so, this late in the year, it was beginning to get dark, and he trod carefully along the path, pulling his cloak around him against the cold. It was only hours since he had been here – just this morning, but it seemed a very long time since he had spoken with Mother Rufus. She was sitting just as he had left her.

"You took your time," she said, without looking at him. "I was expecting you back long since."

"Mother, I must speak candidly," said Pontius. "I have heard the whole story from your daughter. Imminent invasion, indeed. Ye gods! We must put a stop to this before there is bloodshed and mayhem, and I know not what. If there is anything further you can tell me, this would be a good time to share it."

"There is something, Reverend. You had best memorise it," she said, with a little snigger.

"Another history?"

"No."

"A prophecy, then?"

"No. A suggestion."

Set down your shields and set aside your swords
For if you fight the isle shall swiftly fall.
The battle may be fought with honest words;
The common-wealth is common to us all.

Pontius memorised it, as usual, without paying full attention to its possible meaning. "Thank you, Mother," he said, feeling he had been somewhat short-changed. But at least he hadn't paid a brandy-flask for this one. "I shall think on it."

Back at the Sea Poppy Inn Captain Castello had no intention at all of setting down his shield or setting aside his sword. On the contrary, as soon as Young Ferro arrived, riding the brown stallion, Bruno, he was sent straight to the fort to fetch the Captain's sword.

Castello was not absolutely convinced, on reflection, that he was doing the right thing. It was possible the whole story was a ruse, that the tunnel did not reach as far as Arjento Rock, and that no one would be coming through it at all. Could it all be a trick to concentrate their attention, and their firepower, on the tunnel, when the real invasion would come by sea? He thought it unlikely, given the Arjentans' obvious lack of sailing-skills – but who could tell – perhaps they had help. Could Salticus, or his crew, be assisting them somehow?

It was possible. And *their* seamanship was excellent. He felt torn. He couldn't share all these thoughts with Rissa or Ligo, since they both clearly believed Zostra.

"In any case," he said softly to himself, "I'm damned if I'm going to get caught out. If only Ralham and Lineus were back…"

When Rissa returned to report that her network of runners was complete and operational, taking messages all over the island, he called her over. "That is excellent. Very good. We shall need them. But listen, dear wife, do not neglect the lookouts. It is just possible the *Honest Trader* may return and try to take advantage of the situation."

"I have not neglected the lookouts," said Rissa, slightly affronted, and was tempted to shout at him for doubting her. But no. This was all too important to waste time bickering. "But I will make extra sure that all is properly secure, since you think there might be a danger, Hugh." Castello gave a small, worried smile and kissed her cheek, knowing she could be depended upon absolutely to see that they were not taken by surprise. Rissa vanished into the darkness outside.

Ligo came in to say that people were gathering and awaiting orders.

"Right," said Castello. "Organise a work party and get these barrels out of the cellar – I think most of them are empty. We need all the space we can clear for the gun. And get that trapdoor off its hinges. Send for Old Ferro if you have to. Tell the gun crews I will be with them in a moment." Ligo saluted and dashed off.

Castello took a steadying breath. What next? How much more could they hope to do in the dark? It surely wouldn't be possible to get the gun in place overnight. The best they could do was to have the gun ready for transport at first light, and put an overnight guard on the cellar. And where the devil was the Reverend Pontius?

Zostra appeared out of the shadows. "Is there anything I

255

can do, Cap'n dear?"

"Everything is under control, ma'am," said the Captain, carefully. "Master Ligo will begin clearing the cellar now. I am away to the fort – there is much to do, but I will return later, with your permission, ma'am, to set an armed guard in the cellar. I shall command it myself. Just in case the Arjentans should decide to break the door down tonight."

"I thank you, zur," said Zostra. "Then I shall have vittles-and-drink ready for you and your brave crew. To sustain you through the night, zur." Her eyes twinkled flirtatiously in the candlelight.

Castello bowed, and turned to leave. "Oh, and Mistress Zostra – no strong ale for them, if you please. They will need to stay alert."

As he left the inn, Castello met Ligo and his working party coming in, and went to see how many people were still outside. The remaining members of the gun crews stood to attention and saluted when they saw him, but some of the others seemed to be making an evening of it. Some had got hold of a barrel of ale.

"Put that ale down!" bellowed the Captain. The wind was rising, and he struggled to make himself heard. "We are in danger of invasion. Would you be asleep and in liquor when it comes?"

There were sullen murmurs, and a giggle or two. This was a bit rich coming from someone who had been carried home unconscious from the party not so long ago. Nonetheless, they put down the ale mugs.

"You can all come with me to the fort. Young Ferro, are you there?"

"Aye, Captain. Yes, sir."

"Where are the other horses, and the cart?"

"Already at the fort, sir."

"Good. Now listen all of you. We will dismantle the gun and get it packed in the cart, ready to move it over here at first light. Young Ferro, go and find somewhere to stable the horses overnight at the fort. Walk the brown horse down – don't risk him injuring himself in the dark. Arrange feed for them all and see that they are secure. Sleep in the stable with them yourself, if necessary."

"But Captain…" Young Ferro had been hoping for a position a little closer to the action.

"Don't argue, lad, just do it. The horses are vital to this operation. Guard them with your life."

Young Ferro saluted, and vanished into the darkness.

"The rest of you, follow me!" And the Captain walked purposefully towards the fort, feeling that his command of this group was edgily insecure, and hoping that giving them things to do would make less of a rabble of them.

It was late, past midnight, Castello thought, when he finally set out from the fort back to the Sea Poppy Inn. He had promised Zostra an armed guard – but in truth, he hadn't much to arm them with. They had depended so much on the cannon for defence, and he had not thought to get hold of small arms. The musket had been destroyed when he faced the shiny ships, and he greatly regretted not having made more effort to replace it. All that business with Salticus had put it out of his mind. He had been remiss. But it was too late now, and they must do the best they could. The gun crews marched back to the inn with him – he had sent everyone else home – and they had brought knives, hammers, axes, whatever they could find. The Captain could only hope the Arjentans would not choose this night to break through the door.

As they arrived at the inn, Rissa, Pontius and Ligo all rushed up looking worried. "They are here!" said the Reverend.

"Who? Who's here?"

"Why the Arjentans, of course," said Rissa impatiently. "We can hear them on the other side of the door."

257

"Oh, good grief... we're not ready." Everyone tried to get through the inn door at once, and the entrance was quickly jammed with people pushing and shoving.

"STAND ASIDE," yelled Rissa, in her loudest bellow. "Let the guardians through."

The crowd stood obediently back. Rissa stood in the doorway. "We will assess the situation, and then the Captain will tell you all what you should do. Understood?" Everyone was silent. Rissa nodded, content that they were under control. It was important that people didn't panic and flap about wasting their energy.

The three guardians went down into the cellar, as quietly as they could and listened. No doubt about it, there were muffled voices coming from behind the door. And chinks of moving light showing underneath it, too.

"Has there been any sign they are trying to break the door down?" whispered Castello. Before anyone could answer, there was a thunderous knocking. It had no effect on the door, but the three guardians nearly jumped out of their skins.

"Oh," said Rissa, her hand to her heart, "such a noise! Will they break the door down on us?"

"Be easy, be easy, wife," said Castello, his own heart thumping wildly. "I think they are just trying to attract Mistress Zostra's attention."

"I should think they succeeded," said the Reverend Pontius, and promptly passed out on the floor.

When Pontius came to, he was lying on the stone floor of the cellar, but his head was cradled in something soft and warm. He looked up and saw Rissa and Zostra, looking strikingly alike, peering down at him with concerned expressions. Rissa was waving her smelling salts under his nose and his head was in Zostra's lap. He had rarely felt so comfortable. I could get used to this sort of thing, thought the Reverend, but it is not quite proper. And he struggled to sit up.

"Oh, Mr Parson, zur," said Zostra, "I was afeard you were dead-and-gone-to-heaven."

"Not quite yet," said Pontius, gathering his wits. It occurred to him that this sudden passing out was becoming a bit of a habit. "Help me up, will you? Don't fuss, madam, I'm perfectly well."

There was another loud knocking on the door. "Let us all go upstairs away from this racket," said Castello, taking charge again, "and we will decide what to do next. Here, Reverend, let me assist you." But Rissa and Zostra had already firmly grasped an arm each and Pontius was almost lifted off his feet as they took him back up the stairs and deposited him in a chair.

"Now then," said Castello, turning to Zostra, "will they stay thumping on the door like that all night?"

"Oh, no, Cap'n dear," she said, "they will give it up soon. 'Tis a long way back through the tunnel to Arjento."

"Do you mean they are walking all the way from Arjento Rock and back, through that tunnel, every night?"

"Not walking, zur, no. They has horses."

"Horses?" said Castello in astonishment. "Horses in that little tunnel?"

"Little pony-horses, Cap'n dear. We uses them in the mines. They don't mind the dark, zur."

Castello was worried by this. They not only faced the prospect of being overrun by Arjentans, but by Arjentans mounted on little pony-horses. He didn't stop to consider how they would get up the stairs and out of the cellar.

"Well," he said, recovering again. "If you are right, ma'am, we can set up a guard in the cellar, just in case, and begin again with the gun in the morning. With luck we'll have everything in place before they return."

In the event, Zostra was proved right, and the hammering

on the door had soon ceased. Castello had stayed on guard in the cellar with one of the gun crews, and sent everyone else home to rest. At first light, the gun and its carriage were hauled down to the inn by cart and by main force. Young Ferro was concerned about the old grey mare, who stood and shivered from head to hoof, and unharnessed her from the cart. "I should not wish her to lose her foal, Captain," said the young man.

"No, indeed," said Castello. "But we still need powder and shot and other gear brought over here. Will either of the stallions pull the cart?"

"They are not trained for it, sir, but I'll try." Young Ferro saluted, and ran off.

"That young man will be a great asset to the island," said Castello to Ligo, who nodded in agreement.

"Captain, Mistress Zostra has told me more about the Arjentans," said Ligo, blushing as he said her name. "She says they are very organised in their mining operations, but a hopeless rabble when it comes to fighting an organised enemy. Which is how they were defeated by the Larus-men in the old story, despite greatly outnumbering them."

Zostra appeared beside them. "All true," she said. "You have seen the way they fight, Cap'n dear. All fists and nonsense. No arrangement at all. Complete rabble-mess, they are."

"Your crew obeyed you, Mistress," said Castello.

"Ah, zur, I am only half Arjentan. My Mama's family are all Larus-folks. The failing is diluted-weak in me. I can command them easy."

Castello thought that the amount of shouting, foot stamping and cuffing of ears it took was scarcely easy. But he kept this thought to himself.

"Will all the Arjentans obey you, Mistress?"

"Only my crew, Cap'n dear. The rest will not take orders from me, especially if they think me a turncoat-traitor."

It was a considerable struggle getting the gun down into the cellar, but one way or another they had pushed, shoved, rolled and heaved it into the inn and manhandled it down the stairs. There had been something of a scene when someone had suggested widening the main doorway by knocking down part of the wall, and Zostra had declared she would beat their brains out with her broom if they laid so much as a finger on her stonework. But aside from that it was done amicably enough, and the gun was settled back on its reassembled carriage, facing the great door. There was a further kafuffle when a message came to say they had harnessed Bruno to the cart, but that he had reared up, overset the whole cart and a cannonball had rolled onto Master Broad's foot, and that he was hopping about screeching. Zostra went down to the quay to provide medical assistance to Broad, and the shot and powder were laboriously wheeled over to the inn in handcarts.

"You will be a-blowin' of our roof off, zur, if you lets off that great gun-thing in here," said Zostra, later, when she came down to see what they had done to her cellar.

"I hope, ma'am, that it will not be necessary," said Castello. "But better safe than sorry, don't you think?"

"I always feels safe with you, Cap'n dear," said Zostra, smiling, as she climbed back out of the cellar. "Do as you think fit, zur."

Castello ran his finger round the inside of his collar. He invariably felt a little warm when Zostra smiled at him. He sat down on a powder keg and surveyed the precious cannon. They had achieved so much this last twenty-four hours. He was proud of them all. Even Master Broad. And with that he fell fast asleep.

Chapter Seven
Set Down your Sheilds

"Hugh. HUGH. Wake up!" It was Rissa's voice. The Captain was still sitting on the powder keg, leaning back against the cellar wall. But someone had insinuated a cushion behind his head. And there was a blanket draped over him. Daylight was filtering down the cellar stairs.

"I… um… just resting my eyes… how long…?"

"You have slept all night," said Rissa, quietly.

"What? But… didn't the Arjentans…? Weren't they hammering on the…?"

"You slept all through it. They showed no signs of breaking the door down, so we let you sleep."

How could he have slept through all that racket? Through a time of danger? What would people think? He tried to move, but found the rim of the barrel had cut off the circulation and he was numb below the knees. He fidgeted as the feeling returned. He looked at the great door; it was unchanged. He looked at the cannon; that was fine, too. Apparently there was no harm done. A delicious smell of cooking wafted down the stairs, reminding the Captain that it was a long time since he had eaten anything.

"There is news," said Rissa, helping him up. "The *Mergoose* is in the offing." Castello flashed her an anxious look, but she smiled encouragingly and went on. "Ligo is down at the quay with his telescope. He has just sent a message to say that the boat is undamaged. All seems well, so far as he can see. He will

262

send Lineus and Ralham over here as soon as they come ashore. Everything has been done that can be done, husband. Now come and have some breakfast." And she marched him up out of the cellar.

Upstairs in the inn, Zostra was feeding the overnight guard and a raggle-taggle of other people. Broad was sitting in a chair in the corner with his bandaged foot on a stool, snivelling to himself. "Now, now, Master Broad, dear, we must be a brave boy, eh?" said Zostra, handing him a plate. And she patted his injured foot playfully. Broad let out a yelp.

"Is he seriously injured?" whispered Castello, as Zostra swept by.

"Oh, no, zur. A little break-crack of the bone, maybe. But mostly it is all play-acting. He likes the attention, Cap'n dear. I will fetch you a plate. You must be starving-famished."

Lineus and Ralham, when they eventually disembarked, came straight over to the Sea Poppy Inn, as instructed. Ralham was full of a story he had heard as he came ashore. "Alvan said they had hauled the bronze cannon out of the fort and set it up in the cellar of the Sea Poppy."

"They've put it *where*?" said Lineus, in disbelief.

"In the cellar, to guard the door, he said."

"What door?"

"The door that keeps the Arjentans out, so he said."

"How can a door in the pub cellar keep the Arjentans out? And why would they want to get in anyway? He was pulling your leg, Master Ralham."

"But didn't you see, at the fort? Ferro's cart was there, with a broken wheel. Something's certainly going on." Ralham was fairly mortified that he might have missed something exciting while he was away. He had enjoyed his expedition to Arjento Rock, but it had been a sightseeing trip, really. Nothing you could call exciting had happened, unless you counted cleaning out the *Mergoose's* bilges after the seasick Arjentans.

263

Lineus shook his head. "Cannons in the cellar!" he muttered. "Complete claptrap."

"We will explain everything later," said Captain Castello, "but first, tell me about Arjento Rock." Ralham and Lineus, having discovered that the cannon was indeed in the pub cellar, looked at each other in consternation.

"Wouldn't it be best to ask Mistress Zostra, Captain?" said Ralham, cautiously.

"I could," said Castello, "but I am asking you. You have the most recent knowledge of Arjento Rock." Know thine enemy, thought Castello.

"It's a big island," said Lineus. "Much bigger than Larus. We sailed all round it, on the way back…"

"For a proper reconnaissance…" said Ralham, anxious not to be left out.

"The main harbour is smaller than ours, but it's still an impressive port," Lineus went on.

"…And there's no other place to land, not round the whole coast," said Ralham.

"So nowhere you could hide a fleet of boats, then?" asked Castello.

"None at all," Ralham and Lineus said together.

"And you saw nothing of the *Honest Trader*?"

"No, Captain," Lineus shook his head looking even more puzzled.

"Good," said Castello. "Now get the *Mergoose* unloaded, and prepare her for sea again, in case we need her. Ligo will tell you everything that's happened." And he rushed off leaving them none the wiser.

Rissa, Castello and Pontius were holding a council of war seated round the fire in the Reverend's comfortable little room under the bell tower. It was already growing dark, and a bitter wind was trying to find its way under the chapel door and making all the shutters rattle. They had retreated up here to talk in private. It wasn't that they disbelieved Zostra, exactly; more that they felt better able to speak freely when she wasn't listening.

Now that Ralham and Lineus were back, it was easy to keep a gun crew on duty in the cellar at all times. Ralham had immediately volunteered to take the first watch, and Castello had gratefully left him to it.

"I could wish this had not happened in the wintertime," said Castello, fretfully.

"You and me both, colleague," said Pontius. He felt the cold all too keenly these days, and gallivanting about the island in the teeth of an icy gale was not his idea of a proper occupation for a winter's evening.

"I am concerned that Mother Rufus is not here," said Rissa.

Pontius wasn't sure he could agree with this. "We informed her, Lady," he said. "And she says she will not leave the east cliff. But then, neither did her predecessor. We must continue without her, for the time being."

"Yes," said Castello. "Now let us get on. We must agree our plan."

"Could we not simply wait and see what the Arjentans do?" said Pontius. "After all, Ralham and Lineus were not attacked on Arjento Rock. Nothing at all has happened, really, apart from that infernal hammering on the door night after night."

"Nothing?" said Rissa. "Oh, indeed, nothing except sending my sister and a gang of ruffians to find the door and let the whole lot of them in to steal our commonwealth and murder us all in our beds."

"So what must we do then, if not wait and see?" asked Pontius, positive to the soles of his shoes that he wouldn't like the answer.

Castello stood up. "It will be far better, will it not, to open the door and confront them on our own terms, fully prepared, at a time of our own choosing? It will give us the advantage in every respect."

"You mean to fight them?" said Pontius in alarm. "There in that cellar?"

"I mean to *confront* them. Tell them they will not be harmed if they return to Arjento Rock."

Pontius felt this was a good moment to fully apprise them of Mother Culver's song.

"Another prophecy?" said Rissa. "And you didn't tell us?"

"I didn't know we were about to fight a battle in a freezing cellar, Lady," said Pontius, grumpily. "Let me tell you what she said – and it's not a prophecy, either. She calls it a *suggestion*." And he repeated the verse:

Set down your shields and set aside your swords
For if you fight the isle shall swiftly fall.
The battle may be fought with honest words;
The commonwealth is common to us all.

"What are we to make of this?" asked Castello, after a pause. "Is she saying we shouldn't fight?"

"I think she's *suggesting* there's another way," said Pontius. "I think she means we should look to negotiate a truce… an agreement. Perhaps something of benefit to ourselves and to the Arjentans, too."

Castello, though he quavered with fright at the thought of a battle and its horrible consequences, had nonetheless been looking forward to it, in a perverse sort of way. "Well, perhaps," he said, a little flatly, "but what could we offer them?"

Rissa, half-Arjentan as she was, saw the opportunity. "Let's see," she said, thoughtfully. "The old story says the Larus-men raided Arjento Rock and stole the cache of silver, right?"

Castello and Pontius nodded.

"And they not unreasonably want it back?"

"But it's *our* commonwealth," said Castello.

"It was theirs first, brother," said Pontius. Castello was obliged to agree.

"*The commonwealth is common to us all*," Rissa quoted. "Could we offer half of it back, in return for peace between us? Offer to share it? As a gesture of good will?"

"Lady, that is a good suggestion," said Pontius. He turned to Castello. "Do you think we can make it work? Force them to parley with us?"

"Yes. If we can stop them in their tracks, make a show of force, perhaps we can."

"And would they give up their determination to fight, having come so far, do you think?" asked the Reverend.

"I would think anyone, finding themselves nose to nose with the snout of that cannon, all prepared to fire, would think twice about it," said Castello.

"And if they refuse?" asked Rissa fearfully.

"Then I will fire the gun and blow them and their pony-horses and their tunnel back where they came from."

"Oh," said Pontius, and swallowed hard. "And, um, when do you propose this confrontation should take place."

"Immediately," said Castello, decisively. "Tonight."

Chapter Eight
The Men of Silver

Captain Castello was striding through the darkness back down the hill. The Reverend Pontius was trotting along behind him, struggling to keep up. It was desperately cold, and the Reverend was not looking forward to another night in that chilly cellar. Perhaps, he thought to himself, I could sit upstairs by Mistress Zostra's fire. They could call me if anything should happen. But he knew, deep down, that he needed to be in the cellar standing shoulder to shoulder with his fellow guardians. It was his duty, damn it, whether he liked it or no, even if his hands and feet were already numb, which they were.

"I could wish my lady wife had come down with us," shouted Castello, battling with the wind.

"She fears for her children, brother. It is perfectly natural. This is a dangerous moment, after all. She will come down as soon as ever she can."

Rissa had wondered aloud whether she should bring the twins down to the fort, so she could reach them quickly if things should go badly wrong. Castello and Pontius had said that this was not a safe place, with the treasure stowed nearby, and they all agreed, on reflection, that the children and their nursemaid would be safest lodged with a large family living near Rissa's house, and she had gone home to make arrangements.

Arriving at the fort, Castello found Ralham. "Round up all

the gun crews – yes, and send for Ferro and Young Ferro, too, bring everyone over to the inn and meet me there. We need to put on a show of force." Ralham saluted and dashed into the darkness. Castello went to put on his best uniform and fetch his sword. I must look invincible, he thought, insuperable, if we are to have any chance of settling this thing peaceably.

Long before midnight, all was prepared. The gun was loaded and ready to fire. The gun crews had squabbled over who should be in charge of it, and been silenced by Castello who said he would send the whole kit and caboodle of them outside if they couldn't behave themselves. He would take charge of the gun himself. He wasn't entirely sure what would happen to the building if the gun were fired, and he wanted to be sure there was no excitable and unnecessary shooting by an over-enthusiastic crew.

Rissa had returned, looking less anxious for knowing the twins were in a safe place, and immediately insisted that Lineus be sent straight to Mother Rufus to let her know what was going on. "I'm sure she already knows," sighed the Reverend Pontius, listening in to the conversation as he warmed himself by the fire. "She probably knows the outcome, too. But I doubt she'll share it with us." Rissa ignored this and sent Lineus off at the double.

They settled down to discuss tactics. They would keep the cellar as dark as possible; there would be no lights showing under the door to warn the Arjentans. They would let the enemy knock at the door for a while before opening it. Ralham would be stationed at the doorway with the key in place, ready to unlock the door and throw it open at the Captain's word. As soon as the door was open, the lanterns would be uncovered, revealing the cannon, the gun crews in warlike stances, brandishing axes, and Captain Castello in his finest uniform, waving his sword.

"It is to be hoped," said the Captain, "that they will be taken aback. They will see that they have lost the element of surprise, and that we have gained it, and that they will have nothing to lose by talking with us."

He hoped this sounded sufficiently positive. Had he known that bets were already being quietly made, and that the odds against his being flattened by the invading army and run through with his own sword were alarmingly short, he would have been rather less happy.

Finally, the troops were deployed around the cellar, with extra people upstairs and on guard outside in case things didn't go entirely to plan. Castello asked Zostra and Master Broad to keep out of sight upstairs, at least to begin with, as their appearance might confuse the issue. He tried to persuade Rissa to wait upstairs in a slightly safer place, too, but she would have none of it, saying she was a guardian of the isle, and would be standing with the others in the island's hour of need, whether he liked it or not, and that was that.

On the stroke of midnight, the hammering on the door began. The whole pub seemed to jump with fright. Captain Castello drew his sword, which gleamed faintly in the near dark. The hammering ceased and everyone in the cellar was left listening to the hammering of their own hearts. The Reverend Pontius felt his knees shaking and thought that if he wished hard enough for a chair perhaps one would materialise behind him. Rissa, standing beside him, took his arm, and, whether for her benefit or for his he could not say, gripped his elbow tightly. He patted her hand in what he hoped was a reassuring way.

After a long pause, the hammering began again, made everyone jump again, and ceased again.

"Now, Ralham!" said Castello, into the echoing silence. The lock clicked, and the door swung open. "Lights!" hissed the Captain, and the lanterns were uncovered. The open door revealed the turned backs of a group of Arjentans. Their heads swivelled round at the sound of the opening door.

"Good evening," said Captain Castello, civilly. There was a long, tense silence while the Arjentans in the doorway took in the scene. They were clearly too surprised to think of even the most obvious reply. Castello decided to say his piece before they had time to collect their thoughts.

"I am Captain Castello, Commander of Fort Resolute and northern guardian, Isle of Larus." No response.

"This cannon is loaded and we will not hesitate to fire it if you attack us," said the Captain, surreptitiously polishing away a thumbprint on the gun's gleaming flank with his elbow. "But we would prefer to hold talks with you. Will you agree to parley with us?"

Voices could be heard from further down the tunnel, asking what the hold-up was. The Arjentans looked at each other, but seemed incapable of making a decision.

Castello brandished the sword so it flashed impressively in the lantern light. "Where is your leader? Bring him to me and I will speak with him."

Again, the Arjentans seemed undecided, but eventually one of them said, "We will find a leader-man to come talk-parley with you, Mister Captain. Do not be letting off that gun-thing."

Voices were heard again, calling in the tunnel, apparently arguing, and after a long pause, a figure pushed to the front and strode out into the cellar. He was ancient and grizzled, and half a head taller than most of the other Arjentans, who literally looked up to him as he spoke. "We is come to recover back our silver-treasure, as was stolen from us, good and solid, by sneaky-thief Larus-men, back in the long-ago." He looked round at everyone. "And we means to have it, for certain sure. Big gun, or no."

Before Castello could think of a suitable riposte, there was a shriek from the top of the stairs, and something small and fierce came rushing down. "Peregrine!" cried the fierce creature. It was Mother Rufus. She rushed forward and took the astonished Arjentan firmly by the ear. "What kind of a time do you call this to be coming home? Eh?"

"Ow – let go!" said the Arjentan, trying unsuccessfully to release her grip on his ear. "By the… be that you, Lenora?" He looked appalled.

"Of course it's me, you dirty, filthy stop-out!"

There was another shriek, and Zostra came rushing down. Within a moment, she was firmly attached to the other ear. "Daddy – how… how could you have told me such untruth-lies about the Larus-men? They are dear, sweet people," she said, with a glance at Ligo and another at the Captain.

The Arjentan stood struggling to free himself, with the two women dangling like a pair of giant earrings, both shouting incomprehensibly.

Rissa sailed forward and stood before him with her arms akimbo and a very dangerous look on her face. "Am I to understand," she said slowly, "that this PERSON is my father?" Silence fell again, at this interesting question.

Castello, having had time to take in what had happened, and a chance to look carefully at Peregrine, thought the resemblance was pretty striking. He also wondered whether Rissa were about to demonstrate her punching technique again. Mother Rufus and Zostra clearly thought so, and they stood aside a little, without letting go of their respective ears.

"Mother Rufus… sister… I beg you will let him go," said Rissa, quietly. "Come, Father, come and sit by the fire upstairs with me. There is much to talk about. Tell your men to wait here. We will send refreshment down for them." When Peregrine looked doubtful, she added, "No one will be harmed. Come."

Well, you could have knocked Captain Castello down with a feather. She was being nice to the fellow! No matter that he had abandoned her as a baby, betrayed her mother, threatened to overrun the island and make off with the commonwealth. She was taking him to the pub for a drink, forsooth! The gun crews looked at the Captain in consternation. He lowered his sword, shook his head and shrugged to them. He would never, ever, understand women in general, and in particular he would never understand his wonderful wife. Meanwhile, Rissa had tucked her hand into the crook of her father's arm and was escorting him up the stairs, saying, "Did you know, sir, that you have two little grand-children? A girl and a boy. I will introduce you properly to my husband as soon as he recovers his wits and his manners..."

The Arjentans stood with their mouths open in stunned surprise at this curious turn of events. Mother Rufus and Zostra looked bemused. Castello recovered himself and said, "Mistress Zostra, perhaps you would go and arrange refreshments as my wife suggests. For everyone." He turned to the nearest Arjentan, "Sir, will you inform your brave compatriots in the tunnel that there will be no need for any fighting today. We will talk this problem over. And we will send down ale for them all."

"Aye, zur," said the Arjentan. "No fight-squabbling; talk-parley; and drinks all round." And he dashed into the tunnel to spread the good news.

The Reverend Pontius, who had said nothing all this time in his astonishment, realised that he was mortally chilled. Cold as a codfish. And there was a pleasant fireside upstairs. Also, the most interesting conversation was likely to be taking place up there very shortly, so he said, "Captain, will you not go outside and set our troops at ease. Our very extensive troops," he added loudly, for the Arjentans' benefit, just in case. "And Mother Rufus, we are guardians of this isle, too, are we not? We should join the discussions upstairs, don't you think?" He bowed and offered her his arm.

She screwed up her eyes suspiciously for a moment, and then, realising that he had just publicly acknowledged her as a fully-fledged guardian, took the Reverend's arm, saying.

"Don't mind if I do, *colleague*, don't mind if I do." And they paraded out of the cellar.

Castello made a show of handing over command to Ralham, who gave an extravagant salute, and followed them up the stairs. But he did not join them at the fireside. He was not convinced that all was safe. Or not yet, anyway. Instead, he opened the door to go outside. Several people fell in and nearly knocked the Captain off his feet. They had obviously had their ears to the door listening for news. He shut the door carefully behind himself and addressed the troops quietly.

"Listen carefully, all of you, we are holding talks with the Arjentans, and I hope there will be no need for any fighting." Some people looked relieved, others were clearly disappointed. "Nonetheless, for the time being, I wish you all to remain alert. No wandering off. No putting down your weapons. And absolutely no ale. You are on duty here, for the protection of the island, until I tell you to stand down. Do you understand me?" They did.

It was a cold night, but the islanders were hardy folks, and basically very good-natured. They stayed outside the inn, as they were bid, entertaining each other with jokes and old tales, and occasionally peering through the window to see how things were progressing.

For all his precautions, Captain Castello was still uneasy. He spoke quietly to Zostra as she supervised the sending down of the ale. "Mistress, is it wise to send all these barrels down to the Arjentans in the tunnel? We have seen how quick they are to lose their tempers. Might it not encourage them to attack us?" He had been too surprised to argue with Rissa when she had suggested refreshments for all, and too keen to keep up the appearance of a united front among the guardians to question it since.

"Why, bless you, Cap'n dear," she said, smiling, "they will be all fight-squabbling among themselves in the tunnel. Will have clean forgot why they came by now." Castello raised a questioning, worried eyebrow.

"Do not be fret-worrying about it at all," she said, patting his hand. "Now go and join the talk-parley with the others by the fire. I will bring you some ale."

There was a great deal of laughter coming from the group around the fireplace. It didn't sound much like an international peace conference, thought Castello, irritably, as he took his place among them.

"Ah," said Rissa, "here he is. Father, may I present my husband, Captain Hugh Castello." The Captain got up again and bowed. He wondered for a moment what he should call his newfound father-in-law. Father? No, too familiar.

"Master Peregrine, I hope my wife and colleagues have made you welcome," he said, awkwardly.

Peregrine leapt to his feet, grinning, pumped the Captain's hand and slapped him so hard on the back that he overbalanced and nearly fell into Mother Rufus' lap. She shrieked with laughter, and even Rissa appeared to be suppressing a giggle. How can I make them be serious, thought Castello, as he straightened his jacket and took his seat again. This is serious. Very serious. And they are sitting here cackling like a lot of geese.

Zostra leaned over the Captain's shoulder to hand him a tankard of ale, exposing an eye-popping quantity of bosom as she did so. The Captain completely forgot what he had been about to say. He raised the tankard, but received a look of such ferocity from Rissa, that he put it down again hurriedly. "Um, perhaps, Master Peregrine, you will allow my colleague the Reverend Pontius here, our western guardian, to explain the situation and make our proposals for the future?"

Pontius was caught completely off-guard. It was very comfortable by the fire, and way past his bedtime, and he had suddenly begun to feel very sleepy indeed. It wasn't until he became aware of the expectant silence and found all eyes upon him that he took in what Castello had said, and got to his feet, clearing his throat. It's going to be a very long night, he thought.

And a very long night it was, too. When the grey winter dawn broke, they were still talking by the fire. In the early hours, a nasty lumpy sleet had begun to patter on the windows, and they had taken pity on the guards still outside, bringing them indoors to warm up, and leaving just one or two on watch at a time. The inn was full to capacity and had taken on a party atmosphere. Master Peregrine's hearty laugh rang round the building again and again, and could undoubtedly be heard in the cellar, if not throughout the whole tunnel. Happy agreements had been reached. The offer to share the commonwealth with the Arjentans had been happily accepted. Castello and Pontius had doubted this would be the case, but Peregrine, standing between them, had said, "Oh, no, zurs, do not be worrying. It was never about the silver-treasure, as such – we has plenty-much of silver on Arjento – it was more the *principle* of the thing, if you gets my drift. It was ours, stolen away, and we wanted it back, like. My dears, you can keep it if you wish."

Castello and Pontius wouldn't hear of it, saying this was an ancient wrong that must be put right. They had agreed to give half of it back, and give it back they would. Would fetch it and count it this very morning, as soon as daylight permitted. Peregrine said that this was a damned generous-happy outcome and how about more drinks all round?

The possibilities of trade and co-operation between the two islands had been well received, too, with many ideas presented and discussed in depth. As daylight appeared, the Reverend Pontius had decided he could leave the talk to the others, and had just settled gratefully in his chair thinking he might be forgiven for resting his eyelids for an hour, when there was a great worried shout from outside, followed by a messenger bursting in. "The *Honest Trader*, Captain, your Reverendness –

she is in the harbour!"

Captain Castello was fighting down doubt and panic. Had this whole night's work been nothing more than a ruse by the crafty Arjentans after all? A trick to make him take his eye off the cannonball, so to speak? Master Peregrine, Mother Rufus, were they all in cahoots? Even, even… He suppressed the thought, and pulled himself together.

"Are you sure?" he asked the messenger. "Truly sure? This is important, man."

"Yes, Captain. Bluff bows, ruby-red sail. Nice boat. It's the *Honest Trader* all right."

"Very well. LIGO!" Ligo's head popped out of the trapdoor a moment later. He was suspiciously red in the face, and Castello wondered how much ale he might have consumed. But there was no help for it, the Captain must trust his gun captains now, drunk or sober.

"Get your telescope, Ligo, and run down to the fort. Take your gun crew with you, and prepare your cannon. Have a good look at the boat in the harbour. If it shows any sign whatsoever of attacking us, blow it out of the water immediately. Use all the shot and powder you need, as necessary. And tell all the lookouts to be extra vigilant. Understand?" Ligo saluted, yelled for his gun crew, and they all thundered out of the inn.

Peregrine and his two daughters were left looking stricken. Rissa recovered first. "You don't think… you don't think that I… that my father…"

"I don't know what to think!" snapped Castello, and dashed down to the cellar to put Ralham and the others on the alert.

When he came back up, carrying his sword, he found Peregrine had planted himself at the top of the stairs. "This is none of my doing, son," he said, stolidly. "I know nothing of any plan for invasion-fight by boat-thing."

"For all our sakes, sir, I hope you speak the truth," said

Castello. "But I am responsible for the security of this isle and all her people. The *Honest Trader* is known to have been at Arjento Rock not long since, and her owner has every good reason to wish us harm." He stared hopelessly out of the window, feeling that all the good will was now in ruins. "There could be a whole fleet in the offing, for all I know, and the tunnel below is full of your compatriots. With all due respect to you as my father-in-law, sir, I cannot take the risk. I cannot take your word for it."

"Well, since you put it that way, I see you can't," said Peregrine, reasonably. "Suppose I send all my men back into the tunnel, and turn the lock-key on them? Would you feel more safe-secure then?"

Castello was touched by this offer. He said, "Master Peregrine, there is no need. As a gesture of goodwill, we will leave the door *un*locked. But I beg you will not let your people out of the inn." Peregrine smiled and nodded agreement. Castello sighed and hoped to the soles of his boots that he would not regret this spur-of-the-moment decision. A possible attack from the sea was bad enough, without having to repulse another from the tunnel. I can only be in one place at a time, he thought. And which should it be? Before he could make up his mind, it was made up for him by an alarming new development.

Chapter Nine
One Crisis at a Time, Please...

"Captain, oh Captain, sir, there is an island – a great silver island coming in to the beach!"

"What?" said Castello, taken aback. "*Coming in*? Talk sense, man. How can an island be coming in?"

"This one is, Captain, sir. Oh, come and see."

Outside, approaching the beach at some speed there was indeed an island. An island with great, sheer, silver and black sides, and castles on top.

"Is it... is it Arjento Rock?" someone said. "Have they sailed their island here to attack us? What sorcery is this?" Everyone looked round at Peregrine, who had come out with them. But the Arjentan looked just as astounded as everyone else.

Castello looked at the island. It was bearing down on them at ramming speed, as warlike as you could wish. The Captain drew his sword and brandished it, though his hand shook. He hoped it wouldn't show from a distance. "Guardians..." he called. And Mother Rufus, Rissa and the Reverend Pontius came and stood alongside him, united in adversity. There was nothing they could do, Castello knew, except show their defiance and love for their home island in the face of this horror. But show their defiance they would.

The island ran into the far end of the beach with an enormous metallic clang, throwing up a bow-wave of shingle that hissed and clattered and crunched as it fell back to earth.

There was a series of crashes high up on the island, which had stopped moving.

The guardians stood their ground. "We are the guardians of the Isle of Larus," yelled Castello. "What do you do here?"

Rissa, at his side, stared up. "Husband, this is not an island. It is a shiny ship… one of the shiny ships. Just bigger."

Just bigger. You can say that again, thought Castello. But was it friend or foe? Could it have been sent by the Arjentans? What was its purpose? He stared at the mountainous thing.

I am such a coward, thought the Captain, that I am shaking right through to the ground. The Reverend Pontius had exactly the same thought. So did Rissa. They glanced at each other fearfully. "The very ground is shaking!" cried Mother Rufus, in awe. The ground was indeed shaking. The shingle was rattling. And, from somewhere, came a deep, dangerous, shuddering roar that seemed to wash over them, or under them, or possibly through them. It was hard to tell.

When it finally stopped, there were other sounds, yells from the inn. Ralham, who had stayed at his post in the cellar, floating silver island or no floating silver island, came out white-faced. He gaped at the beached ship for a moment and then recovered himself. "Captain! The tunnel has collapsed. Help me!"

Castello was rooted to the spot. He felt that there were only so many crises a man could be expected to deal with at once, and this was definitely one too many. Rissa faced him. "Hugh, my dearest, go and assist Master Ralham. Take charge. People may be hurt. I will stay and face this shiny ship." He frowned and looked doubtful. But she insisted. "I have faced them before, and I do not truly think they mean us any harm. Ship watching is my job, after all. Go and help. I will call you if there is any need." Castello looked at her for a long moment and then turned and ran into the inn, barking orders.

Rissa was left on the beach with the Reverend Pontius and Mother Rufus. The three of them linked arms. United. And

280

before their very eyes the great ship shimmered and was gone. The wave of shingle remained heaped on the beach, the shape of the ship's bow clearly carved into it. The three guardians looked at each other. "Well," said Mother Rufus, matter-of-factly, "no chance of any useful wreckage from that one, then."

The Sea Poppy Inn was in chaos. Captain Castello had real difficulty fighting his way through the crowd of dust-covered Arjentans who were pouring up the stairs into the bar. Zostra was energetically thumping them with a broom handle, trying to protect her dwindling stocks of ale. "Oh, Cap'n dear," she cried, "help us! 'Tis all a muddle-wreck, and no mistake! My cellar is full of pony-horses, and these rapscallion-thieves have designs on my good ale."

"Ralham!" shouted Castello, desperately, peering through the flying dust. "Where are you?"

"Here, sir!" called Ralham, from across the room.

"And here!" shouted Lineus, obviously in the cellar.

"And here, and at your service, sir!" yelled Young Ferro in the Captain's ear, making him jump.

"Right," said Castello. "Ralham, take these people outside. Right out of the inn, please. Tell them no harm will come to them. Tell them anything, but get them out of this building. I want it cleared. Now." Ralham saluted and began rounding up Arjentans. "Young Ferro, come with me." And he pushed through the crush and down the stairs to the cellar. It was indeed full of pony-horses, milling round and whinnying in fright.

Lineus was trying to restore some form of order and obviously failing. "The horses came up the steps out of the tunnel, Captain," he yelled across the dust and din. "But they won't go up the stairs and outside." Lineus' gun crew were being pushed about and squashed by the panicking ponies. More Arjentans were pouring through the doorway.

"Grab the halters, try to calm them down," shouted

Castello, as he was barged out of the way by a stampeding Arjentan.

"Captain – let me," said Young Ferro, pushing forward. "I will take charge of the horses."

I have to admit, thought Castello to himself, five minutes later, when the horses were calmer and being tethered in an orderly group, that lad is pure magic with animals. The rush of people through the tunnel door was steadying to a trickle. One or two more frightened ponies clattered up the steps, and were taken in hand, and a sort of dusty silence descended. It was quiet upstairs, suggesting that Ralham had succeeded in getting everybody outside. Now then, thought Castello, what next?

"Lineus, do we have any idea how far along the tunnel the cave-in has happened. Might there be people trapped?" He was half-afraid to ask. The Captain had a horror of underground places. And of the bottom of the sea, too. An undersea tunnel multiplied the horrible claustrophobic effect, and he was very anxious to avoid going down there, if at all possible.

"I've had no chance to ask, sir," said Lineus, "with all this shaking and shouting and stampeding about."

Castello went into the doorway and listened. "Is anyone there?" he shouted, and listened again. There was a complete, deadly silence in the tunnel.

"There are no calls for help. Let us begin by getting these horses outside. Mistress Zostra, are you there?" Zostra came down the stairs from the bar. "Can you suggest a stratagem for getting these ponies up the stairs and outdoors, ma'am? They are very reluctant."

"Why, bless you, Cap'n dear," said Zostra, "they is afraid of the bright light. They does not come out of the deep-mines much at home. Blindfold them, zur, and they will follow you anywhere. Here." She took off her apron and handed it to Castello, who passed it to Young Ferro, who was

282

simultaneously nodding his understanding and patting a pony soothingly on its dusty behind.

"Thank you, ma'am. And would your father... would Master Peregrine be free to step down here and give us some advice on the tunnel?"

The first pony, with Zostra's apron tied over its eyes, was meekly following Young Ferro up the stairs by the time Peregrine arrived at the trapdoor. He patted the pony as it passed, saying, "Good little Brownie, off you go, now." The pony pricked its ears under the apron and snorted with recognition.

"How did you know its name?" asked Castello, mystified. All the horses looked identical to him.

"Oh, we calls them all 'Brownie', Cap'n," said Peregrine. "Saves time, like."

"Ah," said Castello. "Tell me, have you spoken to your people? Is anyone badly injured? Is anyone missing?"

"No and no," said Peregrine. "Our folks was all at this end, a-waiting, when the quake-shake of the earth happened. The rock fall is way-away down the tunnel, near the middle, we thinks." He looked thoughtfully at Castello, and smiled. "Do not worry yourself at all about it, Cap'n. When the dust settles a bit I will go see for myself what condition-state it is in. There is no danger here, at all."

Ralham appeared at the top of the stairs. "Begging your pardon, Captain, but the shiny ship has gone."

"Gone?" said Castello. "Sailed away, you mean?"

"No, sir. Gone. Vanished. Disappeared into the air, the lady warden says. Just like the other shiny ships. Oh, and Master Ligo says the *Honest Trader* is tied up at the quay, and her captain would like to speak to you, sir, when you have a moment." The *Honest Trader*! Castello had forgotten all about it, what with the shiny ship, the earthquake and the stampeding horses. It had completely slipped his mind.

"Send a runner to say I'll be down as soon as possible,

Ralham."

Outside, Young Ferro had rigged up a little paddock for the ponies and a growing line of them were tied up in a row, their eyes still covered. He had used a selection of aprons, tablecloths, petticoats, and unmentionable items of ladies' underwear. Castello shuddered to think how they had been obtained. "Can they not take the blindfolds off now?" he asked Zostra.

"Oh, no, zur, or they will panic again. We must cover their eyes til it's dark. After that they will be no trouble. When the dawn comes tomorrow, they will be all accustomed and happy." Castello wondered how they were going to feed so many extra animals in the middle of winter.

Master Broad wandered outside, stretching, having been fast asleep all night in a corner with his foot propped on a stool, and looked with surprise on all the Arjentans milling about, and the string of ponies.

"Did I miss something, Mistress?" he said to Zostra.

"Not much at all, Master Broad," she said mildly.

Chapter Ten
Bless all the Spirits

Captain Castello sighed. Everything was going so well here. The Arjentans were all best friends with the Larus people. Plans were already in hand for trade between the two isles, for the benefit of all. Nobody had been hurt in the earthquake, and the shiny ship was gone, and good riddance. But now he had to go down and confront the captain of the *Honest Trader*. Was Salticus at the quayside, waiting to ruin it all with threats of blackmail? Was the whole nightmare to begin all over again?

Castello tried to brush himself down, without much effect. His best uniform was covered in dust. He had lost his hat. And he had put his sword down somewhere and couldn't remember where. Zostra came to his rescue. She had magicked a brush out of thin air, apparently, and she did her best to restore the uniform to its full glory.

"Your hat is indoors, Cap'n dear – stand still now while I clean this epaulette-thing – and I have put the sword in a safe-secure place. I shall fetch them." And she bustled off.

Five minutes later, with most of the dust removed, and cutting a reasonably smart figure, the Captain set off for the quay to face his doom.

As Ligo had reported, the *Honest Trader* was indeed tied up at the quay, her sails neatly furled, looking clean, prosperous and ready for business. Castello's stomach turned over at the sight of her, and he felt the weight of his worries on his shoulders. He stopped and thought: how can I face this? The answer came loud and clear in his head: think of all the terrors and troubles you have faced, Castello. This is one man, no more. Confront him. You can deal with this.

And the Captain threw back his shoulders, straightened his jacket and marched up to the ship and bellowed, "I am Captain Castello, northern guardian, Isle of Larus, Commander of Fort…"

"Yes, sir, yes, we know all that." The speaker was aboard the ship. But it certainly wasn't Salticus. The man was coming ashore. He strode over and saluted. "Sir, I am Callio, Acting Captain of the *Honest Trader*. Formerly first mate," he added modestly.

Castello was perplexed. "Is Salticus not with you, then?"

"Not with us in more ways than one, sir. He stays on Arjento Rock. He cannot be moved, sir." Callio saluted again.

"All right, Master Callio, stand easy. Tell me what has happened to Salticus."

"Well, sir, he never got over that thing with the waterspout, sir. Has retreated into the mines, sir, where he thinks it's safe. His mind is more than a little unhinged. Thinks he's a money-box, sir. The Arjentans treat him kindly. They give him little silver coins – sometimes he swallows them, sir – and they bring him food, treat him as a pet, sort of, sir. Has his own little silver water bowl and all. In the meantime, sir, the rest of us must earn our living, you understand, until such time as Master Salticus should recover."

"Of course," said Castello. "I understand. You and your crew are welcome here, Master Callio."

"Thanking you kindly, sir. We were worried you might not be glad to see us, after that sorry business with the silver. But with your gracious permissions, sir, we should like to continue trading. We see great possibilities of trade and exchange between this isle and Arjento."

"Master Callio, we have just been discussing the self-same thing. And to begin with, we have a cargo of ponies to send to

Arjento Rock. Would that be of interest to you, now?"

Master Callio indicated that it would certainly be of interest, yes indeed, and they set off together to the Sea Poppy Inn to inspect the cargo and enter into productive discussions.

"Such events, Mother!" said the Reverend Pontius, as they stood together on the shingle beach. "Was there no warning, no prophecy of all this?"

"No, colleague," she said. "None that I know of. I was as surprised as you yourself, believe me."

"But, Mother – a shiny ship the size of an island, colliding with our beach; a quaking of the very earth beneath us, and the breaking down of the tunnel. It's just the sort of thing there *ought* to be a prophecy about, don't you think? I, for one, would be glad of some sort of explanation – to know the meaning of it all."

"Well," said Mother Rufus, thoughtfully, "the shiny ship was sent to us by the Spirit of the Sea, I suppose. As the hermit used to say, it's a playful spirit. Likes a joke, you know. Likes to make us jump."

It succeeded, thought Pontius, to himself. "And the quake-shake of the earth, as Master Peregrine calls it?"

"Ah, Reverend, I think that is none of ours."

"None of ours, Mother? What do you mean?"

"I believe it was sent by the Arjentan spirit, the Spirit of the Rock."

"Oh, indeed? Well, I suppose the underground places would be within its jurisdiction," said Pontius, doubtfully. "But why would it shake the earth and break the tunnel?"

"Perhaps it felt the tunnel had completed its task."

Pontius thought about this. "Do you mean... because the tunnel has been the means of bringing together the people of Larus and Arjento Rock?"

"Aye," said Mother Rufus. "When we sat down and reached agreements, the isles were brought together, as you say. The tunnel was built for secret attacks. It is no longer needed. It was destroyed. We must all be above-board, now, Reverend."

"And what part, I wonder, did *my* spirit, the Spirit of the Sky, have in all this?" said Pontius, mostly to himself.

"Ah, Reverend," said Mother Rufus. "If you don't know the answer to that one, then no one does."

"Hm," said Pontius. "Well, colleague, is there anything else you would wish to tell me, eh?"

"There is a history you might like, Reverend." And she settled herself to sing quaveringly:

Men of Silver tunnelled from the south -
The spirits saved us, sent us guardians four
Who built a house of stone at tunnel's mouth
And hid the key, forever sealed the door...

"You see, Reverend, the first guardians came to the fore during the ancient battle with the Arjentans. That's how it began. When it was over they sealed the tunnel. Kept the island safe." She shrugged. "But perhaps it wasn't such a good idea."

"Indeed." said Pontius. "We might all have been spared much trouble and worry had they all sat down and settled it properly at the time." He sat staring at the great wave of shingle left on the beach by the shiny ship, and a voice said in his ear, "History!" And Pontius knew the Spirit of the Sky, that particularly taciturn spirit, had spoken to him at last.

"Mother!" he said, "Look at that wave of shingle. None of us will forget this day so long as it stands there. But the sea will wear it down, in time, will put the beach back as it was. And we will forget. We will forget the lessons we have learned this day, as we always do here on Larus. You must make a history, and so must I. And we must make sure none of it is forgotten."

"Aye, Reverend," said Mother Rufus, nodding. "We must

work together, eh? Bless all the spirits. They will provide."

They sat companiably for a while.

At length Pontius asked, "Will you tell me, Mother, what happened to the hermit and the red horse?"

"The Spirit of the Sea spoke to me, Reverend," she said matter-of-factly. "The spirit sent the red horse to return Rufus the Hermit to the sea. The horse came to me. I led it to Rufus, and helped him onto its back, and the two flew together, back to the sea."

The Reverend wasn't sure that this could be believed. But if it were a mere excuse, it was a comforting one.

Pontius blurted out what was on his mind: "Tell me, Mother, did we do the right thing? Burying Rufus on the cliff? Should we have buried him at sea?"

"You did the proper thing, Reverend," she said. "He is back with the Spirit of the Sea. All is as it should be. All is well." She spoke with such unusual sympathy and gentleness that Pontius was touched. And relieved.

"Come, Mother," he said. "It will be dark in an hour or so. Allow me to escort you back to the east cliff. Our work is done here."

As they turned, they saw Castello and Rissa coming out of the inn. The four guardians exchanged news, and said their farewells for the day.

Castello and Rissa strolled away, arm in arm. When they were out of hearing of everyone else she whispered something in his ear. She blushed, and he blenched. But after a moment he kissed her hand and said, "Then we must finish the new house, quickly. Dearest wife, you make me the happiest man in all of Larus, or the world, indeed the whole universe." And any other universe, too, most likely.

AND WHAT *OUR* WORLD MADE OF IT ALL...

From The Western Clarion:

**Ship damaged in mysterious collision
'Larus' effect strikes again**

The container ship *Ocean Venturer* suffered damage to its bows following a possible collision in the English Channel yesterday. There have been a number of strange incidents in this area of the sea, which is becoming known as the English Channel's Bermuda Triangle. Mysterious vessels, apparently registered to the non-existent 'Isle of Larus', have been reported, along with a number of other unexplained phenomena, the so-called *Larus effect*.

A crewman of the *Ocean Venturer*, who asked to remain anonymous, told our reporter, "I was working in the bow area of the ship when the collision happened – I was thrown to the deck by the impact. I got to my feet and looked over to see what we had hit. There was nothing there. Nothing. I looked around and in the distance there was a small sailing boat. Bluff-bowed. With a ruby-red sail. Yes, I said ruby-red, didn't I? But it could never have stopped a ship the size of the *Venturer*. We'd simply have run it down. And then I looked again and a door opened in the ocean. Yes, a door in the ocean. A big, heavy wooden door. No, I don't know how it got there, do I? But it was definitely a door. And as I looked at it, the sea shook. Yes, I said shook. Have you got cloth ears or something? The sea shook, and the door closed. And disappeared. That's what happened, and that's that."

A spokesman for HM Coastguard stated: "There is limited information available at present regarding this incident. The ship was damaged and several containers were dislodged, but no one was hurt. A minor earth-tremor was recorded in the area at the time the incident was reported, and we are investigating the possibility that it may have caused the accident."

Questioned about the crewman's statement, the spokesman said, "Don't give me all that rubbish about ruby-red sails and a door in the ocean. It's been a long day and I've got a headache. Someone is just trying to cash in on a sensational story. As we said when the earlier incidents occurred in this sea area: there is nothing there, and there is no such place as the Isle of Larus."

THE END

Fantastic Books
Great Authors

Meet our authors and discover our exciting range:

- Gripping Thrillers
- Cosy Mysteries
- Romantic Chick-Lit
- Fascinating Historicals
- Exciting Fantasy
- Young Adult and Children's Adventures

Visit us at:
www.crookedcatbooks.com

Join us on facebook:
www.facebook.com/crookedcatpublishing

Printed in Great Britain
by Amazon.co.uk, Ltd.,
Marston Gate.